I0747542

Arousing AFFAIRS

sinful awakenings

T. M. AMAT

Red Satin Press

First Published by Red Satin Press 2023

This novel is entirely a work of fiction. Names, characters, places, businesses, organizations, events, and incidents portrayed in it are the products of the author's imagination or are used fictitiously and are not to be construed as real. Any resemblance to actual persons, living or dead, events, locales, or organizations is entirely coincidental.

AROUSING AFFAIRS
Copyright © 2023 by T. M. AMAT

All rights reserved. Printed in the United States of America. No part of this book may be reproduced, stored or transmitted in any form or by any means, electronic, mechanical, photocopying, recording, scanning, or otherwise without written permission from the publisher. It is illegal to copy this book, post it to a website, or distribute it by any other means without permission.

ISBN: 978-1-7378693-3-7
Library of Congress Control Number: 9781737869337

For information :
www.tmamat.com

Cover design by Alex Albornoz

First edition 2023
10 9 8 7 6 5 4 3 2 1

Para Mamá...

Por expandir tu mente.

Gracias por apoyarme siempre.

ACKNOWLEDGEMENTS

First and foremost, I'd like to thank my readers for your patience and support in the time it took to get this second book out. I couldn't have done it without knowing you guys were there waiting.

Second, thank you Alex Albornez, my cover designer. You nailed this one. So much better than I imagined!

Also, thanks to Larissa Melo Pienkowski, my editor. For your time and expertise I am forever grateful.

And finally, a big THANK YOU to my family. Your continued support and encouragement mean the world to me! I love you all.

Chapter 1

Ian

"Forgive me, Father, for I have sinned. It has been a while since my last confession."

There was a lot I needed to unpack, but I didn't know how to word it exactly. I let out a shaky breath, concentrating on the priest's silhouette behind the confessional screen as I gathered my thoughts.

"Go on, my child. Unburden your soul," the godlike voice prodded, calming and deep. Not one I recognized.

Clergy from other parishes had been stepping in to help while the diocese found a replacement for Father Anthony. Correction: it was just Anthony now—or Ant, as some liked to call him. In a shocking "nobody saw that coming" moment, the former priest had fallen in love with my BFF, Anna Ward, and left the priesthood to marry her. Now they were expecting a baby.

Yeah, it had been a crazy year so far.

I cleared my throat. "I've, uh, been drinking a lot lately. More than usual. And, um, I have these thoughts . . . of hurting myself. I don't mean suicide. I mean, it's like there's a darkness inside of me that masks anything good in my life. Like, I'm just angry all the time, and there's this rage that screams to be let out. And I'd do anything to numb this feeling. So I drink—sometimes until I pass out. I haven't turned to drugs, but I've considered it. I also think about sex a lot. I don't watch porn because it reminds me of—" Fuck, I almost mentioned *him*, the one who shall not be mentioned. Don't fucking say that bastard's name. "Porn is a sin, of course." I cleared my throat again. "I'm seeing someone. A doctor. We haven't made anything official, but I think we will soon. I don't want to feel like this when we get to that stage. Please help me, Father. Tell me what to do to stop this self-destructive path."

"Do you know the cause of such pain?" the priest asked.

Damn it. I had to talk about him. But I wouldn't reveal his gender. The Church held some strong opinions about being gay. And since I hadn't come out at my place of employment, I'd keep that bit of info out of my confession. "I was betrayed by someone I loved."

"Loved?"

"Yes, past tense. That love has turned to hatred, which is why I'm here. I don't want to feel this anymore. I want happiness again."

"How did this person betray you?"

My jaw clenched and my heart rate quickened, as it did every time I remembered that day—and not in a good way. Maybe this was what I needed. To let it out. To talk about it. I hadn't mentioned the day the love of my life had stabbed me through my heart to anyone. Not even to Anna. At least, not with the depth people talked about shit to feel better. No, it was more of an "I'm fine, I don't wanna talk about it" kind of way.

I swallowed my escalating fury as I attempted to steady my voice. "This person used me. Broke promises. We—" I had to confess the other thing, the thing I was most ashamed of, the thing I most hated myself for. "We had an affair. I'm an adulterer, on top of everything else. I mean, they weren't married, but still—I let myself fall for the charm. I believed in this person, and now they're engaged. Maybe I'm too far gone for God's forgiveness."

"Never, my child. We are all worthy of His forgiveness. All you have to do is repent and be truly sorry for your sins."

"I am. If I could take it all back, I would. Had I been stronger, I wouldn't have fallen for—I wouldn't be hurting like this, and I wouldn't be so angry. I want to feel better."

"Well, I could absolve you of your sins. But in order to truly feel at peace, you must forgive yourself and the person who has hurt you."

That was what I'd been afraid of. "I'm not sure I can."

"With God's help, anything is possible. Now, after I absolve you of your transgressions, I want you to say five Hail Marys and five Our Fathers. Then I want you to go home and work on forgiving yourself and the person who hurt you. Only then can you find the peace you're seeking. Consider counseling to assist you."

"Okay, Father. I'll try my best."

I half listened as the priest rambled on about forgiveness and making an effort for the good of self-love. Blah, blah, blah.

Finally—a prayer of the Act of Contrition, then Absolution.

And freedom.

Well, not really.

Before following through with my penance of prayers at the altar, I made a detour to the bathroom, locking myself in. I braced myself over the sink, took some deep breaths, and splashed water on my face, washing away the heat of my temper. Lifting my head, I gazed at my reflection in the mirror.

The beard was getting out of control. My hair, a tangled mess. The styling products I used to tame my curls hardly did their job anymore. I had twirly locks busting out the seams, indicating it might be time for a trim.

My inner rage began to grow again. Of all the men to fall in love with, why Jake Edwards?

Because he'd always been there. Because he'd protected me and made me feel wanted. And he was sexy AF.

Fuck.

The unfortunate truth was that Jake had implanted himself deep into my heart from such a young age that now I would have to rip my heart out of my chest to get over him.

The priest was mistaken: the only way to survive this was by hating him. Maybe in the future, I could forgive myself for being an idiot. But I'd never forgive Jake Edwards for leading me on, lying to me, using me, and then proposing to Miranda Sullivan.

Tearing my eyes from the mirror, I snatched up a handful of paper towels and dried my face. As I wiped down the water on the counter, I froze.

Memories flooded my vision, taking me back to that night—the night Anna's ex, Phillip, jumped me because he thought Anna and I were involved. Obviously, he hadn't known I preferred dick.

Jake had helped me, cleaned me up in this very bathroom—only he hadn't exactly tended to my injuries. Instead, he had given me an earthshattering blow job, in part to make me forget the pain I was in but mostly to make himself feel better for not arriving in time to save me, as ridiculous as that sounded. And it had happened right here.

For a split second, I embraced the feelings. I allowed my mind to take me back to when I believed Jake's words were sincere. He had been so concerned for me that night; the BJ was his way of making it up to me. He'd even refused a return favor.

That night, he'd told me he wanted to leave Miranda for me.

What a lie. It had all been an act to get me into bed.

So fucking gullible.

My eyes shifted back to my reflection and my heart turned stone-cold again. Clenching my jaw, I crumpled the paper towels and tossed them at my mirror self.

It was that or a fist through the fucking glass.

Chapter 2

Jake

Deep breath.

As I entered St. Pius Church, the comforting smells of incense and holy water hit me like a cascade of encouragement. I paused inside the atrium, listening to the choir I used to be a part of. A familiar voice took over, cutting through the vocals, seizing the reins.

His voice.

Ian Cooper.

The man I loved—and who hated me in return.

Over a misunderstanding.

But it was time to face the music. I had stayed away for almost five months to give the man some space. Scratch that: I'd stayed away because he wouldn't take any of my calls. Or texts. Or emails. Or even house calls. And the only reason I hadn't cornered him at church—until now—was to avoid a scene. I got the picture: Ian was pissed.

Did I blame the guy? Hell no. I wouldn't have expected anything less.

But enough was enough. It was time not only to grow a pair and spill the truth behind the engagement to Miranda but also to make Ian hear me out, whether he wanted to or not.

And yeah, I was risking my father's fate by going against Miranda's demands, but I didn't care anymore. Dad had done nothing these past few months to rectify the situation, so I was taking matters into my own hands, starting with my own happiness.

Rubbing my hands on my outer thighs, I took another deep breath as I opened the doors of the nave and walked in. Ian's back was to me, facing the choir as he instructed.

As I slowly made my way up the aisle, a few choir members noticed me. And the closer I got, the harder my heart pumped.

"Hey, Jake," one member called out.

Ian stiffened.

I expected him to turn around, but he just stood there, rigid and unmoving. A million scenarios had played in my head about how this moment would go. Completely ignored was one of them, but the absolute terror making my heart thunder in my ears was not part of the equation. I opened my mouth, hoping some coherent words would come out, and—

Ian whipped his head around, peering at me over his shoulder.

My breath caught in my throat. The change in him was also not part of the equation. And I wasn't referring to the death stare.

Almost unrecognizable.

A beard shadowed his face now, making him look older. He also appeared thinner. His dark hair, which was usually tamed, was messy, longer. The only thing that hadn't changed were those electric-blue eyes. And right now, they bore into me like daggers, unmistaken frigidness illuminating from them.

"This is a closed rehearsal." His voice matched the iciness of his glare.

I swallowed. It was my fault this beautiful man had hardened and become cold and distant. The reality saddened me—and fucking made me angrier at Miranda and Father dearest.

"Sorry—" My voice cracked. I cleared my throat. "Sorry for the interruption. I came to get my spot back on choir. If that's possible."

His jaw clenched as he turned, facing me head-on. He was like a god peering down at me from the altar steps. A sexy-ass god, holding all the power. And I would do anything he demanded of me.

Anything.

"I'll put in the work," I continued when he stayed silent. "Whatever it takes." There was a double meaning in there somewhere.

"Your spot has been filled. So, if you'll excuse us, you know the way out."

Murmurs erupted among the crew. I scanned their faces. Nobody new, as far as I could tell. Ian was lying.

"Let's take it from the top with music," Ian said, clearly dismissing me as he walked over to the organ.

I was not giving up that easily. Made it this far; the least I could do was wait it out and speak with the guy. In private would be the safest option. I slipped into a pew and waited.

God, I had missed seeing him in action. The strong leadership role as music director was sexy as hell. I'd always loved watching him play the organ and piano. And his singing voice was just as thrilling.

The time flew by. Ian glanced at his watch, then announced, "Let's go over that one more time, then we'll call it a night."

Flawless. No surprise there.

"That's a wrap. Good job, everyone. See you on Sunday."

The group gathered their belongings, mingling as they shuffled down the aisle. Some lingered behind to talk to Ian. A few waved at me, patting me on the shoulder as they passed.

"Hey, man, long time no see. Where've you been?" one of them asked.

"Around. Dealing with some personal issues," I replied, unwilling to provide too much detail.

"Well, we miss you. Hope you're able to join us again."

"Me too. Hey, how's it been here? Has Mr. Cooper been cracking the whip on you guys? He seemed a little tense." I wasn't one to gossip, but any info might help.

The kid shrugged and chuckled. "To be honest, he's been a little on edge lately. I don't know what it is, but we all just do what he says and try to stay out of his way." Because they respected the hell out of him. "Good luck," he whispered before taking off.

When silence followed, I glanced around. We were alone. Ian was still at the organ, jotting down notes.

It was now or never.

Sliding out of the pew, I ordered my knees to stop shaking as I made my way up the altar and leaned on the organ.

"You're still here," Ian muttered without looking up. It was more of an annoyed acknowledgment than a question.

Up close, I got a better view of his unshaven face. My mouth went dry as I took in this new rugged look. It was scarier—and meaner. And a bit intimidating. Not to say he wasn't still hot, but I preferred his boyish, clean-shaven face. I cleared my throat. "Yeah. I, um, wanted to talk to you—"

"I already told you, there's no room for you. If you have a problem with that, you can take it up with Father Kevin. He's in charge of overseeing the music now that Ant no longer works here."

"Okay. But I wanted to talk to you about something else."

"If it's not work-related, I don't want to hear it," he said as he stood and gathered the surrounding papers. "Besides, I don't have time. I have a date."

My heart stopped. "A date?"

"That's what I said. You do know what a date is, right? It's when two people go out, have a good time, connect, maybe get lucky—"

"Yeah, yeah, I know what a fucking date is."

He pointed to the crucifix hanging on the back of the altar. "Watch your language. You're in the house of God."

The possibility of Ian dating other men hadn't occurred to me. A part of me had just thought he'd always be there, at least until I figured out how to get out of the nightmare I was living in with Miranda and Dad.

"Who are you going out with?" I attempted to keep the panic out of my voice and tried not to freak out into a jealous rampage, which had always annoyed Ian. The last thing I wanted to do was piss him off further.

"No one you know."

"How long have you been seeing him?" A few questions didn't mean I was jealous, right?

"That's none of your business."

"Is it serious?"

"You know, you sure do ask a lot of personal questions for someone who isn't even my friend."

Those words hurt more than the punch he'd given me five months ago, the day Miranda had spewed out the engagement news. A punch I'd deserved and had been very impressed by.

Ian finished gathering all the papers in his bag and draped the strap over his shoulder. "Gotta go."

Before he moved past me, I blocked him and noticed the dark circles under his eyes. "Is this guy at least taking care of you? Because from where I'm standing . . . it doesn't look like he is."

He pressed his lips together as his facial features hardened once again. "What is that supposed to mean?"

"You look worn-down, like you haven't been sleeping. And you've lost weight—"

"I can't fucking believe you."

"What?"

"You have some nerve coming in here and—"

"I'm sorry, I just—"

"Yeah, he takes care of me, all right. In every way possible. Every night and morning. Every position. Every room. Every surface. Better than anyone has ever taken care of me."

Ouch.

He stepped around me. "By the way, give my best to your fiancée. I must admit, I'm surprised she'd be okay with you joining choir again—you know, considering I'm the music director. I guess she must really trust you. It's hard finding people to trust nowadays. One moment, you're making plans and whispering nauseating words of love, and next, they're stabbing you in the back and revealing their acting skills. Anyway, have a great night. I sure will." He continued down the aisle. "Oh, and remember to pull the door shut to lock it when you leave."

I stared after him until he was out of view.

That went better than expected. Except for the implied sex thing. I had not seen that coming.

Bile gurgled in my stomach, threatening to project. Explaining things to Ian and getting him to forgive me was going to be harder than I thought. If I could just get him to hear me out.

Fuck. I ran down the aisle to the basement bathroom. Thank God I made it to the toilet before hurling.

* * *

Ian

How dare he.

Jake Edwards was so cocky, coming here and expecting to just hop back on choir like nothing had happened.

I gripped the door handle of my SUV, nearly ripping it off as I jerked open the door and rushed inside. My heart was thundering in my chest. I held the steering wheel, closing my eyes as I willed myself to stop shaking.

His surprise visit was the last thing I'd been expecting. When someone called out his name during rehearsal, alerting me to his standing behind me, I'd concealed all emotion. I'd braced myself before turning to face him. The steel front I'd put on had worked. But inside, I was dying.

Fuck me. I still loved him.

But I hated him.

I'd moved on. The choir had moved on. We didn't need him.

The nerve of him, asking personal questions about Matt. Who the fuck did he think he was? And to assume I wasn't being taken care of? The audacity.

Reaching inside my pocket, I retrieved my cell phone and pulled up Anna's number. My best friend was the only person I could talk to about this.

But just as I was about to press CALL, I stopped. She was a newlywed, barely back from her honeymoon. There was no way I could bother her with this.

I put down the phone and glanced out the window. Jake hadn't exited the church yet, but he would at any minute, and I did not want to be around when that happened. My eyes shifted to Jake's motorcycle as I started up the SUV. A sad, nostalgic feeling—

No. I crushed it.

Never again would I fall for Jake Edwards.

Chapter 3

Ian

I parallel parked about a block away from the bar where I was meeting Matt. We'd frequented this place quite a bit over the past few months since we'd met. A gay club where we could unwind and be ourselves without the pressures of society.

Time for some final touches. I reached into the side pocket of the bag sitting on the passenger seat and pulled out the black eyeliner I'd been experimenting with recently. Using the dim light of the visor, I applied it. The contrast to my blue eyes looked cool.

If only there was enough time to paint my nails. I used to paint them black in high school and had been itching to do that again. Work made it difficult. That level of individuality at the church was not something I was ready for yet.

I unbuttoned the first button of my blue shirt and headed out.

Matt was standing in front of the bar, looking like eye candy. He wore a gray V-neck with slim black slacks, along with a black blazer. We had been taking things slow, but who knew? That might change tonight.

"Hey, sorry I'm late," I said as I caught up to him and gave him a hug.

"No worries. I wasn't waiting long. You look great," he replied, skimming his eyes over me.

"Thanks. You do too. Ready to have some fun?"

"Absolutely."

I was so ready to let loose and forget about the disastrous turn of events at work. On my drive, I had calmed down some, but I was still fuming inside. Nothing a little—or a lot—of alcohol and dancing couldn't fix.

We made our way inside, the music blaring. I took the lead, squeezing through the crowd, and headed straight for the bar. "Wanna do tequila shots?" I asked him. "I'm in the mood for some shots."

"What's the occasion?"

I asked the bartender for four shots of tequila—two for me, two for Matt. "Does there need to be an occasion?"

"No, it's just that we've never done shots."

"Well, I thought we should switch it up."

The bartender placed the four glasses in front of us, along with a small plate of limes and a saltshaker. "Okay," Matt said. "But two is my limit. Remember, we still have to drive home."

I handed him one of the shot glasses. "That's hours away. Here, let's make a toast. To new beginnings. Together."

He smiled, inclining his head. "Cheers."

Salt, tequila, lime.

Matt's face remained twisted as I reached for the second one. "Hold on," he grunted. "Give me a sec. How can you drink it so fast?"

"It's not so bad. Here," I said, handing him the second glass. "One, two, three—"

Salt, tequila, lime.

"Okay, I'm done," Matt said, pounding his chest.

I ordered four more and a beer for him.

"Maybe you should pace yourself. I don't want to have to carry you out of here."

I threw my arm on top of his shoulder. "Relax. We have all night."

After the fourth shot—or was that number six?—I felt good. Well, better than earlier. I reached for Matt's hand. "Come on, let's dance."

He took a long swig of beer, then took my hand. We squeezed passed the sweaty bodies until there was a break on the dance floor. My head felt light as I moved to the beat of the music. The room spun, but not enough. I got lost in the base, letting my body flow.

Two songs in, and it was time for more alcohol. "Let's take a break," I shouted over the music. Back at the bar, I ordered a double shot of tequila, no lime, then turned to Matt. "What do you want?"

"More tequila?" His eyebrows drew together. "Dude, maybe you shouldn't."

"Stop being a doctor for one night." I laughed. "I'm fine. Now, what do you want to drink?"

He pressed his lips together. "I'll stick with beer."

Turning back to the bartender, I put in the drink order.

"Is everything okay?" Matt asked when the drinks arrived.

"Of course. Why wouldn't it be?"

"I don't know. I've never seen you like this."

I placed a hand on his shoulder and leaned forward. "There's a lot you haven't seen."

The hottie gave a side smile. "This is true."

I kept my face close. "What would you like to see first?"

He drew his bottom lip between his teeth. "How about some more of your dance moves?"

I laughed, leaning back. "Okay, but you asked for it."

We finished our drinks and headed back to the dance floor. Now the room was spinning in a good way, light and warm. The booze running through my veins gave me courage as I grinded against Matt, moving to the rhythm of the music. Then I went for it.

Taking the guy's face between my hands, I kissed him. And this kiss was not like the others.

This one had passion. And tongue. Lots of it.

We'd kissed quite a bit over the last few months, but never like this. The kisses had always been sweet and restrained, mostly because of me—because of my lack of power to get over the one whose name I refused to mention. Matt was always patient, never pressured me into anything I wasn't ready for. So, we mostly just kissed, quitting before it escalated into more.

But now, thanks to Mr. Liquor, I was ready. It was time I moved forward. Maybe if I slept with someone else, it'd help me forget *whatshisname.* Sex now, dissipated anger later. Yeah, that was the formula I should have followed long ago.

Brilliant.

"Let's get out of here," I said, taking his hand.

I led my soon-to-be lover across the dance floor to the restroom, shoved him into a stall, and locked us in.

"Ian, what are you doing?"

"What do you think?" I pushed him against the stall wall and kissed him, pressing my body into his.

"Here?"

I continued kissing him, moving to his neck as I slipped my hands under his shirt, feeling his warm skin. Oh, it'd been so long since I had skin-on-skin contact. "Don't you want to?"

"God, yes, but . . . here?"

"Yes," I breathed. I slipped my hands down his ass, then brought one hand around and cupped his cock. "Here."

Finally on board, he grabbed my face, kissing me as he pushed me back to the other wall. He leaned into me, his hard body flush against mine. But when I reached for his waistband, he pulled back. "Wait. We can't."

Damn it.

"Yes, we can. Just go with it."

"You're drunk."

"So?" I managed to get the button undone. The zipper was next.

"Ian, stop," Matt said, grabbing my hands.

"What is it?"

"Look, I want you. Trust me, I do. But not like this. I want our first time to be better than in a dirty bathroom at a gay club."

"Then let's go to a hotel. There are plenty around." I reached for him again.

Once again, he stopped me. "And I want you sober, so I know this is really want you want."

"I assure you, this is what I want."

"We've been seeing each other for almost four months. You've made it clear you wanted to take things slow, and I've respected that. But now you're drunk, and suddenly, it's what you want? Come on, Ian. Something else is going on here."

"The alcohol helped loosen me up." I made a move again and kissed him. "I want you. Please—help me forget."

He pushed me back. "Help you forget what? Talk to me, Ian. What happened tonight at work?"

I straightened, clenching my jaw. The anger from earlier crept back in. "Fine." I shoved him away. "You don't want to fuck? I'll find somebody who does."

Stumbling to the door, I unlatched the lock and stormed out.

* * *

Matt

I was worried. Ian had never acted like this.

After buttoning my pants and zipping back up, I went after him, searching the crowd as I exited the bathroom.

If the sexual advance had happened any of the other handful of times we'd been to this club, where we'd each had two drinks—three, tops—I would've been all over the chance to have sex with him. Well, maybe not in the dirty stall, but I would've totally accepted the suggestion of a hotel.

Ian was a great guy. And he was hot. Especially with the beard he'd been sporting. I'd always had a thing for facial hair.

But there was something different tonight. The tequila shots were the first clue. Ian never did shots—at least, not in front of me. I should have pressed for information, but I didn't want to be that guy. We weren't even officially dating. We were just two dudes who liked hanging out, enjoyed each other's company, and kissed from time to time.

So, when I found him in the middle of the dance floor, sandwiched between two guys, bumping and grinding, I had no right to get jealous.

But I could at least keep an eye on him to make sure he didn't get hurt or taken advantage of. In his vulnerable, inebriated state, that would be easy to do in an environment full of horny, drunk men.

Things went from bad to worse when one guy gave Ian a shot glass of something—and he drank it.

Oh, hell. That couldn't be good.

I could no longer sit on the sidelines. But if I intervened, he'd probably tell me to fuck off.

Time for reinforcements. Reaching into my pocket, I whipped out my phone and called the one person Ian would listen to.

"Hi, Anna. This is Matt. Sorry for calling so late, but . . . Ian needs you."

Chapter 4

Ian

The room was spinning now for *sure.*

Weeeeee . . .

The music pulsated in my bones. No pain. Only good vibrations.

The surrounding bodies guided and supported me as I surrendered to the euphoria running through my veins. Happiness, for the first time in months. Even if it was an alcohol-induced illusion, it was better than what I'd been feeling before. I was aware it was temporary, but at least now I knew what it took to get to this level of nirvana.

Hands were on me. Pleasurable. Lips kissing me. Someone was behind me, tugging at my shirt and feeling my ass. I allowed my head to fall back onto their shoulder as lips slid to my neck. My cock, groped and rubbed.

More tugging.

And grinding.

Yelling somewhere in the distance, or so I thought. It was hard to hear over the booming bass. Everything was a blur. The flashing lights made it hard to focus.

Shoved.

Then—emptiness. No more hands. No lips. Just cold and alone. Nothing to anchor me. I stumbled forward, falling to the floor.

I crawled away from the crowd so I wouldn't get trampled. Heat consumed me. Not the good kind. Succumbing to darkness, to sleep, was enticing.

"Ian!"

Did someone call my name? Maybe I was dreaming. It didn't matter. Nothing mattered. I collapsed onto the floor, letting my eyes close. I wanted to disappear.

Hands again, turning me onto my back, slapping my face. I brushed them away. "Leave me alone," I mumbled, not sure if my words were audible.

"Ian!"

Anna? Now I knew I was dreaming. She wouldn't be here at a gay bar. Silliness.

"Ian, stop shoving my wife."

Ant? Why would Anna's husband be at a gay bar?

"Ian—Ian, wake up. We're taking you home, but you need to help us."

The words didn't make sense.

Ice-cold water. I gasped for air as I wiped at my face. Awareness made its way to the surface, and I widened my eyes. Anna, Ant, and Matt stood over me. "What—what's going on?"

"Thank God," Anna said, caressing my face. "We're taking you home. Matt and Anthony are going to lift you. You need to help them. Okay?"

I nodded but was still confused.

Strong arms hooked under my armpits as I pushed up with my legs. I did my best to walk as they led the way, my arms draped over their shoulders. And I would've fallen flat on my face had they not held me up.

The dizziness intensified. Queasy. My stomach churned. I was going to be sick.

The fresh air didn't help. As soon as the stale, muggy night air hit me, I somehow found the strength to push away from my human crutches, leap to a nearby bush, and let it all out.

* * *

A shiver ran through me as I blinked into the darkness. The jostling and low humming indicated I was in a car. How I'd ended up as a passenger in what I assumed was my SUV remained a blur. I snuggled deeper into the blanket draped over me. I was freezing my ass off, thanks to the ice water that had been dumped on me. That, I did recall.

I rolled my head to the left. Anna was driving. Ant must be following in their car. And Matt had probably gone home. Worst date ever, thanks to me.

Falling back to the right, I leaned against the window and gazed into nothingness. The car was giving me motion sickness, but I swallowed down the queasiness. I didn't want to lose it in my own car.

"How are you feeling?" Anna asked.

"Like shit," I mumbled. My voice was raspy to my ears.

"I bet," she scoffed. "There's some water here if you need it."

"I don't want to throw up in my car."

"Just say the word and I'll pull over." There was a pause. "Ian, what happened tonight?" Before I could answer, she added, "And don't you dare say nothing. This isn't you."

"Matt shouldn't have called you." He'd obviously snitched. How else would Anna have found out what was going on?

"Thank God he did!" she shouted, causing my head to pound. "That poor man was worried sick about you. He said you were doing shots with strangers and accepting unknown drinks from them?"

"I was fine."

"Oh, really? When Anthony and I got there, you were . . . surrounded by men. They were sexually assaulting you on the dance floor."

"No, they weren't. It was consensual. I wanted to let loose and have fun for once."

"That's your idea of fun?"

"They made me feel good."

"Were you aware of what was happening? Do you remember? Because you couldn't even stand on your own."

I didn't have the energy for this.

"They were taking off your clothes. They had their hands down your pants. Were you really going to have sex with strangers in public?"

"What if I was? That's my business."

"You were on a date with Matt."

"He didn't want me."

"What do you mean, he didn't want you? Matt adores you. He respects you. So I find it hard to believe he—"

"Well, it's true. He refused to give me what I wanted."

She scoffed. "Sex? *That's* what this is about? You almost fucked up your life because Matt wouldn't have sex with you?" She let out an exasperated sigh. "Talk to me, Ian. What's going on with you? Because I don't believe for one second that you got drunk off your ass only to risk your health and convictions by having sex with multiple strangers on a crowded dance floor simply because Matt rejected you. And don't get me started on the 'just letting loose' bit because—"

"I saw Jake."

She gasped. "What?"

"He came to the church during choir practice." And this was what happened when the alcohol wore off: reality reared its ugly head, and you remembered. All the pain you were trying to forget resurfaced twofold. "He wanted back on."

"Oh, Ian—"

"He just waltzed in with that smug, entitled attitude, expecting me to let him rejoin. And when I told him his spot had been filled, he stuck around and waited till after practice to talk to me like we were still friends. Like nothing happened. Like he didn't rip my heart out and stomp on it until there was nothing left." My voice shook as wetness fell from my eyes, but I was too weak to wipe it away.

"I'm so sorry," Anna whispered, placing her hand on top of mine.

"I told him I had a date, and he pulled the classic overprotective, jealous, alpha-male Jake. He tried to hide it by keeping his questions casual, but I could see right through him. Then he had the audacity to tell me I looked worn-down and accused Matt of not taking care of me. I implied we were having lots of sex, so he was taking care of me just fine." My chuckle had no humor. "Why can't he just be with Miranda and leave me the fuck alone? Why does he keep showing up in my life? Why does he keep pretending to care about me? And why do I still love him? But I also hate him. That's what tonight was about. I wanted to forget. For one night. I wanted to feel something other than pain, anger, and hatred." I took in a shaky breath and sniffled. "Why couldn't he have chosen me? Why couldn't he love me as much as he claimed to? Why couldn't I be good enough for him?"

"Okay, stop it right there. You *are* good enough. Do you hear me? Just because one guy can't see your worth doesn't mean someone else won't. Jake doesn't deserve you. He's the asshole. You did nothing wrong. And you deserve to be happy."

Anna was right, but—

"I have an idea, but you might not like it," she continued. "Talk to him. Hear him out."

"What? Why? So I can hear more of his lies?"

"You obviously have lots of questions. And he *has* tried communicating with you. He left messages pleading that you hear him out. He claimed to have an explanation for the engagement."

"Probably some elaborate lie, all to keep fucking me while promising to leave Miranda but never really following through. What he wants is a fuck buddy."

"You don't know that. Didn't you say something about her threatening him if he left her for a man?"

I refused to let my mind wander back to the night he said those words to me. The night we made lo—fucked. "Yeah, but he thought it was an empty threat. According to him, she had nothing on him."

"Well, regardless, talking to him might give you closure. You don't have to forgive him or sleep with him or even be friends with him again. But you'll be able to look him in the eye and determine if he's being truthful. And if you think he isn't, it could open an entire conversation to get to the bottom of those questions you have. Then you can move on with your life. Possibly with Matt."

I huffed. "I'm sure the Matt ship has sailed. I really blew it with him."

"I wouldn't jump to that conclusion just yet. He was genuinely concerned about you."

"Because he's a doctor. It's his job to worry about people's health."

"Don't dismiss him. He likes you a lot."

Yeah, Matt wasn't ever going to speak to me again. I sighed. "What if I fall for Jake's lies again? I hate myself enough already. I'm weak when it comes to him."

"You're stronger than you think. And you're smarter this time around. I know you can do this. The goal is to hear him out so you can move on."

She had a point. And the priest at confession *did* say forgiveness was the key to feeling better. Not that I was anywhere near there yet. "I'll think about it."

"Fair enough."

I let out a yawn as I pushed away from the window and lowered my head onto my friend's lap, against her baby bump. She ran her hand through my hair, caressing, nurturing. She was going to be a great mom in about four to five months. Wow, time was flying by. "Thanks, Anna. For being a true friend. For everything."

"Of course. You know I'm always here for you, no matter what. I love you."

My eyelids got heavier. "Love you too."

Chapter 5

Ian

My mouth felt like sandpaper. Worse—like I'd drunk salt water, then gargled with sand.

Water. I needed water.

I pulled the covers back and sat up, groaning as my brain literally moved inside my head and pounded like it had its own heartbeat.

Then my stomach gurgled—

I rushed to the bathroom, making it to the toilet just in time to heave a whole lot of nothing. And somehow it still managed to smell like tequila.

Yuck.

Never. Drinking. Again.

The toilet seat was my leverage as I pushed myself up, shuffled into the kitchen, grabbed a tall glass out of the cabinet, and filled it with water. I downed three of those, along with a couple of aspirin. Dragging myself back into the bedroom, I face-planted onto the bed and pulled the covers over my head.

The doorbell rang.

"Go away," I groaned, knowing full well no one could hear me. It rang again. Damn it.

I kicked the covers off me, glancing down at myself. All I had on were boxer briefs. Anna must've undressed me before tucking me in after she brought me home. Did I mention she was going to be a great mom? Anyway, the boxers were decent enough for early, unwelcome visitors. Maybe they'd scare them away.

I stumbled into the living room and opened the door without checking who it was first. Big mistake.

Matt.

Now would've been a good time to crawl under a rock. I'd hoped for more time before facing him. It didn't help that I was half naked. Honestly, I didn't think Matt would ever want to speak to me again.

"Hi," he said, raising his eyebrows as he gave a small smile.

"Hi." For lack of a better response.

"Can I come in?" He kept his bright blue eyes fixated on mine, almost like he was forcing himself not to look down at my undies. But he was a doctor, so he was used to seeing patients with less on.

"Yeah, of course. Please—come in."

As he stepped inside, he said, "I was on my way to the hospital and thought I'd stop by to see how you're feeling."

"Like shit. And not just because of the hangover."

He pressed his lips together, lowering his lids.

I gestured to the couch. "Have a seat. I'll get some clothes on." Rushing into the bedroom, I threw on the first T-shirt I found and slipped on a pair of sweatpants. When I returned, Matt was sitting with his elbows on his knees. "Can I get you anything? Water, coffee?"

"No, I'm good. Thanks."

I swallowed as I sat next to him. The silence stretched between us until I figured I should be the one to speak. "Matt, I'm so sorry about last night."

He shook his head. "It's all right."

"No, it's not. I was rude to you. We were on a date and I . . . I'm so embarrassed. I'm surprised you're even speaking to me right now."

"It's my fault."

My brows scrunched together. "What? How?"

"I knew there was something up with you the moment you ordered those shots. I should have insisted you talk to me."

"No, don't do that. None of this is your fault."

"And I'm a doctor. I saw you drinking back-to-back shots and did nothing to stop you. I saw those guys pour drinks down your throat and did nothing."

"You did do something. You called Anna. And I thank you for that."

His eyes glistened. "Ian, I swear, you were just dancing with those men up till the moment Anna and her husband showed up. That's when they—I ran over and fought them off the best I could. Anthony helped, but . . . I'm so sorry."

"Hey, it's okay. It all worked out, thank God. I mean, I knew what they were doing. I wanted it."

"You wanted it? Do you realize what they were doing to you?"

"They weren't assaulting me. It was consensual. I wanted to feel good, so I let them."

Matt looked incredulous. "You can't give consent if they drug you."

I hesitated. "You're right. It was stupid. At the time, I thought it was what I needed. But I'm thankful you put a stop to it."

"Why? What happened that made you want that? Was it something I did? Was it because of what happened in the bathroom? I'm sorry about that, by the way. I just didn't want to take advantage of you in that state."

I shook my head. "It has nothing to do with you." I paused and took a deep breath. "Jake came to choir practice last night. Seeing him again triggered me. It's no excuse for how I treated you. I should have opened up to you about it, but instead I took my frustrations out on myself."

"Wow," he huffed. "All because of your ex?"

"I'm sorry. You know how hard his betrayal has been for me. I've been clear from the beginning."

He nodded as he crossed his arms over his chest. "Yeah, I know. What did he want?"

"To rejoin choir. But I told him there was no room for him."

"Did he say anything else?"

"He wanted to talk about something, but I didn't want to hear it. I told him I had a date."

"You told him about me?"

"I didn't tell him who you were. He asked questions, but it was none of his business."

He sighed. "You have to talk to him."

"What?"

"It's been months, and he still has a hold on you. You need to get to the bottom of all this. Get some closure."

"That's exactly what Anna said."

"Well, I agree. It's the only way you'll move on from this." He lifted his hand to my cheek. "I really like you, Ian. I've been so patient. But you'll never be ready for a real relationship until you resolve this thing with Jake. And frankly, I can't be with someone who is this hung up on someone else. Not until it's completely over. And things are clearly not over between you and Jake."

I nodded. "I'm so sorry, Matt. I feel like I've led you on and wasted your time."

"Don't be sorry. It wasn't a waste of time for me. We had some great times, and I really enjoyed getting to know you. If nothing else, I hope to have at least gained a friend."

"You would want to be friends with me, after everything I've put you through?"

"Sure. I'd like to think we are kinda friends already."

"We are. For sure. I'm just surprised you're still talking to me."

"Hey, I've been hung up on exes before. I know what it's like.

And who knows, maybe in the future, after you deal with Jake and get closure, you'll be ready for something more with me. Until then, I'm here for you. As a friend."

I sniffled. "You are incredible. I don't deserve you."

"Oh, stop." He put his arm around me, pulling me close. "You deserve the world."

"Whoever ends up with you is going to be one lucky guy."

He chuckled. "Maybe that'll be you someday."

I smiled sadly. "Just don't put your life on hold for me, okay? I don't know if I'll ever be ready."

Chapter 6

Jake

I couldn't remember the last time I'd paid my old man a visit at work.

It was time I checked in.

The secretary informed me that Daddy dearest was in a meeting, so I waited in his office. Plopped myself in his chair and stretched out my legs onto the desk. The office space was just as plain and boring as the job title he held: Senior Financial Adviser. *Yawn.*

At least the place was well equipped with a large desk, a small couch, a couple of chairs, a bookshelf, and a large window with a view—perhaps to jump out of when things got too boring. No wonder he went into the drug business. One might think it was for the money, but I bet it was for the excitement.

To be honest, I probably would have turned the other cheek to his side hustle, had it not been for Miranda blackmailing me into marrying her. Yeah, over my dead body. But she somehow found out my dad was embezzling from his company to sell drugs to other businesspeople, then pocketing a hefty profit for himself. Sneaky bastard. So it was either marry her or she'd turn him in.

I'd given Dad plenty of opportunities to either turn himself in or quit so that Miranda had nothing on us. But to date . . . *nada.*

My patience had ended.

The glass door swooshed open, and my father entered, pausing when he spotted me. "Son, what a surprise."

"Hello, Father. Why so out of breath? Did you take up running?"

He closed the door and chuckled softly. "When my secretary told me you were here, I couldn't believe it. I had to see for myself."

"Why couldn't you believe I was here?"

"Well, because you never visit me at the office." He came closer, setting his briefcase on top of the desk. "To what do I owe this pleasure?"

"C'mon, Dad. You know why I'm here."

"I'm sorry. Did we have a lunch date I forgot about?"

I swung my legs down and stood. "I want an update."

"Update? Sorry, I still don't follow."

"With the drugs, Dad."

His head whipped to the door, palms up. "Lower your voice. Are you insane?"

"It's been almost five months, and nothing has changed. Mom is still oblivious, you're still working here and not in jail, and I'm still stuck with Miranda."

"Honestly, I thought you let that go. I mean, we just had dinner a couple of weeks ago, and you two seemed happy."

Was he blind? I narrowed my eyes. "Do I fucking look happy? Man, either your standards for good acting are really low, or you're not paying attention."

"Jacob, I don't understand what you want me to do. Do you want me to go to prison? Because that's what it sounds like."

"That's not what I want. But marrying Miranda, being in that goddamn house with her, is like being in prison. And it has locked me up long enough. It's your turn now."

"You don't mean that. Think of your mother."

"I am. She's the only reason I haven't gone to the cops myself. But I'll take care of her. You just need to do the right thing."

"Which is what exactly?"

"Stop doing what you're doing so Miranda won't have anything on you anymore."

"It's not that simple. Even if I stop now, she'll still have proof of my prior dealings."

"Turn yourself in, then. Cut a deal."

He laughed dryly. "You watch too many movies. And frankly, we should not be discussing this here."

I walked around the desk and stood face-to-face with the man I was slowly losing respect for. "Dad, I came here as a courtesy to let you know I'm leaving Miranda. I gave you five months to rectify this situation, and you've done nothing. Whatever she decides to do with the info she has once I break up with her is not my problem. I'm done. This is your mess. Deal with it."

I moved past him, but he caught my arm before I could get to the door. "Son, wait. Please—give me a little more time to sort this out. Now that I know how important this is to you, I want to work this out."

It figured; he hadn't taken me seriously. I snatched my arm from his grasp. "One week, William. I'll give you one more week. That's it."

"I'll need more time than—"

"One week!" I shouted. "You had five months. Too bad if you didn't take me seriously before. You have one more week. And regardless of what you've accomplished, I'm breaking up with Miranda."

I pulled the door open and stormed out.

Chapter 7

Ian

Jake had to be behind this.

It was too much of a coincidence that just two days after he showed up out of the blue, Father Kevin sent me an email, requesting a meeting. The jerk had obviously spoken to the priest about getting his spot back. And it was my fault for suggesting he talk to him.

As I gathered my belongings, I made a mental note of all the reasons I would supply to Father Kevin as to why Jake couldn't rejoin choir. Sure, some may have been overexaggerated, but still. Working with Jake again was not an option.

I couldn't.

It was one thing to work up the courage to hear him out and possibly forgive him for the sake of my own well-being, and it was a whole other ball game to see him every week, twice a week. For my sanity's sake, I couldn't handle that.

Why the hell did Jake want to do choir, anyway? It was most likely an excuse to weasel his way back into my life. Back into my bed.

If that were the case, he was in for a rude awakening. Never again. That ship had sailed and sank.

I'd promised Anna and Matt that I would hear Jake's excuses eventually, but that did not include allowing him back on choir.

Tossing my satchel over my shoulder, I marched across the parking lot toward the rectory like I was heading into battle. If I had to air out my personal laundry to Father Kevin, then so be it.

I let myself in and bore right, heading down the stairs that led to the offices. Rosemary, the church secretary, was sitting at her desk and smiled when she saw me. "Good afternoon, Ian."

"Hi, Rosemary. I'm here to see Father Kevin."

"Oh, yes. He had to step out for a few minutes, but you can wait in his office. He shouldn't be too long."

"Thank you." I went over to the office that used to be Anthony's, opened the door, and—

My heart lodged into my stomach.

Jake stood against the far wall, looking at his phone. He lifted his head at my gasp.

It hadn't occurred to me he'd be present at the meeting. I swallowed back my shock and narrowed my eyes. "What the hell are you doing here?"

He lowered his phone as he pushed off from the wall. "Father Kevin wanted to see me."

"I knew it. I knew you were behind this." I shut the door so Rosemary wouldn't hear the choice words I had for the jackass.

"Hey, all I did was speak with Father Kev like you told me to."

"Of course you did. You just had to go tattle."

"Tattle? What are we, in second grade?"

So like him to make a joke. "Why do you even want to be in choir?"

"Because I enjoy singing."

"Then go to a different church. Why do you have to sing here? At my church?"

"It's my church too. And if you want to get technical about it, it was mine first."

"Now who's in second grade?"

"You started it."

I straightened, staring him down. Back in the day, I would have laughed at our banter, but now I wanted to smack that smirk from his face.

He pressed the corner of his lips together. "Look, I like this choir. I know the way things are done. And no one beats your style of directing."

The compliment was unexpected. But I refused to get sucked in by his charm. "There are other directors out there who are just as good, if not better."

"Doubt it. But let me ask you—why don't you want me here, huh? You say you've moved on. You're dating some other guy now. So, what's the big deal?"

What's the big deal? Did he really . . . ? Where shall I begin?

My jaw clenched, fighting the urge to spew out all the venom he had produced. On an impulse, I closed the distance between us, intending to tell him to fuck off, but he flinched like he thought I would hit him. Made sense, considering I did punch him once. He stood straighter, meeting me eye to eye.

Getting this close to him was a mistake. But I couldn't waver. Otherwise, it'd look like I still had feelings for him.

God forbid. I refused to give him that satisfaction.

Masking any inner revelations, I hardened my expression. "You are a liar and a traitor. And I don't want you here."

He blinked, then inched closer. "Are you sure about that?"

I should have moved away. But as usual, I was under his spell. My eyes lowered to his mouth. Memories of where those lips had been flooded my mind, spreading warmth throughout my body. Goddamn him for still having this effect on me.

This was why I couldn't work with him.

Those lips seemed to move closer, and just when I thought he would make a move to kiss me, the door swung open. I jumped away.

"Oh, good. You boys are still here," Father Kevin said as he closed the door behind him and went to the desk. "Sorry to have kept you waiting. My errand took longer than expected."

I focused on cooling down while regathering my thoughts. Jake would not rattle me.

"So," Father Kevin began. "Ian, Jake has expressed to me his interest in returning to choir. He says he had to take a leave of absence for personal reasons."

I smirked. Personal reasons? "Father, Jake has missed a lot. I don't think it would be wise to bring him back in."

"Oh? But you have people coming and going all the time. I'm sure he'll catch on. Besides, he's been a member for a long time. Surely these last few months he missed shouldn't matter too much."

I had to say something drastic. "With all due respect, Father, I do not want him on my choir for personal reasons."

"Oh, dear. I thought you two were close friends."

"So did I. But the devil disguises himself well, Father."

"Ian, come on," Jake muttered.

I cranked my head over to him. "Just being honest. Unlike some people in this room."

"I've tried being honest, to explain, but you won't let me."

"The time to be honest was before you f—"

"Ian!" Jake cut me off, reminding me where we were.

Yup. That was how messed up in the head Jake made me. *The time to be honest was before you fucked me.* I almost voiced those words in front of a priest.

Jake came closer. "For the record, I was honest up to when I went home that night. I've always been honest about—"

I stood straighter. "I'm not doing this right now. This isn't the time or place."

"Then when?"

"All right, boys, that's enough," Father Kevin scolded. "You obviously have some issues to work out, which is unfortunate, considering what I have to ask of you."

I didn't like the sound of that. "What is it, Father?"

"I want the both of you to play a piano/guitar duet for this year's Christmas program."

My mouth gaped. "What?" That was worse than having Jake rejoin choir.

"Ian, you would help me out tremendously. I'm swamped with my workload plus Anthony's daily tasks. I don't have time to find anyone else. You are the music director of this parish. You should be able to make this happen."

"But that would mean extra practice." And tons of alone time . . . with Jake.

"Yes. I know you can do it. You can use the piano that's in the church hall, but you'll have to coordinate with the other activities going on. The church is always quite busy in the weeks leading up to Christmas. It might be easier to use your own piano."

"My piano? You mean—the one at my house? Are you suggesting I hold practice inside my home? With *him*?"

Father Kevin shrugged, smiling apologetically.

I whipped my head back to Jake. He hadn't uttered a word since this nightmarish request was spawned upon us.

Holy crap. The guy had an amused look on his face. "This is your doing, isn't it?"

He twisted his face. "What? No!"

"I assure you," Father Keven piped in, "Jake had nothing to do with this. This has been brewing in my mind for quite some time. You two are talented, work well together, have a history together, and I know you've played together in the past. All deciding factors, in my book. So, if you two can somehow put your differences aside, you'd be lifesavers."

I'd been placed between a rock and a hard place. If I refused, I'd be the asshole who couldn't play well with others at work. Defeated, I had no choice but to attempt professionalism. "Fine. But I'm only doing this for you, Father."

"Oh, God bless you. Jake? I take it you're fine with this?"

"Yes, of course, Father."

"Oh, heavens, thank you both so much!"

"Does this mean I'm back on choir?"

I snatched up my bag. "Whatever. But since you missed this week's practice, it won't matter if you come on Sunday or not."

"I'll be there."

Of course he would. I shrugged. "I'll let you know about the duet practice. Father, send me the details about the program."

"Will do. Thanks again, Ian."

With a stern nod, I turned and hauled my ass out of there.

Chapter 8

Matt

I was a sucker.

How had I let Ian rope me into this? It must've been his electric-blue eyes. No question. And that fucking beard he'd grown out over the past few months.

When would I learn to say no to cute men with facial hair?

But I owed him. After the club catastrophe a few nights ago, I'd promised I would support him as a friend, and I meant it.

Well, as it turned out, the first thing on the agenda was attending Mass. As his fake boyfriend.

It was Ian's way of getting answers from the ex—by making him jealous.

Wonderful.

To be fair, Ian had wanted to come out at his place of employment for quite some time now. He just didn't know how to go about it without making it a big deal. That was where I came in. Happy to oblige.

But of all places to work, why a church?

I hadn't stepped into a place of worship since I was sixteen years old. Yeah, things didn't go so well for me when I came out—or rather, when I got discovered. But that was another story for a different time.

My only fear was that I'd combust into flames once stepping inside.

Not much I could do about that. I sucked it up and took a deep breath as I stepped out of my Lexus. Nice and steady.

An usher held the door open. "Good morning. Welcome," the guy said, extending a pamphlet out for me.

I took it cautiously, like the thing would bite me. Ridiculous, I know. "Thank you." I passed the threshold, entering at last. No flames. But this was only the atrium. I still had to get to the actual congregation part.

Memories flooded my brain as the smell of incense hit me, memories I'd worked hard to forget. I blinked them away as I attempted to control my heart rate and continued forward. Music played—Ian, no doubt. At the entrance, it was confirmed; Ian sat behind the organ. The song he performed was calming. It almost made me forget where I was.

He lifted his head and glanced my way, smiling when he spotted me. I smiled back and waited awkwardly, not sure if I should find a seat or what. Bursting into flames was still a viable threat.

Ian must've noted my hesitation because he finished up the tune and came over. "Hey, you made it," he said, hugging me.

"Hi. Yeah, um, I wasn't sure if I should sit or if you wanted me somewhere specific or—"

"Are you nervous?"

"A little, but not because of you. I just—"

"I know. Your fear of churches."

"Yeah, bad experience."

"Well, don't worry. Everyone is friendly here."

"I'm worried about catching on fire."

He laughed. "I haven't burst into flames. I think you'll be fine."

If he only knew. I'd never told him the whole story of why churches and I didn't mix; we'd never got that deep into it. All he knew was they didn't accept that I was gay. And that was putting it mildly.

"Thanks again for doing this. I owe you one."

I drew my brows together. "No, this is me making it up to you, remember? You don't owe me anything."

Ian rolled his eyes. "I told you, that night wasn't your fault."

"And I told you I feel responsible. Nothing you say will change my mind."

He shook his head. "Well, thanks again. I really appreciate this."

"It's my pleasure. Does this mean we get to kiss in front of everyone?"

Ian's cheeks turned pink as he chuckled. "Let's keep it PG to start." His smile faded as his gaze lingered on something over my shoulder. I turned.

Ah, the ex. I recognized him from the hospital I worked at. The guy had just walked into the atrium with a tall blonde by his side. His eyes landed on Ian, then me. His jaw clenched.

Let the party begin.

"Are you okay?" I asked.

Ian shrugged, glancing back at me. "Yeah. Are you ready? I'll walk you to your seat."

"Ready when you are. Should we hold hands? How do you want to do this?"

Instead of answering with words, he took my hand and led me down the aisle. Eyes followed us as we passed the pews, which I was used to. People always stared. Some judged; some supported. It was whatever.

We stopped at the third row on the left, the side the organ was on, and I slipped inside. "This is great. I have a perfect view of you."

Ian smiled, blushing again. "And look—no flames."

"Yet. The service is not over. There's still time."

He laughed, shaking his head. "I'll talk to you after and introduce you to the choir."

"Okay. Sounds good."

His hand stroked my arm as he leaned forward, giving me a quick kiss on the cheek. Then he headed back the way we came from, back toward the atrium.

I glanced at the massive crucifix hanging behind the altar. Maybe if I remained perfectly still, God wouldn't notice me.

* * *

Ian

I smiled at those who eyed me as I made my way toward the atrium to huddle with the choir. I'd expected it, and I didn't mind. Although I hadn't intentionally hid that I was gay, I'd never been open about it, either, at least not at the church. It was time I changed that.

The choir members were no different. Their eyes were glued to me as I approached them, and not in a "What's on the agenda, boss?" kind of way. Ignoring the scrutinizing stares, I proceeded like normal. "Any questions before we begin?"

"Is that a friend of yours?" someone asked.

Here we go. "Oh, you mean Matt? He's more than a friend. I was planning on introducing him to you guys after mass."

A moment of silence. Then: "I didn't know you were—why didn't you tell us?"

"You never asked."

Someone else said, "But you don't act gay."

"How are gay people supposed to act?" Maybe I'd missed the memo on proper gay protocol.

"I don't know. Flamboyant?"

Jake smacked the guy on the back of the head. "Don't be a dumbass. And stop stereotyping. Not all gays are the same."

Before I could acknowledge Jake's support, someone else spoke up. "So that guy was right."

"What guy?"

"The one a few months back. The one Jake got in a fight with."

My eyes shot to Jake, who jerked to attention. Anna's ex-fiancé, Phillip, had come causing trouble, and Jake had put him in his place, a result of the beating Phillip had given me. Jake had stuck up for me. What a joke. Another lie. I didn't understand why he would do that if he had been using me, unless the sex was just that good.

Patting myself on the back.

"Oh, yeah," another person said. "I remember that. He insinuated Ian and Jake were involved." They laughed, along with some others.

"Why the fuck is that so funny?" Jake snapped.

"Because—come on, you and Ian? Ian, I can kinda see, but you? No way you're gay." There was a pause. "Wait—are you?"

"Of course he's not," I answered before Jake said something stupid. "He's engaged to Miranda, remember?" I ignored the unreadable look Jake gave me. "Now, let's get back to the topic at hand. Does anyone have any questions that don't have to do with my personal life?"

"Yeah," Jake answered. "Where do you want me?" His voice was rough. I couldn't tell if he was angry or bored.

How about anywhere else but here? "In your usual spot. Just sing the songs you know in your normal range. For the songs you haven't practiced with us, just lip sync. Or stand there. I really don't care."

Father Kevin came over, interrupting our staring contest. "Are you ready? It's about time to begin."

"Yes, Father," I replied and turned to my choir. "Okay, I'll see you out there. Let's do this."

* * *

Jake

I wanted to puke.

But God, not until after mass. Purging in front of the whole congregation, especially in front of Ian's new beau, would be humiliating, to say the least.

He fucking brought the guy to church.

Church.

That meant it must be serious. What kind of fucked-up shit was that?

I'd finally grown a pair to call it quits with Miranda so I could be with Ian, and now it might be too late. This was supposed to be our gig, coming out at church together.

I had been Ian's first for everything. First BFF, first jerk-off partner, first to come out to, first boy kiss, first blow job, first boy fuck. I wanted to be his first in this too. First public boyfriend.

Fuck.

And the only thing preventing me from going across the aisle and beating the shit out of the boyfriend was my love for Ian.

How fucking ironic.

I barely sang, not even the ones I knew. The only thing I could do was sit there watching Ian and the new guy make googly eyes at each other. Well, maybe not googly eyes, but they kept smiling at each other, and I swore there was some winking involved.

The worst part was the boyfriend wasn't that bad-looking. He had dirty blonde, almost light brown hair, which was short but longer on top. He was slim built, about the same height as Ian. Not sure what his eye color was. And he wore a suit. Hard to tell if he was a suit guy like Ian, or if he'd just dressed up for church like me. Yeah, suits were not my thing; jeans and tees were more my cup of tea. But Ian dressed to kill, and he always looked hot.

Speaking of hot, this guy might be good-looking, but Ian was way hotter. No one could beat his shade of blue eyes and dark hair . . . those curls . . .

Fuck. The bastard now had dibs on running his fingers through Ian's soft curls. He got to kiss him whenever and—did someone shut the AC off?

I pulled on my shirt collar as I fought the heat of nausea threatening to explode. Making things right with Ian was more crucial than ever. If only he would hear me out.

I had been ready to spill the truth when the kid on choir asked if I was gay—or at least a "what if I were" retort. But Ian had denied me that chance. Either he was protecting me, or he was scared I would really go through with it.

I hadn't officially left Miranda yet, hence the reason we'd showed up together. I wanted to give my father time to react after my last visit. So far, no.

Ian belonged by my side—*on* my side—when my father went down. Call it moral support or whatever. I just couldn't do this alone anymore. I missed my best friend. My lover. The man I loved.

Communion time already. Mass flew by, thank God.

Looked like Lover Boy chose not to receive communion. Was he even Catholic? Where'd Ian find this clown?

As soon as Mass ended, I beelined to the sacristy and changed out of my choir robe. Thankfully, the bile in my stomach had settled, and the urge to throw up subsided.

Scratch that.

It came back . . . twofold.

In the atrium, Ian was introducing the guy to Father Kevin and some choir members. Everyone was friendly with him, shaking his hand and smiling.

"So, what do you do, Matt?" Father Kevin asked.

"I'm a doctor at Mercy Grace Hospital," Matt replied.

A fucking doctor?

Wait. Recognition slapped me in the face. Mercy Grace was where everything had gone down. Anna had been taken there when a crazy bitch who had been obsessed with Ant shot her. Also, Miranda had announced our bogus engagement, shattering what Ian and I had. The bastard doctor had witnessed Ian punching me and taken advantage of our falling-out.

Asshole.

"Well, well, well," Miranda said from behind me. "I guess he is a homosexual, after all. And looks like he's moved on rather nicely. A doctor? My, my. I think that trumps a teacher and half-assed musician combined, don't you?"

I glanced back at her. "Go to hell."

She stepped closer. "Lower your voice if you know what's best."

"Who's got more to lose here, huh? We're at church, remember? Surrounded by all of your friends."

"Exactly. Do you really want them to know about your father's side business?"

"And do you really want them to know about me? Because I have no problem admitting who I'm actually in love with."

She narrowed her eyes. "You wouldn't dare."

"Try me."

She clenched her jaw. "I'm going to say hi to Lizzy. I'll meet you outside, *honeybun.*"

As she turned to leave, I grabbed her wrist. "Don't fucking call me that anymore."

Yanking her arm from my grasp, she stepped back and stormed away. I turned back to my view and froze.

Ian was looking at me dead-on. Did he witness the exchange with Miranda?

If he had, good. Now maybe he would see things weren't as peachy as they appeared.

The group surrounding them had dissipated. Ian shook his head as he placed his hand on the small of Matt's back and led him toward the doors.

"Ian, wait," I called and caught up to them.

He turned and waited. "What is it, Jake?"

"Can I speak to you a sec?" I glanced at Matt. Eyes, blue. Not as bold as Ian's, more like a sky blue. "Alone."

He hesitated, then faced Matt. "Do you mind waiting for me outside?"

"Are you sure you want me to go?"

Who in the holy fuck did this asshole think he was? Ian did not need protecting from me.

I instinctually moved forward, intending to tell him to mind his fucking business, but Ian's arm came up, blocking me. Like he'd predicted my move. He knew me so well.

"I'll be fine," Ian told him. "This won't take long."

Matt nodded, pausing as he glanced my way, like he was contemplating his next move. Then the motherfucker leaned in and kissed Ian. On the fucking mouth! Not a face-sucking, tongue-down-the-throat kiss, but a soft, dignified, lip-on-lip kiss. Still—a kiss was a fucking kiss.

The guy had a death wish.

I burned to tear the fucker's face apart. But that would not get me brownie points with Ian. The struggle for restraint was real.

When the dead man walking finally left, Ian crossed his arms. "What is it you want to speak to me about?"

It took a moment for my blood pressure to return to normal. I cleared my throat, buying time, and mentally bleached out the image of Ian and Matt locking lips from my head. "I, uh—I wanted to ask about the Christmas program. Did you decide when and where our first rehearsal will be?"

Ian sighed, shaking his head. "That's what you wanted to say? You couldn't ask that in front of Matt?"

I shrugged. "I didn't know if he knew about us having to work together."

"Of course he knows. I don't keep secrets from him."

I quirked a brow. "Really? So he knows about us?"

He stood straighter as his eyes narrowed. "There is no *us*. But yeah, he knows about you. And everything you did. In fact, he was there when I knocked you on your ass. He was rather impressed."

"Who wouldn't be? Heck, I was impressed."

He blinked like he hadn't expected the compliment. "Yeah, well, he checked my hand to make sure it wasn't broken."

So, Matty boy did take advantage of the situation. I ground my teeth together, not wanting to say something to piss him off. "Was it? Broken?"

"Nope."

"Good. I'm glad."

He glanced away. "Tomorrow night. My place. Seven o'clock. Don't be late." He walked away.

I grinned.

Chapter 9

Matt

Family dinners.

Every Sunday, pending the on-call work schedule, I would go to my parents' house for dinner. Tonight was a little different.

I had planned to invite Ian to meet the fam. When my parents and older brother found out I was seeing someone, they'd insisted on meeting him, even though I had explained it wasn't serious. But then Ian's club breakdown happened. And I was once again deep in the single life.

I could've invited him anyway. We were still friends, and I did him a favor by attending Mass and pretending to be his boyfriend. But it was better to sever any expectations now before introducing him to my family.

Lesson learned: never get involved with a guy still hung up on his ex. The realist in me knew that regardless of having told Ian that maybe we'd have a future together after he found closure, it would never happen. Who were we kidding? Ian and Jake were going to end up back together. Just being in the same room as them, I felt the sexual tension looming between the pair. Sure, a lot of hostility and unfinished business, but also attraction—and yeah, I'd go out on a limb and say love was evident.

I was rooting for them. Really. Ian deserved to be happy. But that didn't make our breakup any less difficult. And side note: that kiss I'd given him was meant to trigger Jake into action. He had to move his ass; otherwise, he'd lose a great man for good.

Stepping out of my Lexus, I walked the path to the front door, smelling the aroma of my mother's cooking and the gas from the grill my dad was firing up.

"Hey, little bro." My brother, Luke, had answered the door. "About time you got here. Were you too busy sucking face with—" He stuck his head out, looking left, then right. "Where's the guy you've been seeing? Weren't you supposed to bring him?"

I pushed past him. "I don't want to talk about it."

"And what's with the suit? Did someone die?"

"Don't want to talk about that either," I mumbled as I entered the kitchen and caught my parents in an embrace.

I'd love to have what my parents had. Married forty-some years and still very much in love. There was time, considering I was only thirty, but . . . I was already *thirty*. And not getting any younger.

"Matthew, darling," my mother greeted as she came over to hug and kiss me.

"Hi, Mom. Sorry I'm late. I had this . . . thing. Hi, Pop."

My dad came over and hugged me as well. "Glad you could join us, sport."

"Where's this boyfriend of yours you've been talking about? I'm dying to meet him," Mom asked.

I was lucky to have the support of my parents, but it hadn't always been peaches and rainbows. There was a rough patch there at the beginning, especially with Dad. To be fair, the way I was outed could take credit for that. Yeah, my churchphobia was related to it. And no, I didn't want to talk about it.

"He couldn't make it."

"Did he dump your sorry ass?" Luke asked as he popped a cherry tomato into his mouth.

"Luke, language," Mom scolded.

"No, he didn't dump me. We weren't even dating."

"Could've fooled me. You talked about him constantly and were always doing stuff together."

"We were getting to know each other, taking things slow. But it wasn't working out. So we ended things."

There was a mutual *aww* from my parents. "Oh, honey, I'm sorry," Mom said. "But there are other fish in the sea."

"I know, Mom. It's fine. Really. I'm okay. Besides, we're still friends, so it's all good."

She rubbed my cheeks. "My sweet boy. The right man will come along. I mean, look at you. So handsome. Anyone would be lucky to have you."

"Stop making a big deal of this. I'm fine. I don't really have time for relationships, anyway. I'm in no rush." I stepped away from my mother's coddling. "Why don't you fuss over Luke like this?"

My brother straightened. "Oh no you don't. Don't flip the table on me. You're long-term relationship material. I'm not. Hashtag-single-life all the way, baby."

"That's why," my father muttered, shaking his head.

Mom pointed a finger at Luke. "You just wait. A girl will come along when you least expect it and sweep you right off your feet."

He laughed. "Yeah, right. These feet are firmly planted, Mother. No woman is capable of sweeping them. Get used to having a bachelor son for the rest of your days." There were more protests from our parents, and he turned to me. "Hey, why don't you explain to Mom and Pop why you're in a suit?" He gave an evil grin.

I narrowed my eyes.

My parents turned to me. "Why are you all dressed up, honey?" Mom gasped. "Is it because you wanted to impress that young man you were seeing?"

Well, that was half the truth. "No," I sighed—and dropped the bomb. "I went to church." I opened the fridge to grab a soda as silence followed. "I stopped by the hospital after to check on some patients, then came straight here. So, I didn't have time to—" I turned, and everyone was staring at me.

"And you're still alive?" Luke asked. "I mean, no flames?"

I put my arms out. "Nope. I survived."

"Why the hell would you go back to a *church*?" Pop spat out the word *church* like it was profanity.

"I was doing a favor for a friend."

"What kind of friend would make you go—"

"Pop, it's not a big deal, okay? It was for Ian. He's the music director there and asked me to go, so I went."

Luke guffawed. "Boy, you are whipped. You must have it bad for this guy if you were willing to go to church for him."

"No, it's not like that. Look, I owed him a favor and he collected. That's it. Now we're even. And it's over."

"That's some favor—"

"Can we not talk about it anymore, please? Are we going to eat? I'm starving."

"Of course, honey. Your dad will get started on the burgers now."

Pop took her signal and moved to the back patio while she finished in the kitchen. Luke came over to me, draping an arm over my shoulders. "You know what you need, little bro?" he said in a low voice. "Sex. Lots of unadulterated, dirty, unattached sex."

I side-eyed him. "Really." It wasn't a question. Sleeping around was more Luke's style, not mine. But now that I thought about it, it *had* been a while. I couldn't even remember the last time I rubbed one out. Boy, I must be overworked. Maybe I should make a date with my hand and some lube. And possibly a dildo.

"Yeah. You know, they have these dating apps. You download them on your phone and specify what you're looking for. Relationship, friendship, casual—"

I shrugged him off. "Stop. I know about those apps. One-night stands aren't my thing."

"And that, young Matthew, is exactly why you need to get laid."

"Shut up." I walked to the sliding door.

"Hey, I can give you money for condoms if they're not paying you enough at the hospital. Can't you swipe some for free?"

I flipped him off and joined my dad outside.

Chapter 10

Jake

Finally: the end of the school day.

Just two guitar lessons to give, then it'd be time to head to Ian's house. To say I was excited was an understatement, but I was nervous too.

As I swung my satchel over my head and secured my guitar case onto my back, I reminded myself to keep it cool with the expectations. Ian was obviously still royally pissed at me. I only hoped these private rehearsals would help break the ice between us, a way of getting my foot into the door of his life, which would lead to him hearing me out and possibly forgiving me.

I waved at the secretary as I passed the main office and headed outside. As I walked across campus toward the teachers' parking lot, I noticed a pregnant woman standing by my motorcycle. My steps slowed when I realized who it was.

"Hey, Anna. Wow, you look amazing." It'd been a minute since I'd seen her—since the hospital, to be exact. Her baby bump was now noticeable.

Well, duh. It had been like five months.

She gave a small smile. "Thank you, Jake."

"Were you looking for Ant? I think he left already, but I can check." I had helped her husband get a job at the school after he'd left the priesthood. He worked as a school counselor and religion teacher.

"No, I was waiting for you, actually."

Something in her tone and the way she glared at me told me I was in trouble. And my guess was it had to do with Ian. I was surprised she hadn't paid me a visit sooner. "Okay. What's up?"

"As much as I appreciate what you've done for my husband, you and I still have unfinished business." I nodded, waiting for her to continue. "You need to let Ian go."

My heart sank. "What?"

"What you did to him was a low blow. Enough is enough. You need to stop playing games and be honest with him."

"I'm not playing games. I've tried talking to him, but he won't listen. I mean, I'm sure he's told you I've called him, left voicemails and texts—I even went to his house a few times. He wouldn't answer the door."

"Well, try harder. You need to tell him why you hurt him so he can have closure. And be honest. Then you need to leave him alone."

"Look, I plan on telling him everything, but whether he wants me out of his life will be up to him, not you."

"You're engaged, Jake! You'll be a married man soon. Stop trying to make him your secret lover."

"That's not—"

"You weren't there. You destroyed him, Jake. You broke him with your lies and betrayal. I'm the one who was there for him. I watched him suffer, and I helped him pick up the pieces of himself and put them back together, little by little. He's finally moving on. He met someone who is worthy. Who has been nothing but patient and kind. He was in a good place until you showed up again. And just like that . . . all those months of lifting him up vanished."

"What are you talking about? He seemed fine at church yesterday with his perfect doctor boyfriend."

She shook her head, letting out a dry laugh. "Things aren't always what they seem." She sighed. "He'd kill me for telling you this, but that night you showed up at choir practice, he had a complete meltdown."

"He said he had a date."

"Yeah, he did. They went to this club and—well, let's just say he had way too much to drink. Matt ended up calling me because Ian was out of control. By the time Anthony and I got there, he was on the floor. We had to drag him out of there. He was in really bad shape."

The self-hatred just kept growing. My vision blurred with unshed tears. I hated the doctor even more. Why hadn't he protected him? "I'm sorry," I said. I couldn't think of anything better to say.

"I'm not telling you this to be sorry. I'm telling you so you're aware of the damage you cause Ian. You need to be honest with him, even if the truth hurts him."

"The truth isn't what you think." She gave me a look like she didn't believe me. "You're right about one thing: things aren't always what they seem. All of this has an explanation, and I plan on telling Ian everything. Once I do, if he chooses not to believe me and wants nothing to do with me, I'll leave. For good." Because if I couldn't have Ian's forgiveness or the man himself, then I had to move someplace else. I had already determined I couldn't stand by and watch him form a life with someone else. "I promise."

After a pause, she closed her eyes and nodded. "Okay. That's all I needed to hear. I hope you'll honor your word this time."

As she turned to leave, I called out to her, "I do love him, Anna. More than my life."

"Enough to let him go?"

I hesitated maybe a little too long. Then—fuck that. I closed the distance between us. "If it comes down to that and he truly doesn't want me, I'll walk away. But I love him too much not to fight for him. I did nothing wrong except let myself get bullied. And I'll be damned if I lose the love of my life over a misunderstanding. I'm done being bullied, even by well-meaning friends such as you. I will not give up on him. Ever."

I turned to my bike, put on my helmet, and took off. There might've been a small smile on Anna's face. Or I could've been seeing things.

Chapter 11

Ian

This was a bad idea.

I glanced at my watch for the hundredth time. The closer it got to seven o'clock, the more nervous I became. Something familiar stirred in my stomach. Butterflies? Hell no. I refused to admit those critters were back, especially because of Jake. The feeling was more likely me about to lose my dinner.

Yeah, that made more sense.

I couldn't wait to get this over with. All I had to do was stick to work.

Simple.

As I glanced at my watch one more time, I heard the distinct engine of a motorcycle approaching.

Of course he'd be on time.

I gripped the edge of the kitchen countertop and waited, listening as the bike's motor cut off. Then, alas, the doorbell rang.

And I didn't move.

Was not answering the door an option? Jake would eventually take the hint and leave. I could always say I went out with Matt and forgot about rehearsal. But then I would let Father Kevin down. Besides, Jake wouldn't buy it, and it would just prolong the inevitable—not to mention, it would be unprofessional. And professionalism was the only thing that would get me through this night.

Inhaling deeply, I took my time walking to the door. With my hand on the doorknob, I hesitated one more moment as I attempted to control my heart rate and the damn fluttering in my stomach, which was definitely not butterflies. I swung the door open.

Jake stood there with his cased guitar strapped onto his back, looking so—

Definitely *not* hot.

Cocky—yes, cocky. Facts.

Standing taller, I cleared my throat and narrowed my eyes. "It's about time you got here. We're on a schedule, you know."

Jake drew his eyebrows together. "What do you mean? I got here right at seven. You're the one who took forever answering the door."

"I was busy. Am I supposed to drop everything the moment you come knocking?"

He tilted his head and stared at me. "Um, but you just said we're on a—"

"Just shut up and get in here. I don't have time to argue with you all night."

With a sideways smile, he stepped inside.

Do not fall for his charm. Stay strong. "I set up a chair for you by the piano," I said as he placed his guitar on the couch and took off his jacket. I retrieved the music sheets we'd need from my briefcase. When I turned, Jake was looking around. "Did you lose something?"

He shook his head. "Just remembering the last time I was here."

I stilled, staring at him. So like him to bring that up. Tightening my lips, I shoved the music sheets against his chest. "These are the songs we'll be playing." My voice was as cold as I could manage.

He grabbed the papers and gave a small smile. Hopefully he'd gotten the hint that we were not going down memory lane.

"Which are we working on first?" he asked after glancing through the sheets.

"That first one. Go ahead and run some chords to warm up and we'll get started."

He nodded as he went to get his guitar out of its case, then settled on the chair.

In the meantime, I sat on the piano bench, setting up the music. Then I stretched out my fingers and cracked my knuckles while I waited for Jake to be done.

When he was all set, we jumped right in. We went over the guitar parts and the piano parts separately. Everything was going fine until we put it together.

"You missed it again," I said after the tenth attempt. "It's on two."

And a one and a two—

"You're like half a beat late."

"Ian, I'm doing what you said."

"If you were doing what I said, then you wouldn't be late."

"I'm literally going on two."

"No, you're not."

"Yes, I am."

I let out an exasperated sigh and glanced at my watch. We'd been going at it for forty minutes already. Time flies when you're having fun . . . *not.* "Let's take a break," I said, getting up and heading into the kitchen. "Do you want something to drink?" I figured I should offer the guy something, since we were working.

"Sure. I'll take a soda if you have some."

I stuck my head in the fridge, taking my time and utilizing the low temp inside to cool me down, as though I were infusing energy to keep going with this insufferable practice. Just twenty more minutes, and I'd call it a night.

I closed my eyes, sighing as I grabbed two colas, then straightened and shut the door with my hip.

He had to be fucking kidding me.

I didn't move as familiar notes echoed throughout my house. Jake was playing our song, "A Thousand Years" by Christina Perri. It was the first song we'd played together that didn't have to do with church. We'd also played it at our graduation party.

Son of a bitch.

Clenching my jaw, I marched into the living room. "Here," I said, shoving the ice-cold can against the back of his hand, which messed him up, forcing him to stop playing.

He looked up, meeting my eyes as he took the soda. "Let's play it together. For old times' sake."

I popped my can open, then slid Jake's guitar case over on the couch to make room to sit. "Play what together?"

"Our song."

I took a swig. "If you mean that hideous tune you were just playing, I don't recognize it."

Jake popped open the can and slurped. "Come on, Ian." He set the can on the floor. "Let me refresh your memory."

And he fucking played it again.

"Stop it."

He continued.

I made my voice more forceful. "I said stop."

His fingers stilled. "So you do remember."

"No. I don't want to waste time. We're on a short break, then we have to get back to work. If you want to play, practice one of the songs we're required to know."

After a moment, he stood and gently placed his guitar on the piano bench. He picked up the can off the floor, then came over and sat next to me. I scooted to make more room, which wasn't much because of the damn case. Closing my eyes, I let my head fall on the back of the couch. Maybe when I reopened them, this nightmare would be over.

"Ian, I'm sorry."

"It's just a stupid song," I said, knowing full well his apology had nothing to do with music.

"No, that's not—" He sighed. "I'm sorry for hurting you."

I lifted my head and took a sip of my drink. "Whatever."

"No, it's not whatever. You're clearly upset, and I want to make it right."

Turning my head, I met his eyes. That was a mistake. Jake's gray eyes appeared to be sucking me in.

No!

"You can't." I got up. "Break time's over."

"Ian, please, let me explain."

I had told Anna and Matt that I would hear Jake out for closure or whatever, but something deep within me was preventing me the ability. The truth was, I was scared. The way I saw it, there were only two possible explanations: either Jake had played me from the start and used me to get his gay kicks, or he'd chosen to be with Miranda because, in the end, he'd decided he was too scared to come out.

And I didn't know which version of those possibilities was worse. In the end, I would still end up alone and hurt. So what was the point?

"We have to get back to work. Our session is almost over."

Jake stood, setting the soda can on the end table. "Why won't you listen to me?"

"Because nothing you say will change what you did."

"True, but you'll understand why I did it."

"Oh, I understand already. You're a coward. That's the bottom line. And whether you say it out loud won't change anything between us."

"The fact that you just called me a coward tells me you don't understand anything." He paused. "You know what? You're the coward. You're afraid of hearing me out because you know that deep down, I would never intentionally hurt you, so once you hear the truth, you would have no choice but to forgive me."

"And why would I be scared of that? You think I enjoy feeling this way?"

"Yes. It gives you power so you don't have to trust anyone or admit you were wrong. It's your coping mechanism."

"You made me this way."

"No, *you* made you this way. You're the one who jumped to conclusions from the start. You wouldn't even hear me out. You still won't. We were supposed to be in this together. We were a team, us against Miranda. But you decided to believe what was on the surface. You let her tear us apart again. Instead of trusting in me, in my love, you believed her. Maybe you didn't love me as much as you claimed you did. Who hurt who here, huh?"

"Get out."

"Excuse me?"

"Get the fuck out of my house."

"Ian—"

"Get out!"

Jake hesitated, a stunned look on his face. Then, with a curt nod, he snatched up his guitar and placed it securely in the case. It seemed like forever went by as he zipped up the case, put on his jacket, swung the satchel over his head and across his chest, and looped the guitar case onto his back. I awkwardly stood watching, my arms folded across my chest.

When he was done getting his shit together, he went to the door and paused. "I love you, Ian. And I know you love me too. When you're ready to hear me out, let me know."

And he was gone.

Chapter 12

Ian

Thank God for extra work.

The stack of papers that had accumulated on my desk at St. Pius the last few days was the perfect distraction. Tonight was choir rehearsal. The thought of facing Jake made my insides turn to mush—and not in a good way. With any luck, he wouldn't show.

I'd kicked the guy out of my house. It didn't get any worse than that. So much for keeping things professional.

But Jake had twisted everything and had the audacity to accuse me of betraying him. The sad thing was that he had a point: I'd chosen to believe what I'd seen without giving him a chance to explain. What if there was a good explanation as to why he'd ended up engaged to Miranda?

Someone knocked on the open door and cleared their throat.

I glanced up to see a priest standing there. He was older, maybe in his fifties or sixties. Mostly silver locks covered his head in small, tight curls.

"Sorry for the interruption," the priest said.

"No problem, Father. Please, come in."

The priest stepped forward and extended his hand. "I'm Father John. I've been assigned to this parish."

"Oh, that's great. Nice to meet you. I'm Ian Cooper," I said, shaking his hand.

"Nice to meet you, too, Ian. You're the music director?"

"Yes, that's right."

"Wonderful. I just wanted to come around and introduce myself to the employees."

"Yes, definitely. I'm glad you came by."

"Father Kevin tells me you're working on a Christmas program?"

"Yup. I'll be doing a duet with a choir member who plays the guitar. Jake Edwards."

"A piano/guitar duet. How fascinating!"

"Yeah, it should be awesome."

"Can't wait to hear it. And you also direct the choir? When is rehearsal for that?"

"Tonight, actually."

"Oh, lovely. Would you mind if I stopped by so I can meet everyone?"

"Not at all, Father. You're always welcome."

"Thank you, Ian. I shall do that. See you tonight."

* * *

I was able to get some much-needed work done after Father John left. At about six o'clock, I went to get some dinner, then came back in time to prepare for choir practice. Just as I was warming up the organ, Brad, the youngest member of choir, showed up.

"Hi, Brad. You're here early."

"Hey, Ian. I was hoping to talk to you in private before the others showed up."

"Of course. What's up?"

The kid seemed nervous as he glanced around and fidgeted with his fingers.

"Would you like to sit?" I scooted over on the bench so there was room.

"Thanks," he said as he sat. "I, uh, wanted to say I think it was great what you did. You know, bringing your boyfriend to Mass."

I kept up with the boyfriend facade for now. "Oh. Well, thank you. That's very kind of you to say."

"Can I ask you a personal question?"

"Of course."

"How? I mean, the church teaches us it's okay to be gay but not to act on it. Does that mean you two don't have sex?"

I smiled. "It's true the Catholic church teaches that, but I don't agree. I feel that expressing love between two people, no matter their gender, is a beautiful thing."

"Aren't you afraid of going to Hell?"

"No, because I don't believe it's a sin to love someone."

"I wish I was as brave as you."

"Brad, are you gay?"

The kid visibly swallowed before nodding. "Please don't tell anyone. No one knows. Not even my parents."

"Your secret is safe with me. Trust me, I know how scary it is. It took me a long time to come out to my parents, but as it turned out, when I finally got the courage, they already knew."

"Really?"

I nodded. "You'd be surprised what parents know."

"Well, I know my parents won't accept it."

"Is there anyone else in your family you can talk to?"

"No. They all think like my parents."

"How about talking to someone here at the church? We have counseling here."

"Yeah, but I bet they'll just tell me not to act on my feelings."

The kid had a point. The church needed a LGBTQ+ support group. Real support, not condemnation or repression.

I glanced up to see some choir members arriving. "Listen, you have my number. Give me a call if you ever want to talk."

"Really? You wouldn't mind?"

"Of course not."

"Thanks so much, Ian. I might do that."

As Brad stood, I locked eyes with Jake as he walked down the aisle. He'd showed up. Great.

I checked my watch. Time to get started. I stood and walked over to my choir members. Something was not right. The crowd seemed smaller than usual.

"Who are we missing?" I asked.

There was grunting among them and a bunch of shoulder shrugging.

I took out my cell, checking for text messages from any of the no-shows.

Nothing.

"That's strange. We have, like, six people missing. Nobody knows anything?"

"I think some people might be uncomfortable," Kathy, a middle-aged member, spoke up.

"Uncomfortable? About what?"

"About you, uh, bringing your boyfriend to Mass."

I frowned. Someone cleared their throat behind me. "Father John," I said, unable to read his expression. "So glad you could join us."

"I hope this is a good time."

"Absolutely. We were just getting started. We have a few members absent tonight, but you can introduce yourself to those who are here."

Father John nodded.

While the new priest talked among the choir, I stepped aside and took out my phone. I sent messages to those that were allegedly "uncomfortable," asking if everything was okay and if they were coming to rehearsal. What, they were just going to quit choir because their director was gay?

Wow. Just wow. I hoped that wasn't the case.

I glanced up and found Jake looking at me from where he sat, his lips curled into a tight smile. Kind of sympathetic.

The priest turned. "Okay, Ian, they're all yours. If you don't mind, I'll observe for a few minutes before I go."

"No problem, Father."

This issue with the homophobic hooky members would have to wait. I didn't want to get into it in front of the new priest.

I went on to direct rehearsal as normal. For the most part, there were no major setbacks. I was able to put Jake back where he was before, vocally, and for the sake of practice, we replaced the missing vocals in case they didn't return.

After I dismissed everyone, Kathy came up to me. "Ian, I wanted you to know that what I said earlier about the others being uncomfortable—it was only whispers I've heard. It has nothing to do about what I think."

"I know, Kathy. Thank you."

She patted my arm, then left.

As I gathered my things, Jake came up to me, leaning on the organ. I raised my eyes to him when he didn't say anything. "May I help you?"

"Are you okay?" he asked with a concerned look on his face.

"Yeah. Why wouldn't I be?"

"Because of the no-shows."

I huffed. "I'm sure they have their reasons for not coming."

"Yeah, 'cause they're homophobic assholes."

I shook my head. "We don't know that for sure."

"Have they replied to your texts?"

"Not yet."

He pursed his lips.

"Just don't worry about it. I'll deal with it," I said.

"I'm not letting you deal with this alone."

I snatched up my bag. "Stop trying to be my hero." And walked away.

Jake followed. "Oh, yeah, I forgot. Matt's your hero now."

I whipped around, causing Jake to almost bump into me. "I can fight my own battles. I don't need a fucking hero. Besides, we don't know if there's a battle to fight."

I turned, continuing down the aisle and through the doors into the night. Jake secured the door behind me and followed me across the parking lot.

Something was off as I neared my SUV. It seemed slanted. I got closer and stopped dead.

What the—

Two of my tires were completely flat. And if that weren't enough, the word *sinner* was spray-painted on the side.

Jake gasped, stopping next to me. "Looks like a fucking war to me."

I reached into my pocket and retrieved my cell. "Do tow trucks come out this late?"

"Yeah, I think so."

I called 9-1-1. Someone had vandalized my car. This was not okay. Besides, my insurance might want a police report before they paid for any damages.

While we waited for the police to show up, I turned to Jake. "You don't have to wait with me."

"I'm not leaving you here alone."

God, he kept saying that like he thought he still needed to protect me. It was annoying, but I was thankful. I was a little shook-up. Who knew who could be lurking in the shadows?

"Thanks," I muttered.

Jake smiled and nodded.

Fifteen minutes later, the cops showed up. I gave them my statement. They assessed the damage and filled out paperwork.

"Do you have any idea who might've done this?" the officer asked.

I left out the names of members who were no-shows. "No. Like I said, I brought my boyfriend to Mass this past Sunday, and I think it may have stirred up some personal opinions. But there's no telling who did it. This is a large church."

The officer turned to Jake. "Are you the boyfriend?"

"No," I answered before he could speak. "He's my partner." That did not sound right. "I mean, duet partner. Not, like, domestic partner. He's engaged. To a woman. So, he is definitely not my boyfriend. Especially since he's straight." *Shut up.* I cleared my throat. "He was nice enough to wait with me until you arrived."

The officer nodded with an amused look on his face and called in a tow truck while I avoided eye contact with Jake. When it arrived, the officer asked, "Do you have a ride home?"

"I could take you home," Jake said.

"You don't have to do that. I'll call Anna."

"You're going to make your very pregnant bestie come all the way out here this late?"

"I'm sure Ant will come. Or I could call Matt," I added so Jake wouldn't wonder why I hadn't mentioned him. Damn it, I should have named him first. Matt was probably working, but he would come, considering we were still friends.

"Ian, come on. I'm right here. Let me do this for you."

I hesitated as I glanced at the officer, then back at him. The thought of standing around, waiting even longer, didn't sound appealing. "Fine."

We watched as the tow truck took away my car, then I thanked the officer.

I couldn't remember the last time I'd ridden on Jake's motorcycle. Maybe when he first got it, sometime in college. "Do you have an extra helmet?"

Jake handed me his. "Wear mine."

"What about you?"

"I'll be fine. The passenger is more important, anyway."

"But isn't it the law to wear a helmet?"

He shrugged. "I'll go slow."

I made sure my bag was securely latched, then pulled the strap across my chest, making sure it was snug against my back. Then I pulled on the helmet.

Jake helped me with the chin strap, then grabbed on to the helmet, making sure it was secure. "There. Looks good on you."

"I don't feel right about you not wearing one."

"Does that mean you care about me?"

I narrowed my eyes. "Never mind."

Jake smiled, then got on the bike. I took a deep breath as I mounted behind him. "Hang on tight," he said as he started the motor.

As I brought my hands around Jake's waist, I tried not to focus on his hard abs or how every inch of my body was painfully aware of the closeness of his.

The next twenty minutes were going to be excruciating.

While we were stopped at a red light, Jake's hand covered mine. "Are you okay back there?" Jake shouted over the motor.

"Yeah, I'm good."

And we were off again.

Once we arrived at my house, I couldn't get off the thing fast enough. At least I waited until Jake came to a complete stop and turned off the engine.

As I used Jake as leverage to hop down, I hoped my slacks didn't reveal the semihardness that had occurred along the way. It was like my body knew it was Jake—and missed him.

I took off the helmet and handed it to him. "Thanks for the ride." Why did that sound like a sexual innuendo?

Apparently, Jake noticed it, too, because he raised his eyebrows and smiled. "Anytime."

"And thanks again for sticking around." *Goddamn it.*

Jake's smile turned into a grin. "Glad I was there. I just hope they find the fuckers who did that to your car."

"Me too."

Then he got serious. "Do me a favor and be careful. Don't go anywhere alone."

"I'll be careful."

"And I know you're your own hero, but call me tomorrow if you need a ride to the church or wherever. I want to help you."

"Don't you work at the school tomorrow?"

"Yeah, but I can get a sub to cover for me."

"Okay." As the silence stretched between us awkwardly, I cleared my throat. "Um, I'm sorry I kicked you out last night."

He shook his head. "You don't have to apologize."

"It was unprofessional of me. I shouldn't have lost my temper."

"It's okay. I shouldn't have brought up personal stuff while we were working."

"But you brought up some good points, and you're right. I should've given you a chance to explain. And I will. It's just—"

"It's all right. Like I said last night, when you're ready to listen, let me know. I'm not going anywhere. My promise still stands. I'll always be here for you."

"Thank you."

"By the way, stop answering for me whenever people ask if I'm gay or if I'm your boyfriend. You keep giving the wrong answer."

My jaw went slack as he slipped on his helmet with a side smile, started up the motorcycle, and took off.

Chapter 13

Matt

I was beat.

The hospital had been crazy. It had been the kind of night that made you think there was a full moon out. But as tired as I was, I needed to unwind before hitting the sack. After placing my briefcase on the couch, I sauntered into the kitchen. I wasn't hungry, so I grabbed the red wine off the wine rack and poured myself a glass.

I savored a few sips as I took my phone out of my pocket. The thought of calling Ian crossed my mind. It had become a ritual to call him at the end of my day, but I wouldn't do it. I wouldn't be that guy. Instead, I opened the dating app I'd downloaded the other night and looked through it. Had I taken my brother's advice? Yes. Would I ever admit that to him? Hell no.

A few profiles showed up as recommendations. No one caught my eye, so I kept swiping left.

This was what it had come down to. Looking online for men to fuck. Why not hang out at a bar? Or a street corner? The whole use-technology-to-date thing felt unnatural and forced. It reeked of desperation.

I was about to quit the nonsense when a face popped up on my screen, capturing my attention. The guy looked familiar. But I'd remember that face; he was hot and had a beard. Perfect.

After pressing on his profile for more details, I read through his bio and scanned his other pictures. Hot. So far, I liked what I saw. His name was CJ. Thirty-seven. Six feet tall. Brown hair. Hazel Eyes. No kids. Looking for a good time. No strings. Nothing serious.

Perfect. A stepping-stone, a rebound of sorts. Someone to help get over Ian and relieve all the built-up tension inside me. To help let loose so I could be ready for my future partner.

My finger lingered over the guy's image. It was now or never. Taking another big gulp of wine, I swiped right.

And nothing happened.

Of course not, *dumbass*. This wasn't instant gratification. And there was no guarantee this hottie would be interested in me.

I flipped the phone over, downed the rest of the wine, then headed to my bedroom and stripped. In the bathroom, I stepped under the cool spray of the shower as it washed away the day's stress.

As I soaped down my body, I took extra time on my ass and balls, enjoying the sensation. It'd been too long. Gripping my hard dick with a soapy hand, I leaned against the shower wall and worked myself. I didn't need anybody else for this.

The face from the app entered my mind. That one shirtless pic—with the shorts—

"Ahhh." I came without warning. Did I mention it'd been a while?

I took a moment to catch my breath, then finished washing up, cleaning the shower as well. Feeling a bit more relaxed, I dried myself, slipped on some pajama bottoms, and brushed my teeth. Out in the kitchen, I washed the wineglass and put away the wine bottle.

It was late. I didn't expect any messages on my phone, so I was surprised the light was blinking when I grabbed my cell off the countertop. The notification was from the dating app. Not only had CJ liked me back but he'd also DMed me.

Holy shit.

Chapter 14

Ian

I was working from home today.

Not because I was scared, but because it was getting late.

I'd spent all morning on the phone with the insurance company regarding my car. Bottom line, it was going to take a few weeks to investigate and repair. In the meantime, they'd hit me up with a loaner, which meant I was stuck until then.

Everyone was working. Anna had recently started a new job at the hospital as an office assistant—same hospital as Matt, who was also working. Ant and Jake were also at work. And I didn't care what Jake said; I would not pull him away from his students so he could give me a ride to the church.

Ubering crossed my mind, but in the end, I decided against that as well. So, I called Father Kevin to explain the whole situation with the vandalism and told him I'd work from home.

I shuffled into the bathroom, rubbing the kinks out of my neck with one hand and running the other through my messy curls, pushing them off my forehead. Yawning, I reached for the toothbrush and toothpaste, but paused as I glanced up at the mirror. Leaning closer, I rubbed my face, feeling the overgrowth of facial hair.

Depression and anger had made me stop shaving.

Months ago, when things had gone down with Jake, I hadn't felt like doing much of anything, let alone grooming myself. The beard had grown.

I wondered what Jake thought of it.

Matt liked it, but I had a feeling Jake didn't. Even though he had his own bit of facial hair.

Whatever.

It wasn't like I would shave it off for him. Fuck that.

Grabbing my toothbrush, I proceeded to brush my teeth, but as I rinsed my mouth, my face itched. I supposed it could use a trim, at least.

I dried my face and bent to the cabinet under the sink to retrieve the trimmer. As I reached for it, something fell. I took a closer look.

Black nail polish.

I couldn't remember the last time I'd used it, but I did recall the first time. It was in high school, when I'd realized I might be gay. Painting my nails had been a way to identify myself, embrace who I was. I'd continued in college, where it eventually lessened to once a year, usually around Halloween.

Maybe I should do it. Especially now, with coming out at the church. It might be beneficial for making my statement. I was who I was, and I wasn't afraid of a little vandalism and name-calling.

I set the small bottle on the counter to use later. First, time for a beard trim and shower.

Afterwards, I towel-dried myself as I padded into the bedroom to get dressed. Since I was working from home, I dressed down. Some sweats and a T-shirt.

In the kitchen, I started the coffeemaker, then went to the study and turned on the computer. As it booted up, I fetched a cup of coffee and settled into the desk chair.

The first thing on the agenda: emails—My blood chilled.

Resign! Or die!!

I must have stared at the thing for a good ten minutes before I blinked and swallowed. Shaking my head, I moved on to the next email.

If you know what's good for you, you'll leave St. Pius.

I printed both emails out to show the police. Maybe this was connected to whoever slashed my tires. One thing was for sure: some nonsensical threats would not scare me into quitting my job and going into hiding. I was done suppressing who I was; thought that was clear. I'd have to make it clearer.

Pushing back my seat, I went over to the bathroom and grabbed the nail polish off the counter, then headed back to the desk. I took a sip of coffee, then painted my nails.

Once completed and blowing on them until dried, I clicked to the next email.

Mr. Cooper,
> **Please help! My parents want to send me to conversion therapy. I've heard horrific stories of those places. I didn't even know they still existed. I don't know what to do. No one at the church will help. You're my last hope!**

Conversion therapy? What the fuck? That was still a thing? How could I help this kid? I wasn't trained in dealing with this issue. Still dumbfounded, I moved on to the next email.

Mr. Cooper,
>   You don't know me personally, but I attend St. Pius. I'm usually there with my wife and kids. I don't know why I'm writing to you, really. I feel like it's a lost cause in my case, but I need to talk to someone who understands. You see, I'm a homosexual. But nobody knows. I married my wife because I wanted to be "normal." No matter how much I've tried over the years, I can't fight my attraction to men. I've never had an affair, but I've thought about it. I'm sorry to dump this on you. I guess I just want someone to listen. I'm not even sure I'd have the courage to talk to you face-to-face. But for now, thank you for taking the time to read this. You don't have to reply. Just knowing that you're there, a fellow Christian gay man, is enough.

Wow. I wanted to help these people—but how?

Dear Ian Cooper,
>   I just wanted to let you know how much I admire you for bringing your boyfriend to mass and holding hands with him in front of everyone. That was very brave and very cool. I heard about what someone did to your car. Don't let that stop you. Keep doing you. I'm a lesbian myself. My parents know, but they don't like it. They think it's a phase. But I don't care. Seeing you coming out made me want to be brave too. You're my idol.

I sat back in the chair in bewilderment. There were tons of emails. A lot were asking for help, some were praising me, and a few were threats. I never would have imagined that there were this many LGBTQ+ members at the church. There had to be something I could do. I remembered Brad from choir, also in need of my help. Then it dawned on me.

An LGBTQ+ support group.

This would be something that required approval. I clicked on COMPOSE and began writing an email to Father Kevin, asking for permission to start the group. It wouldn't be anything fancy, just something that we could announce to the parishioners. Something available to those who needed to talk to someone. A safe place filled with like-minded people.

Chapter 15

Jake

I'd been summoned by Daddy dearest.

As I rang the doorbell of my childhood home, I prayed my dad had some good news for me. My mom was at bible study, so we'd have privacy.

Dad opened the door with that same authoritative look he always had. It made it hard to tell what he was thinking. "Son, come in." His eyes followed me as I stepped past him. It was like he was observing me more than usual. Weird. "Let's go into my office," he said as he took the lead.

Once there, Dad shut the door. Doubly weird, considering we were alone in the house. "What's up? Did you take care of the situation?"

He went behind the desk. "Have you left Miranda?"

"Not yet. But I've started packing my things."

"Son, I talked to Miranda. I wanted to dissuade her from following through with this blackmail nonsense."

"And?" I prodded when he didn't elaborate.

After hesitating, he said, "She tells me you . . . you want to leave her for . . . *a man?*"

Son of a bitch.

She outed me to my dad. Fucking bitch.

"Tell me she's mistaken," he continued when I remained silent.

What could I say? Miranda had robbed me of this moment. It pissed me the fuck off, but I shouldn't be surprised. "She had no right to tell you that."

"Is it true?"

"I don't see why it matters. It has nothing to do with this situation."

"It has everything to do with it."

"Why? The point is, I don't love Miranda, and she's forcing me to stay with her because of something you're involved in. Nobody can stop me from leaving her. You got yourself into this illegal business, and somehow Miranda found out about it. Now you get to deal with her."

"You are willing to bring shame to this family?"

Fucking irony. "What are you talking about? You're the drug dealer here."

"Son, are you gay?"

My old man wasn't letting this go. Not exactly the way I wanted to come out to my parents, but whatever. And I didn't want to get into my hatred of labels; it was a moot point anyway. Might as well own up to it head-on. "Yeah. I'm gay. And in love."

"With a man? You're in love with a *man?*"

I tilted my head. "That is kinda the idea behind being gay."

The silence stretched as my words dissipated into the air. My father stared at me like I had something nasty coming out of my nose. "Who? Who is this man you claim to love?"

Yeah, that wasn't happening. "I'm not telling you."

"Why not?"

"Because it's none of your business, and he has nothing to do with this."

"The hell he doesn't. You plan to bring shame to this family because of this man. I have a right to know who it is."

"No, you don't. He's my business. Your business is dealing with your illegal shit."

"You'll give your mother a heart attack."

"Really, Dad? I'm the one who's going to give her a heart attack?" He opened his mouth to respond, but I stopped him. This was getting out of hand—and way off topic. "Look, you're not guilting me into staying in the closet. I'm done with Miranda. And I'm done with you."

I got up and turned to leave, but my father blocked my path to the door. "Do not tell your mother."

"You can't stop me."

"Yes, I can."

I stepped back. "What are you going to do, huh?"

"Son, I have played your game long enough. My business is not something I can just stop. There are dangerous people involved. If something happens to me, they're likely to come after my family and any loved ones. That includes this male lover of yours. I highly suggest you think carefully about how you want to proceed."

"Is that a threat?"

"It's not a threat. It's the way things are. If you ever cared for your mother and me—and this man—you will keep your mouth shut and marry Miranda so that she doesn't get us all killed."

A chill went down my spine. I said nothing else as I walked around my father and got the hell out of that house.

Chapter 16

Ian

Would they show up?

Glancing at my watch, I paced the gathering area, waiting to see if the six who hadn't attended rehearsal would come to Mass. I hoped to speak to them before getting started, which was why I was out here instead of playing soothing music while the parishioners took their seats.

I'd sent word to the other members to meet here as soon as they were ready, so we would have time to go over a few things. So far, there was no sign of the six.

A few minutes later, everyone who had been at rehearsal, including Jake, surrounded me in our usual corner.

"Okay, well, let's get started. Thanks, everyone, for being punctual. I just wanted to—"

The doors opened, and two of the missing members entered, Donald and Andrew.

"Good morning," I said. "Were you planning on joining us today?"

"We are part of the choir, aren't we?" Donald replied.

"I don't know. You tell me. You weren't at rehearsal, and I've gotten no replies to any of my texts."

They smirked as they glanced at each other. "We don't have to answer to you."

"Uh, yeah, you kinda do. I'm the director."

Donald scoffed. "We're not sure how we feel about a queer directing our choir. You know, being that you're a sinner and all."

"Hey, Moses," Jake spoke up. "Before you go spewing your righteous bullshit, take a good hard look at yourself. Are you free from sin? Do you masturbate or look at porn? Feel envy or greed? Here's a good one—how about hatred? Didn't God teach us to love one another? 'Cause I'm pretty sure you're hating on Ian right now just because he's different. He's the same fucking guy he was before you found out his sexual orientation, so how about you show him some goddamn respect and stop being a homophobic asshole?"

Yeah. What he said.

"I'm not saying I'm perfect, but at least I don't flaunt my sins," Donald bit back.

"Flaunt?" I jumped in. "I'm not flaunting."

"You brought your lover to the house of God. If that's not flaunting—"

"It's not like we had sex in front of everyone."

"You might as well have."

"How about you stop flaunting your bigotry!" Jake shouted.

"You stay out of this, Jake. This has nothing to do with you!"

Jake stepped forward like he was going to pounce on the guy. I blocked his path, putting my hand on his shoulder. That's all we needed—a fight to break out right when Mass was about to begin. "No, Jake. I got this." I turned back to face Donald. "You're off this choir."

"You can't do that. You can't just kick me off."

"I just did."

"I'll be speaking to Father Kevin about this."

"Be my guest." As he stormed away, I turned to Andrew. "How about you? Are you in or out?"

The man put his hands up. "I'm out." He walked away.

"Is everything all right over here?" Father John asked as he joined us.

"Yes, Father. It's all under control."

"Good, because we're ready to begin."

I nodded and turned to my choir to review the hymns we would be singing and told them to sing like we rehearsed.

As I turned to head to the organ, Jake grabbed my arm. "You okay?"

"Yeah. We'll talk after Mass."

At the organ bench, I closed my eyes and took a deep breath as I played. The more I played, the more I stopped shaking. I hated confrontations like that, but I felt better knowing people stood behind me—like Jake, of all people.

I didn't understand him.

After everything, he still stuck up for me and made sure I was okay. He surprised me by saying the sweetest things, like last week, when he complimented my directing skills. Why was he marrying Miranda?

The only way I would find out was by letting Jake explain things.

After Mass concluded, Jake appeared at the organ while I gathered my paperwork.

"You wanted to see me?" he asked.

I raised a brow. "Excuse me?"

"You said we'd talk after mass."

"Oh, yeah," I murmured. "Where's your fiancée?"

He narrowed his eyes and pursed his lips. "If you mean Miranda, I don't know where she is. Probably talking with friends, as usual."

"Well, I just wanted to thank you for saying what you did earlier to Donald. It wasn't necessary, but it was kinda funny. You know, calling him Moses."

"That asshole deserves to get his ass kicked. He's probably the one who fucked up your car."

"Maybe. But we can't go accusing people without proof. And you can't go around beating people up for me. We're not in high school anymore."

"I can't help it. I hate seeing people treat you like shit. You know I've always had this thing of wanting to protect you."

"I do, but—"

"Don't tell me to stop. It'll be like telling me to stop breathing."

Aaand there it was: another sweet moment.

It wasn't until Miranda joined us that I closed my gaping mouth and snapped out of the stupor.

"Are you ready to go, hon?"

Jake rolled his eyes. "In a minute. We're in the middle of something here."

"Hello, Ian," she said, turning to me. "It's good to see you. It sure has been a hot minute since we last spoke."

"Yes, indeed," I muttered.

"Where is that cute boyfriend of yours? I didn't see him at Mass this week."

"Working. He's a doctor."

"So I've heard. Nice."

"Miranda," Jake said, sounding irritated. "Can we finish our discussion in private?"

She stared at him for a moment. "What were you guys discussing? It seemed serious."

"It is serious."

I cleared my throat. "It's all right, Jake. You can leave with your fiancée. We're done anyway. Just remember, duet rehearsal is tomorrow. Same time and place." I tried to keep it as cryptic as possible in case Miranda didn't know about the duet and where we were practicing. What could I say? Old habits die hard. But I also wanted to clarify that we were done—and not just about the discussion either.

Jake nodded, then turned, leaving Miranda to chase after him.

Chapter 17

Matt

This was crazy.

I couldn't remember the last time I'd gone on a blind date, but that wasn't what this was. This was a hookup, which was even crazier. And I hadn't had one of *those* since early college years. Even then, I'd done it the old-fashioned way: see a cute guy, talk, flirt, dance, then fuck.

After I received CJ's message, I'd replied and we'd chatted all night. So far, great guy. Easy to talk to. We agreed to meet somewhere in public in case one of us turned out to be a serial killer, then we would see how the night went.

I got to the bar early, picked a table by the wall facing the entrance, and ordered a beer, hoping it'd help relax me. Why was I so nervous? It wasn't like I hadn't had sex with a stranger before. I'd even manscaped for the occasion and armed my wallet with condoms. All I needed now was the man.

And he walked in.

CJ looked even hotter in person. He wore dark jeans, a burgundy button-down, and a brown leather jacket. His hair was more of a reddish-brown, with messy waves, short on the sides, and long on top. And his beard—mmm. I'd been hoping his profile pic wasn't an old picture.

When he spotted me, he smiled and walked over as I stood.

"Hey, nice to meet you in the flesh," CJ said as he extended his arms. "Mind if we hug? I'm a hugger."

"Oh, sure," I replied awkwardly as I let the guy wrap his arms around me. He smelled heavenly, like sandalwood and soap.

"You smell good," he said. It was like we were kindred spirits. "What is that? Musk? Obsession?"

"You know your scents. It's Obsession."

"Nice. One of my favorites."

"What about you? You smell good too."

"Every Man Jack. Sandalwood."

"I like it."

We sat across from each other, and CJ ordered a beer. "So, was your day good?" he asked.

"Yeah, I checked on some patients, ran some other errands, got ready for tonight. You know, typical stuff." I chuckled and took a swig of beer.

He laughed. "That's right. You're a doctor. You must have a crazy work schedule."

I shrugged. "It's not that bad. You get used to it. How about you? You never told me what you do."

His beer arrived, and he took a long drink before answering. "Nothing that exciting, to be honest. I work in a bank."

"Like a bank teller?"

"Among other things. It's not that interesting."

He was clearly uncomfortable talking about his job, so I dropped it. It was probably best we knew less about each other. We would most likely never cross paths again after tonight.

"You're a lot sexier in person, by the way."

I raised my eyebrows. That compliment was unexpected. "Oh? Thank you. I guess."

He licked his lips. "I mean it. On your profile, you have that cute boy-next-door vibe, but in person . . . sexy."

My cheeks grew warm. "Wow. Thanks." I had to remember the guy was here for sex. "Well, you're just as sexy as your profile pic."

His eyes hooded, and he smiled. "You think so?"

"Of course. I'm sure you get compliments all the time."

He shook his head and laughed.

I laughed too. "Come on. Yes, you do. There's no way you don't."

CJ took another sip of his beer and leaned forward. "Wanna get out of here?"

That was fast. "Um, yeah. Sure."

He flagged down our server, and we paid for our beer.

We walked down the block to the nearest hotel. It wasn't anything fancy, but it was neat and clean. CJ handled the booking and payment. Our room was on the fifth floor, and on the elevator ride, he backed me up against the wall as his lips sought out mine. It was a kiss full of promise of the night to come. Slow and sensual . . . and burning with passion.

It was over way too soon. But it was only the beginning.

We rushed down the hall to the room, and it took two tries for the room key to work. Inside, CJ captured me in a kiss again. I breathed into him, savoring his lips, mingling with his tongue. Such a good kisser. We both shrugged out of our jackets, tossing them on the floor. His fingers came up to his shirt, unbuttoning and tugging. I did the same until we were both shirtless.

Coming up for air, he flashed a condom packet in my face. "Do you top? Or bottom?"

"Both," I answered.

A smile spread across his lips. "Verse? Oh, this is going to be fun."

He kissed me again, turned me around, and pinned me against the door. His beard scratched me in an intoxicating way as he licked and sucked my neck from behind. I closed my eyes, tilting my head to give better access. The pounding of my heart increased as my breathing quickened. It'd been so long since I'd been this turned on. My head spun with anticipation as his expert hands slipped into my waistband, effortlessly unzipping my pants. I moaned as he cupped and rubbed my swollen cock. Before I realized it, my pants had come off, and that hot mouth was all over my ass, kissing and nipping. I gasped as he separated my cheeks and fucked me with his tongue.

After a few minutes of exquisite torture, he turned me around again and swallowed me whole. I thought I'd lose my mind. But too quickly, he was gone. No mouth, no kissing.

I opened my eyes. He stood, staring down at me, his erection in his palm. At some point, he'd discarded his pants. "Suck it," he said gruffly.

I gave him a side smile. "I thought you'd never ask." I dropped to my knees.

The guy was massive—I couldn't wait to feel him inside. I went to town, sucking him to the back of my throat. Licking to his balls. Squeezing, jerking. I wanted to taste him, but I also wanted to prolong this. We had the room for the night. Might as well make the most of it.

Fingers in my hair guided me to my feet. More kissing. Then I was flipped around once again, pressed into the door. Behind me was the sound of a condom wrapper fiddled with and torn.

Hot breath on my ear. "Do you want me to fuck you?"

"God, yes."

"Say it," he demanded.

"Fuck me."

As CJ penetrated me, I felt myself stretching to accommodate all his glory. The familiar twinge of pain came and went, then pleasure took over. I moaned and arched my back, meeting the thrusts, wanting to take in all of him. "That feels so good."

"Yeah?"

"Mm-hmm."

Strong hands tightened on my hips. "Tell me."

"Your cock feels amazing. Fuck me harder."

He slammed into me again and again, faster. "Like this?"

"Oh. My. God. Yes. Don't stop."

"Do you want to cum?"

"Yes," I breathed.

The thrusts stopped as CJ got close against my back and gripped my cock. "Don't cum until I tell you to."

Fuck.

My heart hammered in my chest as CJ played with the precum leaking from my tip. I buried my head in my arm, holding back the orgasm threatening to explode.

"You're rock hard. Your cock is oozing."

"Please—"

"Please what?"

"Please make me cum."

"How?"

"Fuck me. Hard. And don't stop until we're both done."

The guy chuckled and leaned in again. "I like you." He rotated his hips, leaning back, regripping my hips as he got in position. "And where do you want it?"

"In my mouth."

A gasp as the guy tensed, like he hadn't expected my response. "Oh, I really like you."

Then he went to town, pounding into me. I was so ready. I braced myself on the door with one hand and grabbed my cock with the other. Shit. The guy hadn't given permission. "Can I . . . ?"

"Can you what?"

This fucking game. "Cum. Please let me fucking cum."

A chuckle. "Yes. Cum now."

He didn't have to say it twice. All it took was one tug, and I cried out as I orgasmed, exploding onto the door. I could feel myself pulsating around the guy's cock.

I was still on an orgasmic high when he pulled out and ripped the condom off. I turned, falling to my knees, not wanting to miss any of it. My mouth watered as CJ jerked his cock in front of my face. With a grunt, he poured himself into my open, waiting mouth. I swallowed as much as I could, loving the way he tasted, wanting more.

It was over way too soon.

Chapter 18

Jake

Duet rehearsal night. That meant I would see Ian again.

I planned to keep it professional. Nothing personal, no matter what. The affirmation bounced around in my head as I secured my helmet onto my bike. If Ian wanted to hear the truth, I'd tell him, but I wouldn't force him to hear it. The last thing I wanted was to get kicked out of his house again.

I would not—*would not*—display any signs of jealousy if, by chance, whatshisname was brought up. I wanted to prove to Ian that I'd changed, that I wasn't an overbearing dickhead who didn't know how to control his impulses. As much as it ate me alive, knowing Ian belonged to someone else—gulp—I wanted to show support. If I couldn't have him, the next best thing was friendship. I'd take whatever I could get. Ian's happiness was most important.

And, for the love of God, no matter how cute Ian looked or how tempting his lips were, I would not make a move on him.

Trust, it'd been difficult up to this point.

But I didn't want to get slapped or punched. The progress I'd made would be severed, if you could even call it progress. At least Ian didn't look like he wanted to murder me anymore.

I didn't want him believing I had only used him for sex. That couldn't be further from the truth.

I let out a deep breath as I rang the doorbell, gaining resolve to stick to the self-promises.

Instant. Hard-on.

Ian stood in the doorway. His hair—oh my fucking God. No styling products. Loose curls. Just the way I liked it.

"Hey," Ian said. "Is there something wrong?"

Why would he ask that? Oh, yeah—*close your damn mouth.* "Um, what?" And wipe the drool off your chin.

This was what Ian Cooper resorted me to: a blubbering idiot. I'd be a happy idiot if only—

"I asked if there was something wrong?"

"Nope. Nothing. Absolutely not. Everything's good."

Act cool.

"Are you going to stand out there all night?"

"What? Oh. Nah, man. Don't be silly," I said, stepping inside and clearing my throat. *Smooth.*

As I untangled myself from my guitar case, I studied the sexy specimen of a human while he skimmed through some papers. The man was casual tonight—well, casual for him. He still wore slacks, but they were casual slacks. Beige. Or khaki? And his white button-down was unbuttoned at the neck, showing off his collarbones and a glimpse of his chest hair. The sleeves were rolled up to his elbows, exposing his sexy forearms.

And his fucking hair.

"Is there a problem?"

"Huh?" I raised my lids, pausing amid taking off my jacket.

"Why do you keep staring at me?"

I drew my brows together, shrugging the jacket the rest of the way off. "What? No. Me? I'm not staring. Me? Nope. I wouldn't"—Ian quirked a brow—"say I was staring. I was just noticing that you trimmed your beard."

"It was getting itchy."

"Why not shave it all the way off?"

He narrowed his eyes. "I don't want to."

"Whatever," I muttered, acting like shaving wouldn't be the cherry on top of this hot, casual look he was sporting this evening. Clearing my throat, I added, "I see you left your hair natural."

"I didn't have time to style it. I worked from home today and got caught up in some things."

"Ah." I turned toward my guitar. His eyes were scrutinizing me. *Play it cool, play it cool.* I began whistling some nonsensical tune.

"Are you okay?"

"Huh? Me? I'm peachy. Why?"

"You seem a little flustered."

"Flustered? Me? No, not me. I'm cool. You're cool. We're— yeah. I'm ready."

"Are you sure?"

"Yup." My voice cracked. Fuck. I put my hands on my hips, smacking my lips. My disobedient eyes looked upward at Ian's curls. But Ian was watching me like a worried therapist, so I shifted my gaze to the floor. And whistled again. *Slick.*

"Is this going to be a problem for you?" Ian asked.

"What? What do you mean?"

"Should I go fix my hair?"

"No!" That came out way too forceful. "I mean, no, of course not. Why should you? It's fine. You look"—I sighed—"fine. It's fine." Who turned off the AC? My armpits were sweating.

Ian's lips curled into a half smile. I wondered if my hard bulge was noticeable behind the confinement of my jeans. I turned to grab my guitar and adjusted myself—*sorry, boy, ain't gonna happen tonight*—and used the instrument as coverage.

When I spun around, Ian was still looking at me. "Do you just want to fuck now and get it over with?"

My eyes widened. Did I hear him correctly? Maybe I wanted Ian so badly that I was hearing things. "What?"

He crossed his arms over his chest and quirked a brow. "I think you heard me."

"Wait—really?"

Ian's lips twitched, spreading into a smile as he shook his head. "Let's get to work."

"Right," I said, deflating as I sat down on the chair next to the piano. What did I expect? Not for the love of my life to look extra fuckable tonight, that was for damn sure.

As Ian prepared the music sheets, his fingers caught my eye. Before I could stop myself, I grabbed a hand to get a closer look. "You painted your nails."

He gasped.

Shit. I was touching him, holding him, feeling his warm skin. I lifted my gaze. Ian was focused on our joined hands, his mouth slightly open. He raised his lids, those electric-blue eyes sparkling.

I wanted to kiss him so bad. All I had to do was pull him toward me and our lips would collide. Instead, I rubbed my thumb over his knuckles, keeping my eyes locked with his. Warmth and softness. His fingers, long and sexy. And because I didn't want to push my luck, I squeezed gently and let his palm slide off.

He blinked and looked away. After clearing his throat twice, he said, "Um, yeah. I, uh, guess I wanted to express myself now that everyone knows who I am."

"That's awesome. I love it." The black nail polish symbolized something Ian believed in strongly, and that made him more irresistible. If that was even possible.

"Thanks."

After another stretch of silence, he cleared his throat once again and went back to sorting out the music sheets. And rehearsal began.

It was a better practice than the first one. We got more accomplished and were able to fix a lot of hiccups we experienced at the last practice. It was like the ice had broken—probably, in part, due to my idiocy earlier. We were more relaxed. Kind of like old times.

Almost.

We had been at it for at least an hour. I rolled my neck as Ian wrote some notes on a music sheet.

"Hey, do you mind if I raid your fridge for a drink?"

"Go ahead."

I placed my guitar down gently on the chair, then went over to the kitchen. As I opened the refrigerator door, I asked, "Do you want anything?"

"A glass of water with ice, please, if you don't mind."

After grabbing a soda, I headed to the cabinet Ian kept the glasses in. Damn right, I remembered that shit. Every memory was engraved in my brain.

I popped the glass over the ice button, filled it with water, then returned to the living room. "Here you go," I said, handing the cup to Ian.

"Thanks."

I flicked open my soda can as I plopped down on the couch and gulped some of the fizzy goodness.

"We'll take a short break. I want to get through this next song."

"Okay. How many songs are we doing again?"

"Four."

I nodded as we fell into a not-so-comfortable silence. Ian stayed on the piano bench instead of the couch. Understandable, considering what happened last time. It was probably a good thing he stayed away from me. Especially while looking like eye candy. No telling if I'd be able to contain myself.

My self-promises stood to attention at the forefront of my brain, but that didn't mean I couldn't admire the view. The man's lips—he tucked them in his mouth, licking them after each sip of water.

Just one kiss.

What? No. Bad idea. Had I not just promised myself to not make a move? God, I wanted to. Question was—how?

Don't do it.

"Why don't you come sit over here?" *Fuck.* "That bench can't be comfortable."

"I'm good. Besides, a couple more minutes, and we'll get back to work."

Damn, he didn't take the bait. Good thing. I took another slurp of soda as I tried to think of another way to get close enough to kiss him. *No.* "I came out to my dad," I blurted.

Shit. So much for keeping things personal-free.

Ian's head snapped up, his eyes wide. "What?"

"Actually, Miranda outed me. What a bitch, am I right?"

He closed his eyes, shaking his head as he put the glass of water on the floor. "Wait, what?" he asked again, clearly not getting it.

Maybe this was forcing him to hear the truth. I had to abort any more info. "I'm sorry. I shouldn't have brought it up. Forget I said anything."

"No—Jake, you can't just say something like that and expect me to forget it. Please, explain."

How much could I spill without mentioning my dad's side business? Ian said he would let me know when he was ready to listen. And now, with my dad threatening me as well, I wasn't sure if I should say anything at all, although I was almost positive that it was a bluff. "Miranda told my dad I wanted to leave her for a man. My dad confronted me about it, and I admitted to him that I'm gay—and that I'm in love with an amazing guy."

If a pin fell onto the floor right now, it would've echoed throughout the house. Moments stretched into minutes, it seemed, as Ian continued to stare at me with shocked eyes.

I scooted forward. "I'll leave," I said as I stood, figuring Ian's next words would be to get out.

Ian put a hand up. "Wait, no. Why?"

"Because I know you're not ready to hear any of this. I'm sorry I sprung it on you. I'll get out of your face."

"No, I'm just . . . surprised and . . . really, really confused." He pushed himself up to stand as well. "But I meant why would Miranda tell your dad?"

"Because she hates me. And wants to cause trouble like always."

"If that's true, then why is she marrying you?"

I wasn't sure how to answer that. If I spoke the truth, then I'd have to tell Ian the whole story.

He must've realized the same thing because, before I could respond, he said, "Don't answer that. Instead, tell me what your father said."

"He told me I was bringing shame to our family."

Ian's shoulders fell. "I'm sorry."

"Don't be. I expected it." I could see in his eyes what he wanted to ask. "Yes, it's you. And no, I didn't tell him it was you. I didn't want him to come at you. Besides, I know you're in a relationship. I don't want to jeopardize that." Yeah, as I literally tried to woo the man close enough to kiss him. Points for keeping the jealousy out of my voice, though. Seemed to be the only promise I'd been able to conquer. Not that it was easy.

He looked away, visibly swallowing.

I stepped closer. "Do you want me to leave now?"

His brows came together as he lifted his head and faced me. "No, I—"

As his words trailed off, our eyes met. Now was my chance. I cupped his jaw, my thumb grazing along the stubble of his beard. He didn't pull away, so I leaned in until our lips touched. Soft and slow. So warm. God, I'd missed him. Inhaling, I moved to deepen the kiss.

Ian gripped my shoulders, pushing me away.

"I'm sorry," I said, putting my hands up. "I shouldn't have done that."

And, in a shocking turn of events, Ian latched on to my shirt, pulling me close, and kissed me. Bruising and punishing, but hot. And I wanted more.

My hands came up to the sides of his face, holding him as my tongue wrestled with his. He pushed me back until I fell onto the couch and he followed, straddling me. Our lips came together again, tasting and exploring. I palmed his ass, pulling him along my cock as he moved his hips against me. It all felt familiar, a void that had been missing these past few months. Ian filled it. This completed it.

Too many clothes between us. I was rock hard, and my body screamed for some skin-on-skin contact. The little voice inside my head told me to let Ian take the lead. Don't be greedy. But of course, my hands didn't listen. Untucking his shirt from his pants, my fingers slipped inside, sliding up his back. Hot skin. Then, coming around the front, I began unbuttoning his shirt.

That's what broke the spell.

Ian moaned in protest and pushed off me.

Coldness. Loneliness. Emptiness.

My life source stood before me, flushed, aroused, and sexy as hell. "You should leave."

I nodded. I couldn't deny I was disappointed, but I understood. "Okay."

I got up, grabbed my guitar off the chair, and went through the long process of putting it away, secured and zipped. Jacket on, satchel over my head, case on my back. Sometime along the way, Ian had sat back down on the piano bench, shirt retucked, arms crossed protectively around himself. He looked neither angry nor happy, just confused. Like he was sorting through his emotions.

"Ian, I really am sorry. For everything."

He blinked, nodding. "I'll see you tomorrow."

Well, at least he wasn't shoving me out the door and telling me to go to hell. Progress.

"Yeah, okay. See you tomorrow." And I let myself out.

* * *

Ian

I didn't move for a long time after Jake left. My mind was reeling from everything that had transpired.

What exactly *had* transpired?

I brought my fingers to my mouth. Jake's essence was still there, lingering as if we were still kissing. The moment our lips touched, there had been a spark. All the angst, self-loathing, and emptiness I had suffered the past few months vanished in that split second before I shoved him away, which was why I had pulled him back for more. I wanted to feel again. To feel alive instead of dead inside. To love instead of hate.

Getting drunk and kissing strangers hadn't brought me to the level of euphoria that Jake brought me to while completely sober. The high I'd been searching for. It was like electrical currents had gone through my body, waking me up and charging me back to life.

Earlier, when I had asked if Jake wanted to fuck, I was joking, of course. Jake had been aroused—the way he acted and looked at me, I could tell. I felt in control for once.

I would have fucked him. Hell, I wanted to fuck him.

God, if I weren't so mad and hurt still—and confused—I would have gone through with it right on the couch.

But I remembered my promise to him. No sex again until he broke it off with Miranda. I refused to be anybody's side dick.

Jake made me feel alive. Did it matter if his life was messy?

Was I actually considering becoming Jake's sidepiece?

I groaned as I buried my face in my hands, lowering my elbows to my knees.

Jake had come out to his dad. That had to account for something, right? And he'd told his father he was in love with me. That could have been a lie. The whole thing—just to get laid.

Or he could have been telling the truth.

The priest I had confessed to might have been right. I wouldn't be able to move on, be happy, until I forgave Jake. And made him mine again.

It was time. Time to hear Jake's side of the story. Then we'd fuck.

Chapter 19

Matt

Turned out, it wasn't over.

After coming out of the bathroom from washing up, I expected CJ to be dressed and halfway out the door, maybe even long gone. It was just a hookup, after all. But when I stepped into the room, the man was sprawled out on the bed, facedown, butt-ass naked. Damn, he had a perfect ass. Like, squats-level perfect. I couldn't *not* touch that ass.

"What are you doing?" CJ asked, muffled into the pillow.

"Huh?" I asked, not because I didn't hear him but because I was too busy staring at the guy's ass.

He turned his head to the side, making his voice audible. "You're not leaving yet, are you?"

"No."

"Good. I'm not finished with you yet."

"Hey, are you verse too?"

"Yeah. Why? You wanna fuck me?"

One would think after the explosive orgasm I experienced, I'd be satisfied for a whole week, at least. But nope, I wanted more. My body was on board, already rising for the occasion. "Yeah. I do."

"I was hoping you'd say that." He turned onto his side and extended his hand.

I took it as I sat on the edge of the bed and leaned down to kiss him.

"Where do you want to start?" he asked.

"I kinda wanna play with your ass, to be honest. I mean, do you do daily squats or something? Looks like you can bounce a quarter off that thing."

He threw his head back and burst out laughing. "I take it you're an ass man?"

I smiled, reaching out a finger along his face. "Actually, I'm more of a beard man."

"Oh yeah?"

I nodded, biting my bottom lip.

"I can see how much you like it." He lowered his eyes to my growing erection.

I smirked and shrugged. "What can I say? It's a fetish of mine."

"Well, let's take care of that for you." He turned back onto his stomach. "Have your way with my ass, Doc."

I hopped onto the bed and knelt between his legs, grabbing two handfuls of butt cheek. So firm yet squishable.

"Damn, boy," CJ groaned. "By the way, I do CrossFit occasionally."

"Ah, that explains it." I continued massaging, separating his ass cheeks, then squishing them together. Pressing up his back, I began a full-blown massage.

"Blue eyes, I think I may have found my fetish."

"What's that? Massages?"

"Hands. Yours are amazing."

"Thanks. I'm glad you're enjoying this."

"A little too much. I might fall asleep."

"Uh-oh. Can't have that." Leaning down, I kissed the small of his back, then lower until I reached his butt crack and licked him. I moved down and spread his legs, kissing and licking as I separated his butt cheeks again and licked his asshole.

CJ moaned. "Now we're talking."

I continued with the ass play until CJ's breathing got heavier and moaning got louder. I pulled back. "Get on your hands and knees." Turnabout's fair play.

"Yes, sir. Is this part of the examination, Doc?"

I grinned. "Oh yeah. And trust me, you'll feel so much better after."

He purred.

I reached between his legs, grabbing his cock. It was hard but had room to grow. A few jerks and tugs took care of that. I buried my face in his ass, sucking where I could. Biting. Licking.

I smacked his ass, unable to resist.

"Oh, shit. Do that again."

Who was I to deny him? *Smack.*

"Again," he panted.

I kept that up for a while, then inserted a finger in his hole. He moaned, so I inserted a second finger. He fell to his elbows as I fingered him, his ass in the air, giving me perfect access. I used my spit to keep him wet for easy gliding. You had to work with what you had when no lube was around.

"I want your cock inside me."

"What was that?" After what he'd put me through? C'mon, I couldn't make this easy on him.

"Fuck me, Doc."

"Are you sure you want it?"

He chuckled softly. "I want it so bad."

I smiled. "What do you want so bad?"

"You," he breathed. "I want your enormous cock deep inside my ass."

I jumped off the bed to the night table and grabbed a condom from the stack CJ had provided. After I slipped it on, I used my saliva, making sure he was nice and slick, then pushed my way in.

"Oh yeah," CJ moaned. "All the way. That's it."

I bit my bottom lip. He felt so damn good. He pushed back against me, indicating the go-ahead. And I did. I fucked him good. Fast and slow, rough and gentle—well, mostly rough. "Does it feel good?" I asked.

"Fuck yes. Your cock feels amazing."

"You feel amazing too."

I flipped him over. I wanted to see his face when he came. He smiled as I hooked one of his legs over my shoulder and reentered him. He grabbed his own cock, jerking. "Give it to me, Doc."

He moaned as I fucked him hard until his asshole spasmed around my cock. And he cried out, cumming all over his stomach and chest.

"Where do you want it?" I breathed as my balls tightened. I was close.

"On my beard," he replied without hesitation.

If I weren't about to erupt, I would've laughed. Pulling out, I ripped the condom off and climbed over him, straddling his face as I jerked off. My fingers gripped the top of his head, holding him still as I came on his beard.

I collapsed next to him, panting, and laughed. "That was wild."

CJ turned on his side with his head on his hand. His other hand slid over my chest to my neck and pulled me in for a kiss. "I'm going to wash up."

My eyes followed his perfect ass as he disappeared into the bathroom. I was so spent. A thousand years of sleep seemed achievable. Checking my phone crossed my mind, but my pants were across the room. No energy to move.

I was dozing off when CJ came out. Grabbing his clothes, he strode closer to the bed and began getting dressed.

"Can I see you again?" I asked before I could stop myself. He paused, his pants halfway past his hips. Immediate regret. "Sorry." I rubbed the sleep deprivation from my face. "I didn't mean it like—forget it. I say stupid shit when I'm tired."

CJ smiled as he zipped and buckled his pants, then leaned over me, supporting himself on the bed. "I'd love to see you again."

"Really?"

"Sure. This was fun." He kissed me. When he straightened, he shrugged. "I was going to ask you first, but you beat me to it."

After he was done getting dressed, he kissed me one last time. "The room is paid for through the night, so feel free to stay as long as you'd like. I'll text you."

And he was gone.

Chapter 20

Ian

I rang the rectory's doorbell instead of letting myself in. With Father Daniel away on missionary and Father John joining the ranks in calling the shots, along with Father Kevin, I figured I'd build that trust first. I didn't want to step on any toes.

The door swung open and a nun answered the door. She seemed young and was wearing a gray skirt and blue vest over a white shirt. She had a white veil over her hair, blonde curls sticking out around her face.

"Good morning, sir. May I help you?" she asked with a sweet smile.

"Hello. I'm Ian Cooper, the music director here."

"Oh, nice to meet you, Mr. Cooper. I'm Sister Mary Jane. I'm filling in temporarily as the office assistant."

Anna's replacement. "I'm here to see Father Kevin."

"Ah, of course. Please come in." She stepped aside. "He's in the back office."

"Thank you. It was nice meeting you. I'm sure we'll see more of each other."

"Yes, likewise."

At the back office, I knocked on the open door. Father Kevin glanced up from the computer screen. "Ian, hello. Welcome. Please come in."

I walked in and took a seat across the desk. "Thanks for seeing me, Father."

"It's no problem at all. How are the duet rehearsals coming along with you and Jake?"

Aside from me practically jumping his bones? "Surprisingly well. We've only had two practices so far, but I think we're making progress."

"Oh, wonderful! I can't express what a relief it is to hear you say that. I knew you two could put your differences aside for this great cause. But I must say, when I got your email, I thought there was a problem."

"Oh no, not at all. I know how much this program means to you, so we're making it work." I supposed it wasn't too far from the truth. We were being civil to one another, at least. Kissing and grinding included.

"I'm so glad. Thank you for that. What can I do for you?"

"I wanted to ask your permission to start an LGBTQ+ support group here at the church."

"Oh," he said as he folded his hands on the desk. "We do have counseling groups in place for that sort of thing."

"With all due respect, Father, those groups are not really support groups."

"Oh?"

"Ever since I brought Matt to Mass, I've been getting countless emails from people—mostly teens—begging me to help them. I've even had people come up to me in person. They are lost. They have no support from their families. They need someplace to go. I'm not a certified counselor by any means, but I want to offer them something. A place to go where there would be like-minded people to share their stories, support one another, make friends. A haven where they're accepted without judgment. A place where they're not told it's a sin to be who they are."

"I see. It's kind of you to want to help these people, but—"

"I can do it all myself. All I need from you is approval and a space."

"Unfortunately, it's a little more involved than that. You're talking about going against what the Church teaches."

"Not exactly. We don't want to protest the Church. It's apparent we all love being Catholics, otherwise we wouldn't be here. We just want to share our stories and be heard amongst each other. Please, Father. We wouldn't be hurting anyone or getting in the way of anything."

"You mean how no one got hurt vandalizing your car?"

"You heard about that?"

"The police came here asking questions."

"I'm sorry. I didn't want to worry anyone. But the police are investigating. It's under control. It was just that one incident. And if anything else happens, I'll take full responsibility."

"I don't know, Ian."

"We can do it under the radar."

"Like a secret support group?" Father Kevin hesitated. "Let me think about it. I'll have to see where you can do this group thing. And I might have to talk to Father John as well."

"Thank you so much, Father. This will mean so much to so many people."

"Well, don't thank me yet. I haven't approved it yet."

"I understand. Thanks for the consideration."

Chapter 21

Jake

When I sauntered into the church for choir practice, I wasn't sure what to expect. Would Ian be pissed? Awkward? Act like nothing happened?

No idea.

He was talking to some members at the organ when his eyes shifted and met mine. Hair gelled, beard still on his face, and suit back on. Looking professional and sexy AF. Sure, I absolutely loved the casual look from last night, but this look was also on point. Ian was an all-around hot guy.

The only guy who'd ever given me butterflies. Come to think of it, not many girls held that power either.

As I neared the front pew, Ian lifted a finger, gesturing for me to wait. Was he going to kick me off the choir? Fuck. He was going to kick me off choir because I couldn't control myself around him. To be fair, he was the one who'd tackled me into a full-blown grinding sesh.

Ian finished up with the other members, then motioned for me to come over. It was like a magnetic pull, which I followed with pleasure, but I couldn't read his expression.

"Wait for me after practice," he said quietly once I reached him. "There's something I need to talk to you about."

"Am I in trouble?"

His lips tightened as he drew his brows together. "Just wait for me. Please."

I had planned on waiting anyway. Not only to apologize again but also to protect him from the hater who had vandalized his car. The idea of him walking into the dark alone with homophobes lurking around didn't sit well with me. But I kept all that to myself as I nodded.

"Okay, people, let's get this rehearsal started," Ian addressed the group.

I half listened as he directed. If he was giving me the boot, why let me stay to practice? That couldn't be what he wanted to talk about. It could be about the duet concert. Or maybe I'd crossed a line last night, and he simply wanted to call me out on it.

Just as I thought I'd die from the suspense—

"Okay, that's a wrap. I'll see you all on Sunday."

I didn't even remember singing, but thank God it was over. I stayed put as everybody took their leave. As a few stragglers grabbed Ian's attention, I moved to retrieve my satchel off the front pew, then slid into a couple of rows back on the organ's side.

Brad, the youngest choir member, was the one up there. Ian put his hand on the boy's shoulder as he spoke to him. I couldn't hear them from this distance, but whatever they were discussing seemed serious. Ian smiled reassuringly to the boy, and Brad smiled back. Then they said their goodbyes.

Finally, we were alone.

Ian's eyes met mine briefly. He blinked and proceeded to pack his papers into his bag. I took a deep breath as I watched him. My nerves increased with each passing second.

After slipping on his jacket, he lifted the bag strap onto his shoulder and made his way down the aisle toward me. My heart quickened as he slid into the pew in front of me, facing me. Moments passed before he finally spoke. "I'm ready."

It took me a second to realize what he meant. "Really?"

He nodded. "Tell me. Why did you ask Miranda to marry you?"

"Oh. You want to do this here? Like, right now?"

"Yeah. The church is free for the rest of the night, so we won't get interrupted. Plus, it's neutral ground. You're less likely to lie if Jesus is staring down at you."

My eyes shifted to the crucifix mounted behind the altar. He had a point. Not that I would lie. Moving my gaze back to Ian, I nodded. "Fair enough. The best way to explain this is to start at the beginning."

"Sounds good to me. Let's hear it."

This was not how or where I pictured telling Ian the truth. Honestly, I never thought he'd give me the chance. I gathered my thoughts and prayed I was doing the right thing. "The night after we were together, I wanted to text you, but Miranda was close by in the bathroom, getting ready for bed, so it wasn't a good idea. When she came into the bedroom, she wanted to have sex. Which I thought was strange because she never initiated—"

He put his hands up, squeezing his eyes shut. "Can we do this without those kinds of details?"

"Nothing happened. I couldn't be with her after being with you. In fact, I haven't touched her since that night."

He rolled his eyes. "Come on, Jake. You agreed not to lie."

"I swear to God, I'm not lying." I pointed to the crucifix. "With Jesus as my witness, I'm telling you the truth. I haven't had sex with Miranda or anybody else since you and I were together."

He stared at me in disbelief, then shook his head. "Just continue."

"When I rejected her, she accused me of having an affair with you. I denied it at first because I was exhausted and didn't want to fight. But she kept at it until I couldn't take it anymore and told her I was leaving and moving out the next day. Still, she wouldn't let things go. So—I came out to her. And confessed everything. That she'd been right all along. That I was obsessed with you, and that we were in love. She asked if we had slept together, and I admitted the truth. I mean, at that point, there was no sense in lying to her anymore. But she went ballistic. Slapped me, yelled, everything you would expect. And I took it. I deserved it for staying with her for so long, knowing I wasn't into her."

"So you felt guilty. That's why you proposed."

"Hell no. I felt free. For once, I saw the light at the end of the tunnel. An exit. Finally. The first thing I wanted to do was call you and tell you I'd done it. At last, we could be together. But then—"

"What? Jake, tell me the truth. I can handle it."

"Ian, what I'm about to tell you . . . it's bad. You can't repeat this to anyone. Lives could be at stake."

The concern in his eyes intensified as he nodded. "Tell me."

"Miranda gave me a manila folder." I paused. "Inside was a list of names and numbers. It looked like a list of clients with financial assets. Then Miranda said they were my dad's clients. But not from the financial institution he works for. Ian, my dad is—my dad is a white-collar drug dealer."

* * *

Ian

Of all the reasons I'd thought up as to why Jake had stabbed me in the heart, William Edwards being a drug dealer wasn't one of them.

The notion was so ridiculous, so far-fetched, I didn't know whether to laugh or cry.

I looked away, then back at Jake and shook my head, sighing. "Really, Jake? That's the best you could do?" I got up. I was done wasting my time. There was my fucking closure. Jake thought this whole thing was one big-ass joke.

He stood, blocking my path out of the pew. "Wait, where are you going?"

"I'm leaving. I've heard enough of your lies to last me a lifetime."

"But I'm not—"

"You know, I was willing to forget everything. To forgive you for my own sanity. I was ready to accept that you chickened out and asked Miranda to marry you because you were too scared to come out. I even considered fucking after this, maybe becoming lovers on the down-low. But this?" I shook my head. "I can't."

I tried to move past him, but he blocked me again. "Hold up. What? You need to back up. Did you say you wanna fuck?"

Of course that was what he got hung up on. "*Considered.* Past tense. Now get out of my way."

"No. You asked for the truth, and we're not leaving here until you get it."

"Are you ready to admit you chickened out and that's why you proposed to Miranda?"

"Not unless you want me to lie to you."

I narrowed my eyes as my shoulders slumped forward. I was really tired of this shit.

"Look," Jake continued. "For some reason, you have it in your head that things went down that way. But I'm telling you, you're wrong. We are in church with Jesus staring down at me. And as much as I'm dying to fuck you right now, I'm not going to say something that isn't true. Either you're ready to hear the truth or you're not. But I'm not going to make shit up just to get laid and because it's easier for you to accept."

Goddamn it. He had a point. "Fine," I said grudgingly, sliding back into the pew. "I'm listening."

"Okay, then." Jake sat as well. "Apparently, my dad embezzles money from his company to buy drugs, then he sells to high-profile businesspeople, puts the money back into the company, and keeps a hefty profit for himself."

"And this is what Miranda told you? She got all of that from a list of names?"

"Miranda owns a business. There were numbers by the names that didn't add up to her. That's why she investigated. She said people talk at the salon, which made her suspicious."

"And since when is Miranda a reliable source of information?"

"She's not, which was why I confronted my dad. He denied it at first, but I got the truth out of him."

"Was that before or after you came out to him?"

Jake snapped his brows together. "Before."

"Mm-hmm. I'm sorry, but I still don't see why you're marrying—"

"She's blackmailing me, Ian. It's either marry her or she'll give the feds the info she has."

"And you couldn't tell me this because . . . ?"

"I was scared. She told me not to say anything to you or she'd turn him in. I didn't want my dad going to prison. I needed time to confront him and process this. That's why I stayed away from you. I knew if I saw you, I'd tell you everything. And I had planned to. But keeping this from you—losing you—has been the hardest thing in my life."

"If that's true, then why didn't you tell me at the hospital?"

"Anna was fighting for her life, and you were worried sick about her. I wasn't going to burden you with more shit. I wanted that moment together to be about you. I wanted to be there for you. I thought I'd have more time. I didn't know Miranda was going to announce our bogus engagement that day."

If only I'd waited when Jake came after me. If only I'd given him a chance to explain. All these months, all this suffering. When I thought of the club that night, what I almost did . . . "So why tell me now? What's changed?"

"When I first confronted my dad five months ago, I gave him the opportunity to fix it, but he did nothing. The only thing he did was talk to Miranda to convince her to let me go. It backfired because she ended up outing me, which got my dad on her side and in her clutches. Now he wants me to marry her, not only to keep her mouth shut about him but also to keep me in the closet."

I swallowed hard. "Wow. Jake, I—"

"But to hell with both of them," he continued. "I told my father I'm leaving Miranda, and I didn't care if she sends him to prison. I really don't. He had plenty of opportunities to stop doing illegal business, to fix this, but he's chosen not to. Now he has to deal with the consequences. I'm tired of being everyone's pawn. Why should I suffer the rest of my life for my dad's criminal activities?"

This was too much. Without saying a word, I got up and slid out of the pew.

"Ian?"

"I need some air." I headed down the aisle.

"Ian, wait—"

I pushed out into the damp night. Raindrops slapped my face, but I barely felt them. Across the parking lot—

Jake caught up and shouted from behind, "Ian, stop. I'm not making this up. Please, I'm begging you. You have to believe me. I'm sorry it took me so long to tell you. But I'm fighting for my happiness now. I want to be with you. I've been in prison long enough. Please, forgive me—"

I whipped around. The rain was really coming down now, biting into my skin, masking my tears. "I'm so sorry, Jake."

Confusion shadowed his features as he squinted through the downpour. "What? Why?"

"For not giving you a chance to explain sooner. God, I'm so stupid. If only—"

He closed the gap between us, his hands gripping my face. "Hey, listen to me. None of this is your fault. You're letting me explain now. That's all that matters."

"Why does Miranda hate me so much?" I cried.

"God, no. Baby boy, it's me she hates. I'm so sorry I hurt you. I'm sorry I let her bully me for so long."

"I'm sorry too. I'm sorry you had to go through all that alone."

"It's okay. You didn't know."

"I've been such a jerk to you."

"I deserved it."

"No, you didn't."

"Does this mean you forgive me?"

Instead of answering with words, I leaned forward and kissed him. And that same electrical current from last night came back. I wrapped my arms around him and deepened the kiss. He moaned as he kissed me back, the urgency rising.

I needed Jake. God, I missed him. So much time wasted—I couldn't waste a minute more. Pulling back, I took his hand and led him to the SUV.

"In the loaner, baby?" he laughed behind me.

I turned, leaning my back against the slick car. "I thought you'd want to see how big the back seat is compared to mine. But if you don't wanna—"

"Are you kidding? Where are the keys?"

I dug in my bag and retrieved them, turning to open the door. Jake distracted me by kissing my neck from behind. More currents ran through my body, waking every cell.

"Baby, open the fucking door," he groaned. "I want you so bad."

I chuckled as I finally got it unlocked. We hopped into the back seat, tossing our bags in the front and removing our soaked jackets. Then we tackled each other. Hands going everywhere. Kissing, tasting.

Jake's fingers found the buttons on my shirt, nearly tearing the fabric to expose my aching skin. His scorching lips connected to my chest, licking and moaning as he peeled the button-down off me. Searching for the hem of his drenched shirt, I helped as he pulled it over his head. I leaned back onto the seat as we came together again, easing him down with me. He adjusted himself on top of me, pressing his cock against me, rubbing through the confines of our pants. I was so hard. We'd been apart too long. My body screamed for every inch of him to make up for lost time.

"Let's get these wet pants off you," Jake whispered as he rose to tug at the button and zipper effortlessly.

He was back over my naked body before the cold registered. Every place his lips made contact with left a trail of fire, warming me. My cock jerked for his touch.

And he did not disappoint.

His hand wrapped around me, knowing exactly what I needed. Perfect pressure. Exquisite teasing. A thumb grazed my tip, spreading the pre-cum until the head was well lubricated. He dipped his head. I died as he took me in his mouth.

I couldn't control the moans that escaped my lips. My hips pumped as he sucked me into his throat. My hands extended to his head, tangling my fingers through his short hair. I was rapidly getting closer, but I didn't want to cum yet. I wanted him inside me. Either that or I wanted to give him the same pleasure.

I tugged on his head. "Jake—"

It was like he read my mind. He leaned back onto his knees on the car floor and stripped off his jeans.

I attacked him, contorting my body to reach his abs, kissing and licking his belly button. I wanted all of him, to taste all of him. God, I'd missed his scent, the way he tasted. He ran his fingers through my still-damp hair, holding me to him as I drew him into my mouth.

Jake moaned above me. "Baby . . . that feels good."

I gripped his ass, pulling him closer, taking more of him in. He gasped as he eased me away and pushed me against the seat, kissing me. I wanted to suck him some more, but my disappointment was short-lived as I realized he was just as close as I was to cumming.

"Should I use a condom?"

"No. Nothing's changed since last time." For a split second, my mind went back to that club. If it hadn't been for Matt, Anna, and Ant, my answer would've been different.

Jake furrowed his brow but didn't ask questions. He just took my word as he positioned himself between my legs and slowly eased himself inside.

I bit my bottom lip as he waited until I adjusted around him. The familiar pressure subsided quickly. Intense pleasure took over, along with an urge to pump. I rotated my hips, giving him the okay to go deeper.

We kept eye contact as he moved, sliding in and out, building up the tension. I dug my fingertips along his back, his muscles bulging beneath my touch.

"I love you," he whispered.

"I love you too," I breathed back.

He rested his forehead on mine. "I missed you so much."

I captured his face in my hands. "I missed you too. More than you know."

He kissed me. "I'm so sorry. For every—"

"Shhh. Just make love to me, Jake."

He closed his eyes and dipped his head into the crook of my neck.

"And—Jake?"

"Hmm?" he murmured as he nibbled at my flesh.

"I want you to cum inside me."

His head popped up. "Really?"

I nodded. "I want to feel everything."

Jake kissed me again as he moved against me, beginning to pump faster. I moaned as I wrapped my arms around him, gripping his ass, encouraging him to pump harder. His cock swelled as our bodies caused friction, bringing us closer.

He lifted himself onto his hands, looking between our bodies. Balancing himself, he reached down and grabbed my cock, jerking me slightly. "Are you close?"

"So close."

Lowering back down, he continued to pump. Faster.

"Yes, like that—don't stop." I was so ready to cum. My intent was to reach for my cock between our bodies, but before I could touch myself, I exploded.

"Holy shit," Jake grunted in surprise, then tensed up. "Fuck!" He stilled as his cock pulsated inside me, filling me with warm fluid. As the pulses subsided, his head snapped up. "That was hot."

I laughed. "Oh my God, yes. I loved feeling you cum inside me."

"I fucking made you cum hands-free," he replied, grinning from ear to ear.

I laughed harder. "Yeah, that was a surprise."

He nudged my neck. "When can we do that again?"

"Oh, I don't know. Maybe ten minutes?"

Jake chuckled. "For sure."

Chapter 22

Jake

Fuck ever moving from this position.

As it turned out, the back seat of the loaner was hella spacious. Yeah, we got to test it out twice—and it only took five minutes, not ten, like Ian had predicted.

Now my love lay nestled between my legs, his back to my chest, both of us still butt-ass naked. I tightened my arms around him. I couldn't believe this was real. We were in a good place again. Thank God. For the first time in months, I felt happy. Relieved. Like I could breathe again. I didn't want this night to ever end.

The rain outside had stopped. Because the heat from our lovemaking had faded, it was getting chilly. "Are you cold?"

Ian shrugged. "A little."

"Here, let me reach my jacket. It's on the floor somewhere." I smirked, leaning forward and reaching blindly for it. I found it, then draped it over us like a blanket. "It's a little damp."

"It's fine. Thanks," Ian said, sinking into my arms again. I kissed the top of his head as I wrapped my arms around him once again. "It's getting late. When do you have to leave?" he asked.

I sighed. "I don't know. Never."

"Are you really going to let Miranda send your dad to prison?"

"Yes. I told you, I'm done with them."

"What about your mom? Does she know about any of this?"

"Nope. Clueless. My dad kept begging me not to say anything to her while promising me he'd take care of it. He hasn't, so my mother's wrath will be unleashed."

"You don't care that she'll be hurt?"

"Of course I do, baby. But I can't protect her from this. My mom is a strong woman, and I'll be there for her. If anything, she'll probably be pissed that I've kept it from her this long."

Ian leaned his head back and looked up at me. "I'm so sorry I wasn't there for you."

I dipped down, brushing my lips to his. "It's okay. You're here now. But we have to make a pact to always communicate and listen to each other, no matter what. I can't lose you again."

"I promise."

"Me too." And as much as I hated to bring up whatshisname at a time like this, I had to ask. "What about Matt?"

"What about him?"

"Are you going to let the guy down easy or—"

"Oh, we broke up a while ago. Actually, we were never really official. We just hung out, went out on a few dates—you know, nothing serious."

"What?" Not that I wasn't happy. Hell yeah, I was, but— "When?"

"The day after you showed up at choir practice."

"But that was before you brought him to Mass."

"Yeah. He was doing me a favor."

"What favor? Making me jealous?"

He laughed. "Not only that. He helped me come out. I didn't want to just announce that I'm gay. I wanted to do it naturally, without making it a big deal."

"That's awesome. I'm proud of you."

"Thanks."

"I was so jealous. Especially when he kissed you in front of me. I wanted to rip his face apart."

"I know," he chuckled, then looked up at me. "Nothing happened between us, by the way. Except kiss."

That was bad enough. "Did you use tongue?"

"Um—"

"Wait, don't answer that."

"But he wasn't you, Jake. Nobody beats your kisses."

"Nice save," I said, lowering to kiss him. I hoped I never saw the guy again. "Hey, why did you decide to stop seeing him? Was it because of what happened at that club?"

His head snapped up. "How do you know about that?"

"Anna came to see me the day of our first duet rehearsal. Don't be mad at her. She was just looking out for you."

He pulled away as he sat up. "What exactly did she tell you?"

"She wanted me to be honest with you and tell the truth, which I had planned on doing already. And she told me to let you go, which is ridiculous because I would never—"

Ian shook his head. "What did she say happened at the club?"

"That seeing me again messed you up and you drank way too much. Matt couldn't stop you, so he called her. And when she and Ant showed up, you were on the floor nearly passed out."

He let out a shaky breath as he turned away from me.

"Hey, baby, what's wrong?" I asked, rubbing his back.

"I have to tell you something."

I didn't like the sound of that. "What is it?"

"You won't like it, but since we made a pact to be completely honest with each other, I have to tell you."

I nodded. "You can tell me anything."

"It was a gay club, and I was more than drunk." He paused. "Seeing you again messed me up. I'd been so angry and hurt for so long, I had this hatred inside me . . . I just wanted to feel good for once. I wanted to forget. I did a lot of shots. When I started feeling good, I took Matt into the bathroom and tried to get him to have sex with me. Since we'd been taking it slow, he knew something was up. He rejected me, saying he didn't want to while I was drunk. I got mad and told him I'd find somebody else to fuck. I don't remember much after—"

"Oh my God. Did you—"

"No, thank God. But I danced with a bunch of random guys who offered me drinks. I'm sure they were spiked with drugs. I was pain-free for the first time in months." He paused again. It was obvious he was struggling to tell me something that I wasn't sure I even wanted to know.

Leaning forward, I grabbed his hands. "Baby, it's okay. You don't have to continue talking about this."

"I have to get this off my chest. I was aware a few of the guys I was dancing with—they were"—his voice shook—"feeling me up. Undressing me. Had their hands down my pants." He swallowed. "And I was letting them."

What. The. Fuck. I let go of his hands, staring at him in disbelief. I huffed as I ran my fingers through my short hair, my eyes burning. Rage. Dropping my elbows to my knees, I pressed the heels of my palms into my eye sockets. What the fuck had I done to him?

"I'm so sorry. It was the lowest point of my life. If I could take it back, I would. I was just in a really dark place—"

My head popped up, my vision blurry. "Because of me."

"No. I should have never doubted you."

"Miranda is going to pay for this. And what the fuck was Matt doing when you were being manhandled?"

"He called Anna. Apparently, things didn't get bad until just before Anna and Ant showed up. Matt fought them off, and when Ant got there, he helped."

"Did you press charges?"

Ian looked confused. "What?"

"Did you call the police on those guys who did that to you?"

"No. Jake, it was consensual."

"You were drunk and drugged. There's nothing consensual about that."

"Yes, it was. I knew what they were doing. I wanted—"

"We are going back to that bar and staying there until those fuckers show up. You'll point them out to me so I can kill them."

"Jake, no!" Ian grabbed my wrists, full-blown tears coming down his face. "Baby, please, I just want to forget that place. I never want to go back. Please don't make me. I'm so ashamed. I don't even remember what they look like."

What was the matter with me? The situation with my father had made me an insensitive prick. I leaned forward, taking him into my arms. "Okay. I'm so sorry, baby. We won't go back. God, I'm so sorry. Forgive me."

"Please don't think less of me," Ian cried.

"Never." My voice shook. "Baby boy, I promise you, you will never feel that low again. Do you hear me? I will never hurt you again." Tightening my hold, I drew Ian down with me as I leaned back on the seat. "I love you. I'm so sorry for what I put you through."

"I love you too. And in case it wasn't obvious, I forgive you." He lifted his tearstained face. "Do you forgive me?"

There was nothing for me to forgive, but I knew what Ian needed to hear. "Of course, baby. I forgive you." I cupped his face, wiping the tears with my thumbs, and laid his head back down on my chest.

We remained silent in each other's arms for a while. Now, more than ever, I was adamant about not getting bullied by Dad and Miranda. And as much as I was glad Ian and I were clearing the air, unfortunately, it wasn't over. "Baby, there's something else I have to tell you."

Ian's body deflated into mine. "What is it?" When I hesitated, he said, "It's okay. Tell me. Remember—no more secrets."

"The list Miranda showed me had your dad's name on it."

Ian pushed himself up once again. "What does that mean?"

"I'm not sure. It was supposedly a list of my dad's drug clients, but—"

"No."

"I'm not even sure if that's what the list really is. That's just what Miranda said, and I know damn well not to trust anything that comes out of that woman's mouth."

"Where did she get the list?"

"She stumbled across it in my dad's home office one day when she was hanging out with my mom. She claims there's a ton of ledgers with names. Since she's a business owner, she got suspicious of how the numbers didn't add up."

"Something about this doesn't sound right."

"I agree. I did some research, and I think that even if those are my father's clients, they won't necessarily go down. They have to be caught in the act of buying or have drugs on them. Also, I haven't done shit to help her with wedding plans. I've been rude, doing my own thing, even told my dad I'm leaving her. And yet nothing has happened."

"I need to ask my dad about this."

"Of course. You have every right. Just be careful. I've discovered my dad is almost as scary as Miranda."

"Why do you say that? Did he threaten you?"

"Sort of. He said he deals with dangerous people, which is why he can't just quit. And he insinuated that people we care about can get hurt. I'm scared he might hurt you in some way once he finds out about you." Ian stiffened. "I want to keep you safe from all this for as long as possible."

"Don't you think Miranda will tell him eventually?"

"Yeah. That's what I'm worried about. But she hasn't yet. There has to be a reason for that."

"Jake, we should talk to someone about this. And I think I might know somebody."

"Who?"

"Matt's brother. He's a federal agent. DEA, I think. But I could ask and maybe get his number."

"Seriously?"

"Yeah, I had forgotten about it till just now."

"No, I mean, can you trust Matt?"

"Yes. He's a good guy."

I smiled. "Okay. It might be worth it to talk to him off the record. It's one thing letting Miranda and my dad hash this out, and another thing completely for me to turn him in myself."

We fell silent again as Ian settled back into my arms. I relished the feel of him. I wished I could freeze time.

"I'm scared, Jake."

"Oh, baby, don't be. I got you."

"I have a bad feeling."

"It'll be okay. Our love will survive this, I promise you. We're stronger than ever. I'm not gonna let anything or anybody stand in our way. Never again."

I held him, letting my words sink in. Some time passed, and Ian's lax body indicated he'd most likely fallen asleep.

"Baby?" I whispered.

"Hmm?"

"We should probably get going. It's getting late."

"No," Ian moaned.

I smiled. "Trust me, I don't want this to end, either, but imagine Father Kevin finding us like this."

"I don't care."

"Really?"

Ian popped up. "Oh, God, you're right. We should leave."

We laughed as we gathered our clothes, which were still damp, and got dressed. I kissed him when we were done and again when we stepped out of the car. "Hey, promise me you'll take a warm shower when you get home. I don't want you getting sick."

"I will. You too."

"I will."

"Do you think you can come over tomorrow night?"

"I'll make it happen." I put my hands on either side of his face. "I love you."

"I love you too."

I kissed him. "Text me when you get home."

"I will. Be careful riding that thing. The roads will be slick from the rain."

"I promise."

Chapter 23

Jake

I was so busted.

Did I give a fuck? That would be a big fat negative. Nothing—and I meant *nothing*—could bring me down from the natural high I was on.

By the time I walked into the kitchen, Miranda was sitting at the table with her witch's brew—aka coffee, to us normal folk—and whatever breakfast witches ate, along with her phone.

Last night, after I got home, my good luck had continued to roll. The evil queen had already gone to bed. I had taken a hot shower, replied to Ian's "I'm home" text, then sauntered into the guestroom and went to bed. And slept well, I did. The best I'd gotten in months.

"Where were you last night?" Miranda asked as I reached for a mug.

"None of your business."

"Were you with *him*?"

"Who?"

"You know who."

"I was with a lot of people, so you'll have to be—"

"Ian, damn it."

"Of course I was with him. We had choir practice last night."

"All night?"

The best night of my life.

"Why did you take a shower when you got home?"

I sighed. "In case you weren't aware, it rained last night. Pretty hard." Wow, if that wasn't a double entendre, I didn't know what was. "I hung out at the church till it slowed. I was cold and drenched by the time I got home, so I took a hot shower. Happy?"

"You better not have had sex with him."

"Isn't he dating some doctor?" I couldn't believe those words came out of my mouth—and with a straight face. Better the sacrifice than her blabbing to Daddy-o the identity of who I was in love with.

"That's right, he is. And they look happy. Besides, I don't think I have to remind you what's at stake here."

"Nope, you don't. But like I told my dad, I don't care what you do with the info you have. I'm out. This is between you and him."

"You don't care if your father goes to prison?"

"I do, but he's done nothing to help himself. I don't care anymore. You wanna turn him in? Go for it. But I'm not marrying you. I'll move out as soon as I find a place. Oh, and by the way, low blow, outing me to my dad. But now that he knows, all I have to do is tell my mom. Then it's a matter of time before everyone knows. So, thanks for that. You put me one step closer to being free from this nightmare I've been living."

"There's no way Ian will forgive you for what you've done to him."

"That's none of your concern. But FYI, even if he doesn't, I'd rather be single for the rest of my life than spend another second with you. I'm extending you the same courtesy I gave my dad. I'm breaking up with you, so do whatever you need to do to prepare your social circle for the big tea. Because I'm done with you and my old man."

"You can't leave me for a man. Please, Jake. What would I tell people?"

"I don't care what you tell them. Make me the bad guy. Tell them I died. I don't care. But honestly, in the end, I can guarantee nobody will give a flying fuck who I'm banging."

She was still yelling bullshit as I walked out.

I couldn't stop smiling.

For the first time in months, I awoke content and happy.

Jake hadn't betrayed me. Had I trusted him and heard his explanation sooner, I would have saved myself a lot of heartache. But no more dwelling on it. We'd agreed to put the past behind us and start fresh. If only he wasn't dealing with all the dad stuff. I felt helpless.

Which reminded me that I should pay my dad a visit. No way my dad could be one of Mr. Edwards's regular drug clients. It didn't make any sense.

I grabbed my phone off the nightstand to call him. There were two text notifications. Butterflies invaded my stomach as I read the one from Jake. **Good morning, gorgeous. Miss you.**

Smiling, I texted back. **Morning. Miss you too. BTW, you're the gorgeous one.**

The second message was from Father John, asking to meet. It probably had to do with my support group pitch. I sent a quick reply, letting him know I'd be there.

Another text from Jake came in. **Have you looked in the mirror??**

I chuckled. **Have you???**

LOL. Love you.

Love you too.

Hey, mandatory duet rehearsal tonight. We could use the extra practice *winky face*. Any excuse to get him to my house.

After a minute, Jake replied, **Yessir… I'll be there.**

I smiled, then sent Anna a quick message. **I have something to tell you. Call me when you get off.**

Enough with the texting. I put the phone down and got ready for work. An hour later, I was ringing the doorbell of the rectory.

The same nun from last time answered the door. "Sister Mary Jane, so good to see you again. I have a meeting with Father John this time."

"Hello, Mr. Cooper. Father John is expecting you. You may go down."

The office door was open, but I knocked anyway. Father John was sitting at the desk when he lifted his head. "Ian, come in," he said. "And close the door behind you, please."

I did what I was told but couldn't shake the feeling that I was in trouble. The vibe from Father John was hard to read, but it didn't seem positive.

"Is there something wrong, Father?" I asked, sitting in the chair across from him.

Father John folded his hands on top of the desk and leaned forward. "Ian, Father Kevin tells me you want to start a support group for homosexuals."

"Actually, it would be an all-inclusive LGBTQ+ group."

"Uh-huh. But you are aware we already have support groups for those people in place."

"We don't have support groups. We have counseling, which

counsels those people into living a *normal* life without ever experiencing the joys of being in a relationship. Teaches that it's okay to be who you are, as long as you don't share intimacy because premarital sex is a sin. Which is not fair if you think about it, since heterosexuals are allowed to get married in the Catholic church, whereas same-sex couples are not. So, following the no-premarital-sex rule, means we can't have sex. Ever."

"Sex is for procreation. Two men can't procreate."

"Really, Father? Are you saying that every person who attends this church has sex for the sole purpose of having kids?"

"But it's all true, is it not? It's what we Catholics believe."

"No, not every Catholic."

"So, you want to, what, tell these people it's okay to sin? That it's okay to go against God's will?"

"Not God's will. The Church's will."

"I beg your pardon?"

"Look, I'm not trying to convince you or change the teachings of the Church. But I do want to offer these people, these Christians, a place to come together for real support. In the past couple of weeks, I have received tons of emails from people asking for my help. They aren't getting support from their families. I feel this is a good way to be surrounded by like-minded people, so they don't feel alone."

Father John leaned back in his chair. "You are a homosexual yourself, are you not?"

The cat was out of the bag, so no sense in hiding it anymore. "I don't see what that has to do with anything, but yes, I'm gay."

"And are you in a joyful relationship, committing acts of sin?"

My eyebrows drew together. Creepy question, but okay. "With all due respect, Father, that's none of your business."

He pressed his lips together into a straight line. "Ian, I've been receiving emails as well. And I must say, they are not in your favor."

"What do you mean?"

"Many people are not happy with you. They feel that having an openly gay music director is not the kind of leadership St. Pius needs."

"I see. And what do you feel?"

"I'm afraid I'm going to have to agree with them."

"Are you firing me?"

"I'm sorry, but yes."

"You can't fire me because I'm gay. In all my years of working here, I have never flaunted my sexuality. I've always kept my personal life personal. I just want to let these people know they're not alone, like I thought I was."

The priest's eyes bore into me intently as he fidgeted, making me uncomfortable. "Perhaps we can work something out."

I narrowed my eyes. "Work something out how?"

"Would you be willing to do me some favors?"

I swallowed as a sick feeling crept in. "Favors? You mean, like, help write your homilies?"

The priest laughed. "I was thinking something a little more personal."

I raised my eyebrows. "Like dry-cleaning your uniforms?" God, please let it be dry cleaning.

Father John pointed a finger at me. "Funny, but no. Think something more . . . intimate."

Creepiness overload. Now was not the time to beat around the bush or jump to conclusions. I had to be clear about what this asshole priest was implying. "Are you saying that if I give you a blow job, you'll let me keep my job?"

Father John quirked a brow, smirking as he stood. "Of course not. That would be unethical." He came around the desk and parked his ass on the edge right in front of me. His legs spread, one foot between mine and hands folded over his lap. "But Ian, how badly do you want to keep your job?" His eyes skimmed over me like they were undressing me, then he licked his lips, taking the bottom one between his teeth.

Ew.

I huffed as I looked down. This was nasty. The man's cock was too close for comfort. Practically at eye level. And I swore the perv had a semi underneath his folded hands. I forced a smile as I pushed back the chair, creating some space, and rose to my feet. "Father, go fuck yourself."

I held it together as I stormed out of the office, not even acknowledging Rosemary or the young nun as I fled past them.

Once I got into my car, I gripped the steering wheel. "Holy shit. I just lost my job," I whispered to myself. My hands shook as I reached for my phone. This would not end like this. Did Father John even have the authority to fire me?

I dialed Father Kevin's number, waiting with my heart in my throat as it rang.

Voicemail.

"Hello, Father Kevin, this is Ian. Please call me as soon as you can. Something just happened. Please—it's urgent. You can call me anytime. It doesn't matter how late it is."

I sent him a text message saying the same thing.

Glancing at the rectory, I thought about what else I could do. I had just gotten fired for my sexual orientation. Was there a law against that in the state of Georgia? I would have to find out. And a priest had implied sexual favors. Wouldn't that fall under sexual harassment?

Before I paid a visit to the precinct for answers, I decided to wait until after I spoke to Father Kevin. This could all be a misunderstanding. Hopefully, Father Kev pulled rank.

As I sighed, I looked at my phone and found Jake's number. **Come over sooner if you can.**

Jake would not be happy about this. Not the losing-my-job part—well, yeah, of course he'd be upset over that—but the fact that Father John propositioned me? I feared for the priest's life. We'd promised no more secrets, so I had to tell him.

I had yet to mention the death threats. But that might be a moot point now, anyway.

By the time I got home, Jake had texted me back. **Is everything okay?**

I didn't want to worry him but also wanted him to know it was important. **Yeah. I just need you.**

There. Something to let him know nobody had died, but it was important. I had just lost my fucking job. The job I loved. The job I'd spent the last five to six years dedicated to. The only real job I'd had.

A few seconds later, my phone rang. It was Jake.

I sighed as I answered it. "You didn't have to call."

"What's going on?" he asked. "Are you sick? Did someone do something? Did Miranda or my dad—"

"No, it has nothing to do with them."

"What is it, then?"

"I don't want to tell you over the phone. Besides, shouldn't you be teaching a class right now?"

"I stepped out into the hall."

"You left your students alone just so you could call me?"

"I was worried. And they're fine. Just tell me one thing—are we still good? Does it have to do with us?"

"God, baby, no, it has nothing to do with us. And yes, we're good."

"Promise?"

"Yes, promise. Something happened and I just need you."

Jake drew a shaky breath on the other end of the line. "But you're physically okay?"

"Yes."

"Okay. I have a guitar lesson to give today, but I'll reschedule it."

"You don't have—"

"You need me. And you're more important." Even after we'd made up, Jake still managed to leave me speechless. "I'll come over as soon as I get out of here."

"Okay. Thanks, Jake."

"I love you, babe," he whispered. "I'll see you soon."

"I love you too. See you later."

As I ended the call, I noticed a text from Anna, responding to my earlier text. **Good or bad??**

Great. I forgot I'd told her to call me after she got off work. This was not something I wanted to share over the phone. **Both. Can we meet tomorrow?**

Sure, but do you still want me to call you?

I'd rather tell you in person.

Okay. Can you come to the hospital at noon? We could have lunch in the cafeteria.

Sounds good. See you then.

Chapter 25

Jake

I went through hell and high water to get to Ian's house quickly. It wasn't fast enough.

Something had happened. And although it had nothing to do with Ian changing his mind about us, it was enough for me to drop everything and run to him. Nothing in this world was more important than him.

Hopping off my motorcycle, I secured my helmet and rushed to ring the doorbell.

A second later, Ian opened the door. He was a mess. His hair was disheveled, like he'd been running his hands through it.

"Hey, baby," I said as I stepped inside. "I got here as fast as I could." I reached for him, my hand behind his neck, and kissed him.

He threw himself into my arms. "Thanks for coming."

I tightened my arms around him. "Of course. I said I would. Now, tell me what's wrong."

He pulled back, wiping at his face. "Well, put your guitar down first and make yourself comfy because it's a doozy."

That didn't sound good.

Ian sat on the couch, elbows on his knees, as I unstrapped my guitar from my back and took off my jacket.

Once my gear was off, I dropped to my knees in front of him, placing my hands on the sides of his legs. "What is it?"

He let out a shaky sigh. "I got fired."

My eyes widened. That was the last thing I'd expected him to say. "What? Why? Was it because of last night? Did they find out what we did in the parking lot?"

He shook his head, smiling a little. "No. Nothing like that."

"Then why the fuck did you get fired?"

"Because I'm gay. It was Father John. He says he's been getting emails complaining about me. Something about how having an openly gay music director was poor leadership."

"What the fuck?"

"But I don't even know if he's authorized to fire me. I'm waiting for a callback from Father Kevin."

"Good. I'm sure Father Kev will fix this."

"I hope so. But there's more."

"What is it?"

"First, promise not to freak out."

I didn't like the sound of that at all. "I'm already freaking out, but I'll do my best not to lose my shit."

He looked away, taking in a deep breath. "Father John—he propositioned me."

Heat overtook my body as every muscle tensed. I narrowed my eyes, trying my best to keep my promise. "What the fuck do you mean, propositioned you?"

"He told me I could keep my job if I did favors for him. I hoped he meant maybe write his homilies or take care of his dry cleaning. But no, he said *personal* favors. And even used the word *intimate*."

"Oh my fucking God," I muttered through clenched teeth. I dropped my head into my hands, squeezing my eyes shut to the scenario no man wanted their significant other to experience. Ever.

"I wanted to make sure I wasn't reading the situation wrong, so I asked point-blank if he was implying that I could keep my job if I gave him a blow job."

I bolted to my feet. "No. Are you fucking kidding me?"

"He laughed, saying that would be unethical. But he stood in front of me suggestively and—the way he looked at me—it made me really uncomfortable. And I'm pretty sure he was aroused." He shuddered.

I put my hands on top of my head in an attempt not to explode. My eyes blurred as rage blinded me and the urge to hurl increased. "What did you say to him?" He hesitated, and I panicked, jumping the gun. "Please tell me you didn't."

His head snapped up. "What? Ew, hell no! I told him to go fuck himself and got the hell out of there." It took a second for relief to sink in. "How could you think—"

"I'm sorry, I—" I fell back to my knees in front of him and took his face between my hands. "I'm sorry. I didn't mean it. I know you wouldn't. I just—I'm so sorry you went through that." Anger resurfaced as I looked into his sad eyes. That bastard had humiliated my boy, and he was going to pay. "I'm going to fucking kill him." I leaped to my feet, lunging for the door.

"Jake, no!" Ian jumped in front of me, blocking the exit.

"Baby, get out of my way."

"You can't beat up a priest."

"The hell I can't! That sick motherfucker is a dead man!"

"You said you wouldn't freak out."

"I said I would try. Now move."

"Please, baby, no. I don't want you to end up in jail. I need you. I lost my job. What am I going to do?"

Fuck. I was an insensitive prick—and wrapped around this man's little finger. He could ask for the world, and I would deliver it on a platter. I drew in a deep breath and clenched my jaw as a burning question nagged at my brain. "Did he touch you?" Ian's confused eyes searched mine. I repeated the goddamn question. "Did he put his fucking hands on you?"

"No!" His hands came up to my face, easing me away from the cliff, grounding me like he always had a way of doing. "I swear to God, babe, he didn't touch me. I told him to fuck off and I left. That's it."

I blinked, some of the anger dissipating, then nodded as tears filled my eyes. Bringing my hand to Ian's cheek, my thumb caressed the scratchiness of his beard. "I'm so sorry." I fell into his arms, pulling him close.

"It's okay," he said, tightening his hold. "I'm okay. As long as I have you, I'm good."

I pulled back, resting my forehead on his. "You'll always have me."

He nodded. "This is all I wanted. For you to hold me and tell me everything's going to be okay."

"Everything will be okay. We'll deal with this together." I leaned forward and kissed him. "And if Father Kev doesn't hire you back, we'll get a lawyer and sue for unlawful termination and we'll get Father Sicko for sexual harassment."

"There were no witnesses. It'd be my word against his. And he's a priest. I'm just the homo music guy."

I clenched my jaw. "No. You are a respected music director who's passionate about his work and has at least six years under his belt at St. Pius with no complaints. He is a fucking closeted pervert. Lord knows how many innocent people he's used his power over and sexually assaulted."

"I *was* respected, right? Until I came out."

"Baby, come on. There are plenty of people who still respect you at that church and you know it."

He sighed as he shrugged out of my embrace and dropped onto the couch, slumping down. "All those people . . . I feel like I'm letting them down."

"What are you talking about?" I asked as I sat beside him.

"I haven't had a chance to tell you, but I'm—well, I was trying to start an LGBTQ+ support group at the church. Like, a real one. With real support and full acceptance."

"Really? That's a great idea."

"You wouldn't believe the number of emails I've gotten asking for my help. People who don't have family support. Gays and lesbians. It's crazy. Some are teens, others are grown-ass adults hiding behind a marriage or a life that's a lie. I went to Father Kevin and pitched my support group idea."

"And what did he say?"

"That he'd think about it, and it would require approval."

"You are amazing, you know that?"

"Why?"

"It's a brilliant idea. My God, baby, if people can't see the compassionate, hardworking, smart, talented man you are—well, then they don't deserve to know you."

He rolled his head on the back of the couch to face me. Those gorgeous blue eyes searched me like he was pinpointing something. "How do you keep saying things that render me speechless?"

"What do you mean? I speak the truth." I reached for his hand. "I love you. These last months without you have been pure hell. Now that you've forgiven me, I don't want to waste one second not saying what I feel when I feel it."

His eyes glistened as he reached for my neck, pulling me toward him until our lips touched. I kissed him back and slid my fingers into his hair. Leaning back, he whispered, "These past months have been hell for me too. Thanks for forgiving me. I love you too."

A phone's vibration interrupted us. It was Ian's. "It's Father Kevin." He sat up and answered. "Hello? Yes, thank you, Father, for returning my call. Father John fired me today." There was a pause. "Yes, he did. He contacted me, asking that I come in for a meeting. When I got there, he started asking about the support group I talked to you about." Another pause. "Right. He was clearly opposed to it." Pause. "No, he didn't fire me because of that. No, it was because apparently, people have told him they disapprove of me because I'm gay. Bad leadership."

I tapped him on the shoulder to get his attention. "Tell him what he did to you," I whispered.

He put his finger up to hush me. "I appreciate that, Father. I mean, have you received any complaints about me?" Pause. "So, why would people contact him if he's new? I don't understand . . . Okay . . . Father, is there any way we can meet before you talk to him? There's more that happened, and I would rather not say over the phone." Pause. "Oh, um, okay, well, while I was in his office, he, uh— he said I could keep my job in return for personal favors." Pause. "Yes, Father, I believe he was referring to sexual favors. I left after that . . . Okay . . . Okay, thank you Father... I will wait for your call. Bye."

"What did he say?" I asked as soon as he ended the call.

"He was appalled. I think he believes me."

"Of course he does. Why wouldn't he?"

He shrugged. "He's going to talk to Father John to get his side of the story."

"Why?"

"Courtesy, I guess. But he doesn't think that was a good reason to fire me. And he's received no complaints about me."

"Ha! I knew it. Father Sicko is full of shit."

He leaned toward me, placing his hand on my chest. "I don't know what I would do without you."

I took his hand and kissed it. "The feeling is mutual. Thanks for giving me another chance."

"I don't want there to be any more secrets between us, no matter how crazy you get."

"Hey, so I'm a little overprotective."

"A little?" He laughed, popping his eyebrows up.

I laughed, too, then got serious. "I just don't like it when people mess with you. Never have, from the first moment we met. You know that."

"Yes, I do. I never understood it, but I do appreciate it. Which is why I have to tell you something."

"There's more?"

"Just one more thing. I was saving it because I didn't want you to freak out, but I know you're going to freak out anyway, so I might as well get it over with. And, like I said, I don't want there to be secrets between us."

"Tell me." I pressed my fist into my palm, trying to control freak-out mode.

Ian stood and walked across the room, disappearing around the corner. After a moment, he returned with some papers in hand. "It's better if I show you."

I took the papers and began reading.

What the fuck? "Death threats? Are you fucking kidding me?" He remained quiet as I continued reading through the papers. "How many are there? Oh my God, Ian."

"I've already taken them to the police. They added them to the investigation."

"I sure fucking hope so!" I was scared. "Fuck this shit. Baby, you can't go back there."

"What happened to fighting for my job with a lawsuit?"

"That was before the mega stack of homophobes you were hiding from me!"

"I wasn't hiding it from you. There hasn't been time to bring it up. Plus, I was trying to avoid dealing with this reaction."

"Oh, I'm sorry. How am I supposed to react to the news that my boyfriend is being threatened with death?"

There was no comeback, just wide blue eyes staring at me. His mouth hung open like he'd seen a ghost or heard something whacked out. I retraced my words. Did I say something wrong?

"You called me your boyfriend."

Oh. "Did I?"

He smiled. "Yes, you did."

"Isn't that what you are?"

"Am I?"

"Aren't you?"

He laughed. "Jake, I believe you technically still have a fiancée."

I sucked my teeth. "Nope, I don't. Not anymore."

"What?"

"I broke up with her this morning."

"Are you serious?"

"Yup. She was asking why I was so late coming home last night and why I took a shower. I didn't come out and say we're back together, but I did say I was done being the middleman for her and my dad. I'm giving her some time to prepare her social circle, but as soon as I find a place, I'm moving out."

He didn't say anything for a long time. His mouth still hung open. "Is this for real?"

"Yup, baby. It's real. I'm free."

He let out a half sob, half laugh, then threw himself into my arms.

I held him while he cried—tears of joy, hopefully. "I'm sorry I didn't have the balls to do this sooner."

He pulled back and sniffled. "I don't care. You did it. That's all I care about." He kissed me. "But you realize you can stay here, right?"

I smiled. "That's what I was hoping, but I didn't want to assume."

"But you assumed we were boyfriends?"

I chuckled. "Don't you want to be?"

"Is this your way of asking?"

"Yes."

"I want to hear the words."

I took his hands in mine. "Ian, baby, will you do me the honor of being my boyfriend?"

He grinned, raising his eyebrows like he was trying hard to think it over. "Um, yeah, okay."

"Okay?"

He nodded. "Babe, I've been wanting to hear those words for a long, long time, so yeah, okay. Either that or it's me running around this house screaming like a little girl because the hot guy I've had a crush on since forever just asked me to be his boyfriend."

I busted out laughing. "Option number two, please." He smacked my shoulder and laughed. I put my arms around him as I kissed him. "For the record, I had a crush on you too. I just didn't realize it till later."

He smiled, taking my bottom lip between his teeth. "I know."

I kissed him again and pushed him back against the couch. "So . . . hot, huh?"

"Oh my God, you know this." He chuckled.

"I like hearing you say it."

"Jake Edwards, you are sooooo fucking hot. The hottest guy I know."

I grinned as I kissed him, coaxing his lips open as I slipped my tongue inside to mingle with his, tasting him thoroughly. "So are you," I whispered against his mouth. "And you're all mine."

He slipped his hands underneath my shirt. "Yes. And you're mine."

I bent my head to his neck, licking and kissing, then began unbuttoning his shirt. "You and these fucking button-downs."

He smirked as he took over, undoing most of the buttons, then pulled it over his head. "There. Better?"

"Fuck yeah," I grunted as I kissed his chest, swirling my tongue over his nipple and nipping at the tight bud.

His hands glided through my short hair, then he stood, slipping from my hold. "Let's go to the bedroom."

Ian's wish was my command. I rose, following him as I took off my shirt and tossed it along the way.

In the bedroom, he removed his pants, boxers included, and laid back on the bed. What a fucking glorious view. His impressive cock jetted out from his hips, just begging for attention. And I was happy to oblige.

Off with my pants. I climbed onto the bed, crawling over him, supporting my weight on either side of his hips, then dipped down, taking him fully into my mouth. He moaned and thrust his hips. I continued to suck him to the back of my throat, loving the way he responded beneath me, rock hard and swollen. Just how I liked him. Bonus that it was because of me.

Dipping further, I licked his balls and sucked on them, one by one, until they became tight. I raised his legs for better access and licked his ass, sticking my tongue in his hole.

"Oh my God, Jake—"

I fucked him with my tongue, feasting and lubricating, resulting in more moans from my boy.

"Please—I want you inside me," Ian pleaded. "Fuck me."

I wasn't one to deny my baby. Sliding off my boxers swiftly, I climbed on top, positioning myself between his legs and slowly pushing into him, waiting for him to adjust. I closed my eyes to the warm sensation, engulfed in his tightness. "Fuck, baby. You always feel so good."

He moaned and lifted his hips. "Go deeper. I love the way you feel inside me."

I slid in more. "We're a perfect fit." I leaned forward and kissed him as I pumped. "I love you, baby."

"I love you too."

I pushed back onto my knees, still joined with him, and gripped his stiff cock. I jerked him, bringing him closer. He threw his head back into the mattress and moaned, licking his lips. I kept up a good rhythm, sliding his dick up and down in my hand.

"Cum for me, baby."

His hole tightened around my cock as the pulses of his orgasm came, spilling onto my knuckles. After squeezing him dry, I leaned forward and pumped into him, hard and fast, until my own orgasm came. Grunting, I buried my face in his neck, holding him tight as I came inside. The vibrations went on forever as I thrusted all of myself into him.

Once the waves of ecstasy subsided, I lay still on top of him as I caught my breath. "Oh my God, baby. That was intense."

Ian ran his hands over my back. "Hell yeah, it was."

Lifting my head, I asked, "Did you like that?"

"Which part?"

"All of it."

"Of course I did. You couldn't tell?"

I shrugged, kissing him. "Just making sure."

I pulled him into my arms as I rolled onto my back. He draped an arm over top of me and rested his head on my shoulder.

We remained silent as I played with his curls lazily. The elephant in the room was nagging at my brain to say something. "I was thinking—maybe you could look for a job at another church. Other churches need music directors too. Even if it's another denomination like Episcopal or Lutheran. And they'll probably be more accepting of us."

"I don't know. Maybe. Let me just see what Father Kev says, then I'll decide. Okay?"

"Okay. But if you decide to go to another church, just know that I'll follow you wherever you go. Even if it's to a different city or state."

"I know, babe. That means a lot."

I kissed the top of his head.

"Are you hungry?" He yawned. "I just realized I haven't offered you anything."

"Oh, I think you offered me plenty," I joked.

He laughed softly as he nudged his lips against my neck. "I meant food."

"Nah, I'm good. I'd rather stay like this."

"Me too," he mumbled as he tightened his arm around me.

* * *

Jake

I gasped as my eyes adjusted to the darkness. We must've dozed off. I angled my watch so the moonlight hit it. Shit. In a few hours, I would have to be at the school. I gently pried myself away from Ian, trying not to wake him. The movement caused him to stir, and he tightened his arm around me.

"No," he groaned. "Don't go. You live here now."

I caressed his head, tangling my fingers through his hair. "I know, baby. But all my stuff is still at Miranda's. I need to get ready for school."

"Get ready here. You can borrow my clothes."

I was tempted, but Miranda was capable of burning all my shit if I didn't come home. I needed to tread carefully with her. Yeah, I'd broken it off with her, but she was still bitter. Leverage was something I did not want to give her. "Baby, this is the last night I'll be away from you."

"Promise?"

"Absolutely. After school, I'll start bringing stuff over. It's just since I gave Miranda the courtesy of a head's up, I don't wanna not show up at all. That would make her know for sure that we're together, and I don't want her running to my dad."

Ian grunted as he rolled onto his back. "Fine."

"You're so cute when you pout." I gave him another quick kiss, then slid off the bed. I grabbed my boxers, then went into the living room to find my clothes and get dressed.

After a quick stop in the bathroom, I went back into the bedroom. "I'm going to leave my guitar here."

Ian nodded as he yawned. "Okay."

I chuckled as I leaned down and kissed him. "Get some sleep. I'll talk to you later."

"Mm-hmm," he mumbled and closed his eyes. Just as I stood,

he grabbed my arm. "Text me when you get there so I know you made it."

"I will," I said as I gave him another kiss, lingering longer this time.

"Love you."

"Love you too, baby."

I shut the door firmly, locking it behind me. As I put on my helmet, I glanced down the street and cursed to myself. The fog was thick as shit.

And it was late.

Fucking fog.

I rushed down the street, but then slowed. Visibility was a bitch. Good thing the roads were pretty much empty.

Coming upon a green light, I sped up. Almost cleared it.

A fucking truck turned out in front of me and—

"Oh, shit!"

Chapter 26

Ian

I woke with a start.

My eyes adjusted to the bright light coming through the blinds.

A gasp escaped me as I glanced at the clock on the nightstand. Past ten o'clock. Well, good thing I didn't have to go to work, otherwise I'd be late.

I rubbed my face and slid off the bed to go in search of my phone. Found it in my pants' pocket and went straight to my messages. Nothing from Jake.

He was supposed to text me when he got home. What if Miranda had found out about us and smashed his phone? That wouldn't be a surprise.

Honestly, that would be better than thinking the worst. If he hadn't texted, it must've been for a good reason. And he was in a rush this morning, so maybe he hadn't had time to text me.

Yeah, that was most likely it. But I decided to send him a quick text anyway. **Hey, boyfriend, you didn't text…hope everything's** okay. Love you.

Setting the phone down, I headed into the bathroom to get ready to meet Anna. After my shower, I stood in front of the mirror and towel dried my hair. Time to say goodbye to my beard, especially since Jake didn't like it. Besides, it represented a low time in my life, and things were looking up. It made sense to get rid of it.

I gathered my shaving supplies and went at it, shaving until my face was smooth again. The thought of letting my curls flow naturally today crossed my mind, but if I met with Father Kevin, I wanted to look as professional as possible. Gel it was. I worked it lightly into my hair.

Back in the bedroom, I checked my phone. There was a voicemail from Father Kevin, asking that I meet him at three o'clock. I quickly returned the call and left a message confirming that the time worked.

I glanced at the phone again. Still nothing from Jake.
Weird.

He was at school. He couldn't whip out his phone whenever he wanted. I wouldn't panic yet. Suppressing the bad feeling in the pit of my stomach, I got dressed.

After some coffee and reviewing some emails on the computer, I was on my way to the hospital to meet with Anna.

* * *

At the hospital, I was lost on where to meet Anna, so I texted her and let her know I was parking.

After two minutes, she responded saying she would meet me in the front lobby. Hopping down from the loaner SUV, I made my way inside. I only had to wait a few minutes before I saw her walking toward me.

"Hi, Ian," she squealed as she threw herself into my arms.

"Hey, you. How are you feeling?" I asked, returning the hug.

As she pulled away, she rubbed her swollen baby belly. "Oh, you know, we're hanging in there."

"Well, you look beautiful as always."

"Thanks. And look at you," she said as she ran her hand across my cheek. "You shaved."

"Yup. It was time."

"I love it. You look like Ian again."

I laughed as I stroked my jaw. "Yeah, it was getting itchy. It feels weird but nice. I'm glad it's gone."

"And you look happier."

"That is actually part of the good news I wanted to talk to you about."

She grinned. "Okay, well, come on. Let's go to the cafeteria. I want to hear all about the good and the bad."

As we headed down the hall, I asked, "How's the new job?"

"It's good. I really like it. It's in administration, which is good because it's what I know. And I'm grateful it's a sit-down job because my back hurts right where I got shot if I'm on my feet too long."

"Oh no. Are you okay now?"

"I'm fine as long as we go slow. I think the baby just puts that extra strain on my back around that area. I plan to bring it up to my OB at my next appointment."

"Good. I bet Ant is happy with the location of the job."

"Oh yes. If I go into labor, all I have to do is contact him and hope he gets here on time."

"I'm sure it'll be fine."

"Yeah, I'm sure too. I read that first-time moms can take a long time in labor, anyway."

When we reached the cafeteria, we selected our food and stood in line to pay. "Here, I'll pay," I said as we got to the register.

"No way. I got this. I'm the employee, it's my discount. My treat today. You'll get it next time."

"But you don't have to do that. You need to save your money."

And actually, I needed to be frugal as well, now that I was jobless.

"I think I can spare some change to treat my friend to lunch. Besides, you've given up a chunk of change for me when you paid Phillip my debt. It's the least I could do. So shut up and say thank you."

I put an arm around her and kissed her temple. "Thank you."

We picked a table and sat. After we ate in silence for a while, she said, "Okay, you've left me in suspense long enough. Spill it."

I smiled. "What do you want to hear first? Good news or bad?"

"Bad. That way, we can end it on a cheery note."

"Okay," I took a bite of the Caesar salad in front of me and swallowed. "I got fired."

"What?" Her eyes widened as she leaned forward. "Oh, Ian. When? Why?"

"Yesterday. Because I'm gay."

"No. You're kidding."

"I wish I was."

I told her the whole story about my LGBTQ+ support group pitch, the emails, and the proposition by Father John.

"You have to report him."

"But it's my word against his. Now that I've come out, I don't know if the Catholic church would even back me up on this."

"You have to try. I think they'll want to know if one of their own clergy is a sexual predator."

"I told Father Kevin everything. I'm meeting with him this afternoon. After I speak with him, I will decide on the next course of action."

"Okay. Let me know what he says." She shook her head. "My God, Ian. I'm so sorry. I can't believe this is happening. I know how much you love that job."

"Yeah, well, maybe I'll have to look for a job elsewhere."

She tilted her head, drawing her eyebrows close. "I'm sorry."

After a moment, I couldn't help but spread into a smile. "Are you ready for the cheery news?"

She sat straighter, smiling as well. "Yes, please. Let's hear it."

I wasn't sure how she'd take it. She'd had my back since the moment I thought Jake had betrayed me. "I talked to Jake. He explained everything."

"And?"

"First of all, I know you went to see him. And I can't thank you enough for having my back."

Her eyes glistened as she reached for my hand. "Of course. You're my best friend. I just wanted you to have closure. I hated seeing you suffer. And I thought if he talked to you, it would shed some light."

"Well, it did. Anna, we were so wrong about him. It was Miranda all along. She was blackmailing him."

"With what?"

I didn't think it was my place to reveal Jake's dad's illegal business, so I kept the details to myself. "It's a long story, but it has to do with his dad—she has incriminating evidence against him. She threatened to turn it into the police if Jake didn't marry her."

"Do you believe that?"

"Yes. He's been trying to get his dad to do the right thing, but he has done nothing. Jake says he's done being threatened by everyone, so he's stepping aside and letting Miranda and his dad duke it out."

"That all sounds crazy."

"I know. But I believe him. Plus, my dad might be involved. I haven't had a chance to confront him yet, but I plan to. Anna, not only could I see the pain in Jake's eyes but he's been proving to me he really loves me. He's putting me first this time."

"Ian—"

"He broke up with Miranda."

"Are you sure?"

"Yes. And he asked me to be his boyfriend." I paused. "He came out to his dad."

"Be careful. If he hurts you again . . . I'm scared you won't recover."

"I know." I hesitated. "I told him about the club. Everything. What I did—what I almost let happen. You should've seen him. He blames himself. He even cried. But this is all my fault for not giving him the chance to explain sooner."

"Why didn't he confide in you?"

"When it happened, he was torn on what to do. He confronted his dad and got the truth out of him, but Miranda warned him not to tell me. He was going to anyway. He was just trying to figure out how and when. That's why he distanced himself from me. Then the shooting happened, and when we were in the hospital, he was going to tell me, but I was a mess. And he didn't want to worry me with yet another thing, on top of you fighting for your life. He didn't expect Miranda to blurt out the news of the engagement that day. But you know her."

"Yeah, I know her." After a moment, she said, "And for some strange reason, it all makes sense. Okay—if you're giving him another chance, then so will I. But you are my priority, not him. All I care about is your happiness. You deserve nothing less. So, if he hurts you again, I swear to God, Ian, I might just kill him."

I put my hand on my heart. "Thank you. I couldn't have asked for a better friend."

"Ian?"

Matt stood in front of our table. "Matt. Hi," I greeted and stood to give him a hug.

"Hello, Anna," Matt said.

"Hi, Matt. How are you?"

"Good. Sorry for the interruption. I saw you over here and thought I'd come say hi. I haven't heard from you in a while. Hope everything is okay."

"Yeah, sorry. Everything's good. Just busy."

"Same here. I'm guessing you're here to see Jake?"

My heart dropped. "What?"

"Oh, sorry. I assumed you guys made up, and that's why you were here. I thought you knew."

"Jake's here?"

"Yes. He was brought in early this morning. Motorcycle accident, I think."

My head whipped to Anna as my hands went to my head. "Oh my God!"

"Go! Ian, go!" Anna said to me. "Don't worry about me. Just go to Jake!"

I bolted out of the cafeteria and to the first help desk I encountered to ask what floor Jake was on. Then I raced to find him. I didn't care if his room was full of people or if Miranda was with him. I needed to see him. He had to be okay.

Please, God.

After the slowest elevator ride ever, I ran down the hall and skidded in front of Jake's room. He was alone.

I tried catching my breath as I walked in. Jake was lying on a slight incline with an arm draped over his face.

He was alive.

"Jake?"

His arm shot down as his head lifted. "Ian, thank God. I've been demanding they call you."

"No one called me. I was in the cafeteria having lunch with Anna. Matt told me you were here. What the hell happened?" I asked as I went over to the bed.

"I'm so sorry I didn't text. My phone died, and I knew you would worry—"

"It's okay. Just tell me what happened."

Jake closed his eyes and swallowed. "It was so foggy. I was trying to be careful and going slow, but I guess this truck didn't see me and pulled out right in front of me. I swerved to try to miss it but ended up skidding."

I drew a shaky breath. "Oh my God."

"I'm okay. They insisted on bringing me in because they wanted to check for neck and head injuries. They said it's standard, even though I was wearing a helmet. That's what's been taking so long. These damn tests. And my leg got a little messed up because of skidding and my bike fell on it. But it's not broken, just sprained, I think. It hurts like a mother, so they got me on some meds."

I covered my mouth. "I knew it. I've had a bad feeling since this morning. You should have stayed over last night."

"You're right. I should've." He grabbed my hand and pulled me down to him. "But I'm okay."

I shook my head as I sat on the edge of the bed. "I was so worried when you didn't text me."

"I knew you would be. I'm sorry, baby. Ask the nurses if you don't believe me. I was yelling at them to call my boyfriend. They kept telling me they were looking for your number. I even told them to call down to Anna. Everything around here takes so damn long."

"Baby, it's okay. I believe you. Just calm down, okay?"

"I just want to go home. With you."

I ran my hand over Jake's forehead. "You will soon enough. Have they called the school, at least?"

"I don't even know."

"I'll find out."

But as I moved to get up, Jake grabbed my hand. "Wait. You okay?"

"I just—you could've died, Jake," I whispered, letting the tears fall.

"Oh, baby, no." He tugged on my hand until I fell across his chest. "I'm okay. I'm not leaving you anytime soon, especially now that I have you back. Please don't cry."

I nodded, burying my face in Jake's neck. When I finally had control over my tears, I pulled back, wiping at my eyes. Jake's gray eyes were red-rimmed and filled with tears as well.

Jake reached up and stroked my face. "You shaved."

I nodded, sniffling. "Yeah. I did it for you."

He smiled. "I love it. Thank you."

"Just don't shave yours."

He chuckled. "Mine isn't quite as full as yours was, but I won't. I know you like it."

"Hey, Father Kevin got back to me. I have a meeting with him this afternoon."

"Okay, cool. Hopefully it'll be good news. I wish I could go with you."

"Why? So you can beat up Father John?"

He laughed. "You know me too well."

"Yeah, I know."

"What time do you have to be there?"

"Three. I have to get going soon."

"Be careful. Remember to check your surroundings."

"I will."

"You'll call me when it's over?"

I nodded. "What are you going to do for transportation?"

"That's a good question. I'll probably have to rent a car while my bike is in the shop. Or use Uber."

"I'll come back here after the meeting. We'll go home together."

"Home. I like the sound of that."

"Me too." I stood. "I'll talk to you later, then."

Jake nodded. "Give me a kiss before you leave."

"What if someone walks in?"

"I don't care who sees us."

"Really?"

His eyebrows shot up. "Do you still doubt me?"

"No, of course not. It's just that you're not publicly out—"

"Baby, I was shouting at the top of my lungs for these people to call my boyfriend. I think I'm publicly out."

I laughed. "You have a point."

"Of course I do. Now, come here."

I sat back down on the edge of the bed and bent, brushing my lips against Jake's as I placed my hand on the side of his neck. Jake gripped my wrist as he deepened the kiss, holding me to him. A moan escaped him as I dipped my tongue inside, mingling and tasting. I savored the feel of him, not wanting it to end. And for a second, I considered rescheduling the meeting with Father Kevin.

Someone cleared their throat behind us.

I jerked back, turning toward the sound. Jake's dad stood at the entrance with a scowl on his face.

"Dad, what are you doing here?"

Ignoring the question, Mr. Edwards took a step closer. "This is who has been brainwashing you?"

"Ian hasn't—"

Mr. Edwards turned to me. "I should've known it was you rubbing your gayness off on my son."

"Don't talk to him that way."

"Have you no shame coming between Jake and Miranda? You homewrecker."

"Dad!"

I stood and glanced down at Jake. "I should go."

"I'm sorry," he whispered.

"It's okay." I gave a small smile. "I'll call you after the meeting."

Jake nodded, squeezing my hand before letting go.

I met Mr. Edwards's eyes as I passed him. "Mr. Edwards, so good to see you."

No response as I kept on walking.

I refused to be intimidated by my father.

As the man stood there with his arms crossed, looking down at me with that look of disapproval, I gave it right back, staring with the same intensity.

"I'm quite disappointed in you, son."

"Right back at ya, Dad."

He came closer. "You're lucky your mother didn't come with me. She would've had a heart attack on the spot."

"Why are you even here?"

"I have friends at the hospital. They informed me of your accident."

"Of course you do. What are they, your clients?"

"Lower your voice."

"Your informants told you I was here. So—what? It's not like you care about me."

"How can you say that? You're my son. I love you."

"Right, as long as I shut my mouth and marry a woman I can't stand just to keep your secret. Please. It would've been better if I died."

"We might all die if you let Miranda talk."

"I don't believe you."

"Stop being so selfish."

"You have the audacity to talk to me about selfishness?"

"Son, I'm telling you the truth. Do you really want blood on your hands? They could go after your friend."

"Ian is my boyfriend. And don't you dare threaten him."

"I'm not. I'm just explaining—"

"Instead of warning me, why don't you talk to Miranda? She's the one you should convince to keep her mouth shut."

And just what I needed. The bitch walked in.

"What is going on in here? I could hear you two yelling down the hall."

"What the fuck are you doing here?" I demanded.

"They called me. I'm still listed as your emergency contact. This was the first opportunity I had to come."

"Wonderful. I'll be sure to change that as soon as I get out of here."

"What happened, Jake? I was worried."

"Bullshit. Save your damn tears. I'm fine."

"Son, that's no way to talk to your fiancée."

"She's not my fiancée. I broke up with her."

"Jake, this has gone on long enough. What you feel for that boy is not love. You are confused."

"That boy has a name. And he's the love of my life."

"You sound ridiculous."

"Wait, you know who it is?" Miranda asked my dad.

"Oh yes. They were locking lips when I got here."

She gasped. "In a public place? Have you gone mad?"

"Are you fucking serious right now? You and my father are blackmailing me, and I'm the crazy one? Fuck you both."

"I am your father. Show me some respect."

"The way you respect me? You won't even back me up on this, Dad. I told you I'm gay and your response is that I'm confused? That you're ashamed of me? And your solution is for me to marry a woman who's blackmailing me? The cherry on top being that we'll all die if I don't?" My eyes burned with tears as I reached for the call button. "Get out."

"Son, I realize you're upset, but we need to talk about this."

"No, you two need to talk about this because, like I've said a billion times, I'm done being the middleman. And I'm done being the sacrificial lamb."

When the nurse came in, she said, "What can I get you?"

"First, you can tell these people to leave. And second, you can get my discharge papers."

"The doctor is making his rounds now. He should be in with your test results soon."

"About time. And make sure you tell the staff that the only visitor who is allowed to see me is Ian Cooper."

Chapter 28

Ian

As soon as I got to my car, I pulled out my cell and sent Anna a text. **Jake's fine. Thank God! They're running tests to be safe. We'll talk later. Thanks again for lunch!**

On my way to the church, I thought of the encounter with Jake's dad. It was true; Jake had come out to him. Not that I had doubted him—but it proved Jake's commitment.

The bad thing, my boyfriend's dad hated me. Great.

I arrived at St. Pius just before the meeting time. After parking the loaner, I rang the doorbell of the rectory, and Rosemary answered this time. After a quick exchange of pleasantries, she moved aside and told me Father Kevin was waiting in the back office.

The door was open, and he gestured for me to come in.

"Hi, Father."

"Hello, Ian. Please have a seat. And close the door."

I did not like the grim look on the priest's face. He leaned forward as he folded his hands on the desk. "I spoke to Father John," he began. "He confirmed that he's received complaints about you, which I've asked to see, but he says that the complaints were from word of mouth."

"What? He told me he received emails."

"Yes, I found that odd. But there's something else."

"What is it?"

"Father John seems to be under the impression that it was you who solicited favors in exchange for your job."

The blood drained from my face. I became lightheaded. This was what I had been afraid of: my word against the priest's. "What?" My stomach clenched. "I didn't—it was him—"

Father Kevin put his hand up. "Relax. I believe you."

I let out a sigh of relief as I closed my eyes and silently thanked God. "Thank you, Father. You know me. I would never do something like that."

"I know. There were some inconsistencies with his version of things that just didn't add up. Plus, I just find it hard to believe that you would do something like that. Therefore, I will be going to the bishop for counsel on how to handle this. In the meantime, I ask that you be patient and stay low for now. I want to let him think I believe him and agree with you being fired."

"I'm not getting my job back?"

"For now. Until this situation is settled."

I leaned back in my seat. "This isn't fair."

"I know. I'm sorry, but it's the only way I can think of that won't raise suspicion. At least until I speak to the bishop."

As I stood, I nodded. "I can't say I'm not disappointed, Father. I shouldn't have to sacrifice myself for someone else's lies about me. I did nothing wrong. All I tried to do was help people. And I think I will pay a visit to the bishop myself, on my own behalf."

"You have every right to do so. In fact, I encourage it."

"What about the Christmas program?"

"I hope your job will be reinstated well before then, but if you don't mind continuing your duet rehearsals with Jake, I would be forever grateful."

I nodded again. "I will wait to hear from you then." Then I turned and left.

I dug out my phone as I stepped into the loaner and did a quick search for the hospital's number. When the operator answered, I asked for Jake's room and was connected. "Hello?"

I sighed in relief once I recognized Jake's voice. "Hi, babe. It's me."

"Baby, how'd it go?"

"Not great but not bad either. I'll explain when I get there. When can you leave?"

"They're drawing up the discharge papers now. All the tests came back good."

"That's a relief."

"I told you I was fine."

"What happened with your dad when I left?"

"I don't wanna talk about him."

"That bad, huh?"

"Worse. Miranda showed up."

"Oh my God."

"Yeah. Hurry up and get here. I miss you and need you to cheer me up."

"On my way. See you soon."

"Okay. I love you."

"I love you too."

Chapter 29

Jake

I sat on the edge of the hospital bed, dressed and ready to blow this popsicle stand. My shredded jeans barely covered my bandaged leg, and the crutches the hospital had given me were on the bed next to me. Walking with crutches was going to suck, but at least it wouldn't be for that long.

When Ian walked in, I perked up. Like, the way a school kid gets excited when their crush shows up. Yup, I had it bad.

"Oh my God, babe, your leg," Ian said as he rushed inside.

I reached for his hand and pulled him down for a kiss. "It's not that bad. The doc confirmed it was sprained, not broken. It just sucks that my good pair of jeans got fucked up."

"How long are you going to need crutches for?"

I shrugged. "One or two weeks, maybe."

Ian shook his head. "Are you in pain?"

"I'm fine. They gave me meds. But tell me, what happened with Father Kev?"

He sighed as he slipped his hands in his pockets. "For now, I still don't have a job."

"Why the fuck not?"

"Father Kevin needs to talk to the bishop."

I narrowed my eyes, not liking where this was going. "Why?"

"Babe, don't freak out."

"Every time you say that, I swear—what the fuck happened now?"

"Father John told Father Kevin that I'm the one who offered favors in order to keep my job."

The motherfucking priest was a dead man. "And Father Kev believed him?"

"No, he says he doesn't, but he wants him to think he does to buy time to speak with the bishop."

"Why do you even want to work there anymore?"

I listened as Ian told me everything that was said at the goddamn church. By the time he finished, I was ready to hop over there and teach them a lesson with my fists. But I was also proud of Ian for telling Father Kevin that how he was handling the shit was not fair. And as far as I was concerned, they could take the fucking Christmas program and shove it up their ass.

"What are you thinking?" Ian asked when I remained silent.

I shrugged. "I think you know what I'm thinking."

Ian smirked. "You want to beat them up, don't you?"

"Fuck yes." I sighed. "But I'm also impressed by how you're handling it."

Ian huffed. "I feel helpless. Like I have no control over my fate."

I took his hand. "If you really want this job, stick with it. If it doesn't work out, do what we talked about."

"Yeah. I want to talk to the bishop first. See what he has to say about all this."

"Maybe he'll kick everyone's ass for me."

Ian laughed. "Now that would be funny." I smiled as I rubbed my thumb over his knuckles. "What happened with your dad and Miranda?"

I rolled my eyes. "I told them I was done being the sacrificial lamb. You know my dad had the nerve to call me selfish?"

Ian sat next to me and put his arm around me. "I'm sorry, baby."

"I don't need them. You're my family now."

"Absolutely. And I'll always be here for you."

I brought my hand to the side of his face. "Thanks. Just like I'm here for you." I leaned in and kissed him.

"Oh," someone said, clearing their throat. "Sorry for the interruption."

We pulled apart. It was the nurse.

"That's okay. This is the boyfriend I was telling you about. See, I wasn't making him up," I told her.

"I'm sorry we couldn't reach him. Nice to meet you. I have the discharge papers."

I signed where she told me and listened as she gave the discharge instructions.

"Is the doctor prescribing pain medicine?" Ian asked.

"Yes, the prescription is right here." She indicated on a piece of paper. "Only take as needed."

"What about the tests you guys ran? Is everything okay with those?"

"Yes. A summary of what was done and the results are included in his copy of the discharge papers. The brace on his ankle can be removed to shower."

"Does he need to come back for a follow-up?"

"Only if he has any problems, like his leg doesn't improve or he develops headaches or any other issues."

I smiled as I watched Ian listening intently to the nurse's responses. I liked him taking over and making sure I was okay.

When Ian was satisfied and had no further questions, the nurse gave the okay to leave. Ian held the crutches for me as I stood.

"Thanks, babe."

"You got it?"

"Yup."

"You sure?"

I paused as I glanced at him and smiled. "Yeah, babe, I'm sure. Now gimme a freakin' kiss."

Ian smirked as he kissed me.

"You're so cute, the way you fuss over me."

"I just don't want you to fall on your face."

"I'm not gonna fall on my face, silly."

Ian gathered the paperwork and my other belongings, and we headed out into the hall toward the elevator.

The elevator doors slid open, and we smiled like we both remembered the last time we were in an elevator together. We quickly hopped in before anyone else did. Ian attacked the CLOSE DOOR button before anyone else had a chance to get on.

As soon as the doors closed, Ian came to me, pressing me against the wall and crashed his lips against mine. Holding the crutches with my armpits, I grabbed his ass, squeezing him close as I savored his lips. He moaned as I twirled my tongue with his, tasting and sucking.

The bell of the elevator dinged and Ian pulled away but stayed close as the doors opened. I would've kept kissing him; I didn't care who saw us. I kept my hand on Ian's waist until he moved to exit.

I followed him, excusing myself past the crowd, careful not to trip the crutches on anyone's feet. Ian waited for me to catch up, grinning.

Then Matt appeared out of nowhere.

We all stood awkwardly before Matt greeted us. "So, you're going home," he said to me.

"Yup."

"I'm glad you're okay."

"Are you?"

Ian gave me the death stare. Excuse me if I was being snarky with the ex-boyfriend. Even though nothing had happened between them didn't mean I wasn't still jealous as fuck of the time they got to spend together . . . and the kissing.

Oh, and not to mention how Ian had gotten drunk, drugged, and almost raped on a crowded dance floor under the doc's watch.

Matt smiled. "Yes, Jake, of course I am."

Ian put his hand on my back. "Babe, Matt's the one who informed me you were here in the first place."

Okay, okay, I'd be nice—only because Ian called me *babe* in front of the guy. "Right. Thanks for giving my man the head's up." I met Ian's narrowed gaze as I held back a smile.

Matt quirked a brow as he smiled. "I see you guys worked things out. That's great. I'm really happy for you."

"Thanks, Matt."

"You are a lucky guy, Jake."

I stood straighter. If the damn crutches weren't in the way, I would've gone right into the guy's face. "I know. You don't have to fucking tell me that."

"Jake," Ian said as he got in front of me, placing his hand on my chest. He shook his head in warning.

I sighed as I looked into Ian's blue eyes and got the message. Lifting the right crutch slightly and pressing it into the floor, I clenched my jaw. "Sorry. Yes, I am lucky. I'm grateful he gave me a chance to explain things. He told me you and Anna both played a part in that. So . . . thanks."

Matt nodded. "No problem. I could tell things weren't resolved between you two, so talking was a logical call." After a moment, he said, "I should get back to work. It was good seeing you both again. Jake, I hope you heal quickly. Ian, let me know if you need anything."

"Thanks, Matt," Ian replied.

I cleared my throat as Matt walked away. "Hey, Matt," I called. "Thanks for being there for him."

Matt blinked and smiled. "My pleasure." He winked at Ian before walking away.

His pleasure? What the fuck? And did he just wink at my boyfriend?

I was about to launch toward him and demand what he meant, but Ian grabbed my arm. "Baby, no."

"He fucking winked at you. And what the fuck did he mean by *his pleasure?*"

"Nothing, Jake. He was just trying to get a rise out of you." He laughed. "Look at you being an overprotective, jealous boyfriend. You're ready to beat up a doctor. On crutches. It's kinda funny. And cute."

I smirked. "Cute, huh?"

Ian began backing up. "Yup. So cute."

"Imma fucking show you *cute*," I said as I began moving my crutches toward him.

"You gotta catch me first." Then he turned toward the doors that led outside.

I hobbled toward him, moving the crutches as fast as I could. I kept my eye on him as he crossed the parking lot. He reached the loaner SUV and leaned against it, waiting.

When I finally got to him, I trapped him between the crutches. "You are gonna get it when we get home."

"Am I? What are you gonna do? Hop around me to death?"

"Wow. Yeah, maybe I will do that 'cause you're killing me. I'm exhausted."

Ian perked up, getting serious. "Are you really? I'm so sorry."

I laughed. "Oh, now you're sorry?"

"Here. Let's get you in the car so you can rest." Ian opened the door and held the crutches while I pulled myself into the passenger seat. He placed the crutches in the back seat, then went around to the driver's side. "Are you okay? Are you feeling any pain? I'm sorry I didn't think—"

"I'm fine. I was messing with you."

"Are you sure?"

"I am a little tired, but not because of you."

He leaned over and kissed me. "Let's get you home, then. Did you want to stop at Miranda's to get your stuff?"

"Nah, I don't have the energy to deal with her right now."

"Okay. Let's go to the pharmacy to pick up your meds."

I dropped my head back onto the headrest and watched as Ian started the engine. As he pulled the car onto the road, I reached up and ran my fingers along some escaped curls. "I love you."

He smiled as he extended his hand to my thigh. "I love you too."

* * *

Ian

As I parked the SUV in the driveway, I glanced at Jake. Sound asleep.

I undid his seatbelt and leaned over, caressing the side of his face. "Hey, babe," I whispered. "We're home."

He stirred and groaned as his eyes fluttered open.

"We're here. We're home."

His head popped up, then he covered his face and rubbed his eyes. "Did you go to the pharmacy?"

"Yeah. You slept through it all."

"Sorry. I guess I was more tired than I thought."

"It's okay. You need the rest. Come on. Let's get you inside."

I hopped out and went around to the passenger side. I took out the crutches and the bags with Jake's medication and belongings, then I helped him get out and onto the crutches.

Inside, I instructed Jake to rest in the bedroom. As he sat, he gripped his hurt leg and rubbed. "Fuck."

"What's wrong? Are you in pain?"

"Yeah, it's like a sharp, pulsing pain. It just started."

"It's about time for more medicine. I'll get it." Seconds later, I returned with a glass of water and a pain pill.

"Thanks, babe." He popped the pill in his mouth and chased it down with water.

"Let's take these torn jeans off so you'll be more comfortable."

He smirked as he laid back on the pillow. "Are you trying to get me naked?"

A smile spread on my face as I knelt on the bed between his legs and undid the jeans. "You caught me." Off they went—carefully as they slipped over his injured leg—along with his one shoe. "I'm going to throw these away. There might be a pair in the dresser you could wear."

"You actually own a pair of jeans?"

"Ha-ha. It's been a while since I've worn them, but yes. You can also wear anything else of mine. Sweatpants, shorts, whatever."

"Okay, cool."

I pushed up and kissed his lips. "Get some rest."

"You expect me to sleep after you stripped me?"

"You were really tired in the car."

"Well, I'm wide awake now, thanks to you."

I laughed. "Sorry."

"Don't be sorry. Come here." Jake slid his hands to my jaw and pulled me toward him, brushing his lips against mine. I kissed him back, coaxing his mouth open, dipping my tongue to his.

"Are you sure you're feeling up to this?" I asked against his lips.

He raised his eyes and smirked, sinking into the pillow as he moved his hands down my backside to my ass and yanked me down to him. Yup, up indeed.

"Yeah. I'm sure."

Moving my hips against him, I smiled, sucking in my bottom lip between my teeth. He kissed me again, then trailed kisses down my jaw, heading to my neck, and licked and sucked. My shirt slipped free from my pants and warm hands seared my skin. Eager to feel him too, I found the hem of his shirt and spread my hand wide along his rib cage. A little maneuvering and his flat stomach was exposed. Perfect for hot kisses, which I happily gave as he removed his shirt.

I licked my way up to his chest, sucking on his nipples, then up to his mouth. My lips lingered on his, mingling, tasting, savoring. He brought his good leg up around mine as he tried to flip me so he could take over like he always did, but I wouldn't allow it. I'd almost lost him. I wanted to savor every inch of him, so I was in charge.

Kissing my way back down to the waistband of his boxers, I teased him with my mouth. Jake's fingers tangled in my hair. "Baby," he whispered. "You're killing me."

Smiling, my mouth covered the cotton fabric of the boxers and I kissed his hard cock, nudging with my lips. He moaned, moving his hips. I reached for the waistband, adjusting it so the tip of his cock peeked up past the band. I tasted him.

"Fuck," Jake breathed.

I rose to my knees and took the boxers off, watching as his gorgeous cock jerked free. Tossing the underwear aside, and lowering once again, my hand wrapped around him, gliding up and down, then eagerly took him in my mouth. I relished the taste of him, swirling my tongue around the tip, then licking down the length of him to his balls and back up. As I sucked him deep, I glanced up. His bottom lip was tucked between his teeth, his head thrown back. I loved giving him pleasure, and he was obviously pleased. With my eyes closed, I deepthroated him. When I popped my eyes open again, Jake's hooded gaze was on me. Our eyes locked as he licked his lips.

"Yeah, baby, that feels good," he moaned as I continued to work him, building him up with my mouth and hands.

His fingers slipped through my curls, and he rocked his hips. His breathing intensified as his body tensed. "Fuck, baby. I'm cumming—"

I swallowed as much as I could. Once the pulses subsided, I licked him clean, then rose over him and kissed him.

He gripped my head, holding me as he kissed me back. "Mmm, baby." He reached his hand between us, rubbing my arousal.

"You really should rest," I whispered.

"Not until I do you," he said, smiling as he undid my button and zipper.

I covered his hand. "You don't have to."

"Are you kidding? I want to. I've been looking forward to this all day."

"But—"

"Baby, shut up and let me suck your dick."

I chuckled at his boldness.

He smiled. "It's not like I have some debilitating injury. My leg is just bruised a little. My mouth works great, so come here and let me please you."

I buried my head in the crook of his neck and laughed. "You say the most romantic things."

"Oh, it's romance you want? I can do romance. Baby, please stick your gorgeous, big, thick penis in my mouth so I can taste you and give you pleasure until you spill warm, delicious medicine down my throat. Is that better?"

I burst out laughing again and kissed him. "Uh, since you put it that way—"

He unzipped my pants and dug inside, releasing my cock and rubbing me. After removing the slacks, I got on my knees and climbed over him so that I straddled his face.

"About time, baby. Come. Here," he said as he gripped my cock, jerking me and then taking me in his mouth.

I braced myself against the wall as he held on to my hips, urging me deeper into his mouth. He worked me with his tongue, building me up. I moaned, fucking his mouth as he expertly brought me closer and closer to the edge.

"Jake," I breathed.

He deepthroated me as I rocked my hips, unable to slow down the fast build. The grunt escaped me as I exploded into his mouth. His grip remained on me until the pulses subsided, swallowing all of me.

Hot.

"My God, babe," I said. He sucked me clean as I eased out of his mouth.

"Mmm," he said as he pulled me down to him. "I love you."

"I love you too." I stretched out beside him as he wrapped an arm around me and pressed his lips to the top of my head. "Are you still in pain?"

When there was no answer, I glanced up. My man was fast asleep.

Chapter 30

Matt

Was I crazy? I must've been crazy.

Why else would I cook dinner for a guy I barely knew . . . in my penthouse? A guy who was only coming over for sex . . . *in my apartment?* Did I mention this meal and sex would take place in the home I lived in?

The guy needed to eat to keep his energy up. Yup, that was the answer I was going with. Why not, you know, two-birds-one-stone it?

And it was just pasta. It wasn't like it was a five-course meal or anything. Pasta and salad, that was it. And sex for dessert. Okay, and some wine.

Whatever.

The doorbell rang. Don't ask why I was so nervous. Maybe it was because I was pretty much letting a stranger into my house. It had nothing to do with wanting to make a good impression so he'd stick around—for sex, of course. Duh, what else would I want him to stick around for? Definitely not a relationship. That would be ridiculous. He was hot. And the best sex partner I'd ever had.

Period.

I swung the door open and thought of jumping straight to dessert. He smelled like sexy man and dressed like a *GQ* model.

"Hey, what's up, Doc?"

I drew my eyebrows together. "Never say that again."

"Sorry. It just came out." He smiled.

I reached for the back of his head and dragged him inside. "You could make it up to me tonight." I captured him in a kiss. Was it weird that I'd missed him? Kissing him was all I'd been thinking about since the last time we hooked up. He was that great of a kisser.

His arms came around me as he kissed me back. "You bet," he said as he pulled away. "What smells so good? You cooking?"

"Yeah. Just a little something I threw together in case you hadn't eaten."

He grinned. "You trying to fatten me up?"

"Nah. Just want you to keep your strength up. You know, for the evening's festivities."

His eyes hooded. "I like the way you think. Let's eat."

"Great." I pointed to the table. "Have a seat. I'll bring you a plate."

"Can I help with anything?"

"Nope. Everything's done. Actually, you could open that bottle of wine."

He removed the cork and filled the wineglasses while I brought two plates of pasta to the table. I left the salad in the middle of the table so he could take as much as he wanted.

"I hope you like it. I figured pasta was a safe dish, considering I don't know what foods you like. Unless you're gluten-free, then I'm sorry."

He laughed. "I'm not gluten-free, and I love pasta. I lived in Italy for a while, so pasta is a staple of mine."

"Oh? What part of Italy?"

"Mostly Rome and a little bit in Milan."

"Nice. I would love to visit Italy someday. With med school and my residency, I've never had the chance, but it's definitely on my bucket list."

CJ held up his glass. "Let's make a toast. To someday."

I smiled. "To someday."

Clink.

"So, what's your specialty, Doc?" he asked.

"Internal medicine."

He swallowed. "An internist, huh? Impressive. Do you work in the hospital, or do you have a practice somewhere?"

"Only the hospital. I see both inpatients and outpatients. Occasionally, I follow my patients to nursing homes, but that's only a handful of them." I paused as he nodded. "Why? Are you looking for a provider?"

He laughed. "Not at the moment. But I'll let you know if that changes." He glanced around. "You've got a nice place here. You live by yourself?"

"Yeah, it's just me. It's big, but I like it. The views are amazing."

"I bet. From what I can see from here, it's a nice place."

"Well, you'll be seeing more of it after we eat. Specifically, the bedroom." Hint, hint.

He smiled, hooding his eyes. "Can't wait."

We must've both been eager for dessert because we ate in silence for a while. "How is the pasta, compared to Italy's standards?"

He chuckled. "Not bad at all. It's perfectly al dente."

My breath caught in my throat as he slipped into a perfect Italian accent. "Do you speak Italian fluently?"

"Maybe not fluently, but I can hold my own, I think."

Something told me he was being modest. "Well, makes sense, since you lived there. That's super cool."

"Does it turn you on?"

"I don't know. Say something else in Italian and I'll see."

"Questo pasto è delizioso. È stato così dolce da parte tua. Ma anche tu sembri piuttosto gustoso. Voglio succhiarti il cazzo. Sei così sexy e non vedo l'ora di fotterti."

I bit my lip. "That was so hot. I'd say your Italian is on point. Definitely a turn-on."

He side-eyed me. "You understood what I said, didn't you?"

I chuckled. "Yeah, sorry. I caught most of it, thanks to my years of studying Italian in school."

A blush crept up to his cheeks as he huffed, smiling.

I replied in English, "I'm glad you enjoyed the meal, and that you thought it was sweet of me. I wanted to do something nice for you. You also look rather tasty. My mouth waters just by looking at you." I put a finger to my chin. "Hmm, what were the last two things you said? Oh, yeah, I remember—I want you to suck my dick too. But I also want to suck yours. You're sexy, and I can't wait to fuck you too."

He stared at me with intensity. The humor faded from his face. "You certainly don't need to speak a different language to turn me on. The sound of your voice holds that power."

I smiled. "Are you ready for dessert, then?"

"If dessert includes you, then hell yeah, I'm ready."

I stood and extended my hand to him. "Shall we?"

Pushing back, he rose to his feet and took off his brown leather jacket, draping it on the back of the chair. Then he placed his hand in mine. I led him to my bedroom. "So, this is my room."

What was wrong with me? What the fuck?

He chuckled. "Nice. I love the king-size bed. Looks roomy and comfy."

I cringed inwardly. "Yup. That it is. Want to try it out?" What was I? Fourteen?

He jumped up and bounced onto the bed, landing on the edge. "Oh, this is nice. I like it. Not too soft, not too firm."

I covered my face with my hand. "I'm sorry. I don't know what's wrong with me."

He reached for my hand, drawing me closer until I stood between his legs. "Are you nervous?"

"Me? Nervous? No way."

"It's okay if you are. I'm a little nervous too. Not sure why, though."

"Really? I mean, what do we have to be nervous about? We've done this before."

"I know, right?"

"I think it's because it's been a while since I've had a guy in my bedroom."

"And it's been a while since I've been in a guy's room. So, we're even."

I had a hard time believing that, but I went with it. I brought my hands to the sides of his face and kissed him, coaxing his lips open, gently demanding entry. He was quick to comply. His arms came around me, pulling me on top of him as he laid back onto the bed.

I lifted my head. "Wait. I have an idea." I rolled off him and sprinted to my closet, trying to remember where I put the—ah, yes. Found them. When I got back to CJ, he was sitting up. I held up the handcuffs I'd never used.

"Whoa, am I under arrest?" he asked with a hint of humor in his voice.

"I swiped them off my brother years ago as a joke but ended up keeping them. I thought they'd come in handy someday."

He visibly swallowed. "Your brother's a cop?"

"DEA agent." When he still looked confused, I clarified, "Drug Enforcement Administration."

"Ah," he said as he looked down at his hands.

I was an idiot. "Look, we don't have to play if you're not into this sort of thing. I just thought it'd help break the ice a little."

"Do you have the key?"

I searched the cuffs and saw it inside the hole. "Yeah, right here."

He gave a side smile as he held up his hands together, wrists up. "In that case, arrest me, Doc."

I smiled and accentuated my Southern accent. "That's Officer Doc to you."

He chuckled. "What are the charges, Officer Doc?"

"You're under arrest for being so damn sexy. Now I demand you take off that fucking shirt before I cuff you."

"Yes, sir."

When he was done, I slapped the cuffs on his wrists, making sure they weren't too tight. "Now lie down in the middle of the bed."

As he crawled onto the bed, he said, "You wouldn't happen to have a police uniform lying around anywhere, would ya? I feel like that would make this even hotter."

I smacked his ass right before he fell onto his back, then I got face-to-face with him. "Oh, I promise you, you will get boiling hot. Now scoot up toward the headboard until your arms reach." I paused when he didn't move. "I'm sorry. Was that too much?"

He shook his head. "Not at all. My pants just got immensely tighter, is all."

I quirked a brow. "Well, then, I guess we'll have to remove them."

"I was hoping you'd say that, Officer Doc."

I smirked and ordered him to scoot up more. When he did, I grasped the links of the handcuffs and pulled his arms over his head and hooked them to the post at the headboard. "It's not completely secure, so try not to move."

He smiled. "I'll do my best."

Sitting back on my heels, I unbuttoned, unzipped, and pulled down his jeans. I leaned over him, cupping his dick over the boxer briefs I'd left on him. "Are you concealing a weapon under here?"

He let out a laugh. "Why don't you check for yourself, Officer Doc?"

"I think I will. Let's see what you're hiding under here." I peeled away the underwear. He was deliciously hard. "Well, well, well, would ya lookie here?" I leaned over him again. "That's a mighty fine-looking piece of equipment you got there. But I suggest you be careful where you point that thing."

"Sorry, Officer Doc."

"Are you trying to shoot me with it?"

"Not yet."

I got close to his face. "Good boy. I'll tell you when."

He smiled, licking his lips, and I couldn't resist. I kissed him but quit before it went deeper. The guy tried to suck me in. I placed a finger over his lips. "Uh, uh, uh . . . not so fast." I quickly glanced at his wrists and checked that the cuffs weren't aggravating his wrists. "Are these hurting you?"

"I feel no pain."

"Are you sure? Here." I grabbed two pillows and stacked them under his elbows so that his arms didn't dangle and the pressure was taken off his wrists. "Is that better?"

When he didn't answer, I looked down at him. He had a grin on his face.

"What?"

"I'm literally lying here naked, at your mercy, and you're making sure I'm comfortable?"

"Of course. Only the best for my prisoner."

"Oh yeah? Then I would like your police stick in my mouth, Officer Doc."

My eyebrows shot up. "Patience, prisoner."

I jumped off the mattress and stood at the foot of the bed so he could see me as I stripped, shirt first. I just so happened to be wearing a button-down; it helped with the dramatic effect of the striptease. He got harder, and I, in turn, got hard as well.

He was a beautiful man—bronzed from the sun, slim and toned from CrossFit, hair on all parts of his body where a man should have hair, even a happy trail that led to the neatly trimmed bush around his cock. And tonight, he was all mine to do with what I pleased. The possibilities were endless. Although I'd never tied anyone up before, I'd watched enough porn to get the gist of what went down.

CJ's eyes were on my cock as he bit his bottom lip. I gripped myself and lightly stroked myself. "Is this what you want?"

"Yes."

"Yes, what?"

"Yes, sir, Officer Doc."

"And where exactly do you want it?"

"In my mouth."

"Anywhere else?"

"In my ass."

"Well, now you're just being greedy." I climbed onto the bed, straddling his legs as I paused at his cock. I couldn't pass it without admiring it—and playing with it a little. I wrapped my hand around him, sliding along his length and back down to his balls. I cupped them as they tightened. "This is indeed a mighty beautiful weapon. We'll have to put it to good use later."

"It's loaded, Officer Doc, so be careful where you point it."

I smirked. This was so much fun. "Don't you worry your pretty head over that. I'm quite capable of aiming and discharging this bad boy in the right direction."

He laughed. "You're killing me, Doc."

I slid over his body until we were face-to-face. "There shall be no killing under my watch, prisoner. Only torturous pleasure." And while I was in this position, I engaged us in a little frotting. He moaned and moved his hips up, grinding back.

Enough of that.

Back on my hands and knees, I crawled up his body, straddling him until I hovered over his torso. I gripped my cock just out of his reach and stroked myself. He lifted his head to reach me, but I shifted out of his grasp. "Don't move."

I put the tip of my cock on his lips and rubbed as we kept eye contact. I could feel his breath on me. The anticipation was building, not only for him—I could see it in his eyes—but for me as well. I'd never done anything this erotic.

"Lick it," I demanded.

His tongue touched my tip, slowly at first, then he eagerly swirled his tongue as far along as he could reach.

"Suck me," I breathed.

He didn't hesitate or disappoint. He groaned as he took me inside his mouth. It was exquisite, but I had to pace myself. I couldn't cum before my captive.

Reluctantly, I pulled out from his mouth and—fuck me—the guy actually whimpered in protest. I bent and kissed him thoroughly, sucking on his tongue and lips, a full-fledged, hungry kiss. I rotated around him into a sixty-nine position and took his cock into my mouth while I made him look at my ass without being able to touch it.

He moaned loudly, I think partly because of pleasure and partly torture for not being able to touch me. He mumbled something—then, suddenly, I felt hands on my ass.

I bolted away like I'd been scorched. "What do you think you're doing?"

"Sorry, Officer Doc. I couldn't help it. This is beyond torture."

I grabbed the link and hooked it onto the post again. "Do you want to stop playing?"

"What I want is for you to sit on my face for a while, just so I can get a taste. Then I want you to fuck me until we both cum."

"Hey, who's calling the shots here, prisoner?"

"You, sir, of course."

"You're lucky I'm an accommodating officer."

He smiled as I climbed up on him once again. I flipped around and lowered my ass onto his face. I gasped as he licked me, then proceeded to feast on me. I concentrated on his cock. I reached for it and rubbed on him, making him super hard.

After a few minutes, I pulled away, twisting to the nightstand, and retrieved a condom and some lube. I slipped on the condom and slathered him with lube, fingering him until he was nicely lubricated and squirming for me to fill him.

I lifted his legs and penetrated him. It felt so good; I would not last long. I gripped his cock and began working him. He was stiff as a board. "Are you ready to shoot?"

"Yes," he breathed.

I slammed into him until the tip of his cock glistened. Then I stilled as I jerked him. He squirted beautiful cum onto his chest. When he was finished, I resumed pumping into him, reaching for my orgasm. My balls tightened as I pulled out, ripping the condom off, and came onto his cock and stomach.

I was still on an orgasmic high when I reached for the key off the nightstand and uncuffed him. Then I collapsed onto my back.

Neither of us said a word as we floated back down to earth. I could see him rubbing his wrists through my peripheral vision. I closed my eyes. Oh, if only the bed would suck me in like in *A Nightmare on Elm Street.*

He was the first to speak. "Wow, Doc. That was . . . interesting."

I huffed. "Was it? Was it really?"

He chuckled. "Yeah. I mean, there were some intense moments. But it was fun overall."

"You don't have to lie. It was a hot mess."

He laughed as he moved onto his side, propping his head up on his hand. "I'm not lying. It was fun. And you're cute when you're a hot mess."

I rolled my eyes. "Cute? Now I know you're lying."

He brought his hand to my chest. "I'm serious."

I pressed my lips together. "I'm sorry." I reached for his wrist. "Did you get marked up?"

"It's fine. I've never been tied up like that. I mean, I like role-playing, but I'm a hands-on type of guy. And I love to give pleasure as much as I like to receive."

"I'm the same way, which was why I thought that by tying you up, I'd be able to give you all this pleasure, teasing you until you literally exploded. Except you kept wanting to give me pleasure."

He laughed. "Sorry I ruined your plans."

"It's okay. At least now I know for next time—if there's a next time."

"Why wouldn't there be a next time?"

"Because I freaked you out with the whole tying-you-up disaster." Duh. "In fact, I'm surprised you're still here. I'd totally understand if you wanna split."

His hand came up to the side of my face, nudging me to face him. "Hey, look at me. I'm not freaked out. Amused and entertained? Hell yeah. And I mean that in a good way. So, unless you don't, I want there to be a next time."

"Really?"

"Bet. The sex is too good to pass up."

I laughed. "I'll have to agree with you on that."

He drew me in for a kiss, and things got serious again. "Hey, do you mind if I use your shower?"

Okay, so maybe he was going to split. I'd hoped he'd stick around for a chance to erase the handcuff catastrophe. "Sure. There's a linen closet inside the bathroom. Just help yourself to a towel."

"Is your shower big enough for the two of us?"

I raised my eyebrows. "Is that your way of asking me to join you?"

He nodded. "Is that weird?"

"Not any weirder than handcuffing you to my bed."

He chuckled. "Is that a yes?"

"Yes."

As we headed into the bathroom, CJ added, "Oh, and don't forget the condoms."

Chapter 31

Ian

“Thank you, Bishop, for seeing me on such short notice.”

I sat in front of the grand mahogany desk across from the man who held my career in his hands. When I called this morning to make an appointment, I was surprised that there was an opening in an hour. I’d quickly showered, dressed, and left Jake sleeping in my bed—*our* bed.

“It’s no problem,” the bishop replied. “I actually wanted to speak with you as well. You seem to be the hot topic of discussion over at St. Pius.”

“Yes, unfortunately, I don’t think it’s all good, which is why I wanted to meet with you. To clear the air.”

“Well, yes, of course, that’s what I’m hoping. I want to get your side of things so I might get a clearer picture of what’s going on.”

I started from the beginning, from taking Matt to mass, to fellow LGBTQ+ parishioners reaching out to me, to my idea for the support group, to my car being vandalized, to Father John firing and propositioning me, to the conversation with Father Kevin—including how unfairly I was being treated when I did nothing wrong. All I wanted was to help people.

The bishop listened intently and took notes, interrupting only to ask questions where elaboration was needed. "And you've been at St. Pius for, what, five or six years?"

"Almost seven. Before that, I helped during summers and when I could throughout the year. I've been involved with St. Pius since my teen years."

The bishop nodded as he wrote some more notes, then he dropped the pen and folded his hands over the desk. "Okay, well, I think I have enough information here, unless there is anything else you'd like to add."

"Yes, there is, Bishop. I take my work seriously. Being a music director is my life, and playing God's music gives me fulfillment I can't explain. I would never do anything to jeopardize that. I have never intentionally kept my sexual orientation a secret. It never was questioned, so I didn't think it mattered. My work has never been affected by it in any way. Everything Father John said to me was completely uncalled for, unprofessional, and appalling. And I find it offensive that he—or anyone else, for that matter—would even think of saying those things to me. And the fact that I could lose my job over it is—"

The bishop chuckled as he put his hand up. "Okay, Mr. Cooper, I believe you've made your point."

"I'm sorry. I didn't mean to go off like that. It's just that I feel strongly about this issue. I mean, it's my career we're talking about. A career I'm passionate about."

"I'm aware. Which is why you are not losing your job."

"Really?"

The bishop waved a hand through the air. "This meeting was more of a formality. I wanted to speak to you in person to gather your take on the situation, but it is clear to me that you did not act inappropriately. Father Kevin also agrees with me and speaks highly of you. In the time that you have worked at St. Pius, there have never been any complaints, only excellent feedback. Therefore, on behalf of St. Pius, I would like to extend an apology and reinstate your position as music director, effective immediately."

I exhaled as I dropped my elbows to my knees and covered my mouth. I closed my eyes, blinking back the tears of relief and joy. "Oh my God, Bishop, thank you so much. You have no idea what this means to me."

"Oh, I think I do," he laughed.

"Thank you, thank you. Oh my God."

"You're very welcome. You're an important asset to St. Pius, and we'd hate to lose you."

"What about the LGBTQ+ support group? Do you have any problem with me moving forward with it?"

"Not at all. I don't see why that should be an issue. If anything, it's admirable, what you want to do."

"Thank you so much. And what's going to happen to Father John?"

"Don't worry about him. He won't be bothering you again."

"But what if this happens again? I mean, there are people at the church who don't want me there. What if they try to get me into trouble again by spreading lies about me?"

"Now that I have a better understanding of what's going on over there, we can prevent things from escalating. Accusations such as these will not be taken seriously unless proof can be provided. I have asked Father Kevin to keep me informed of things there, and I ask of you the same."

"I will, Bishop. Thank you for your help and trust."

"You're very welcome."

Chapter 32

Jake

"Ian!" My heart was racing as I bolted upright.

It had only been a fucking dream. Goddamn it. That woman had managed to infiltrate my subconscious.

I rubbed my eyes, erasing the image of her evil laugh from my head. The details of the nightmare were foggy, but I did recall Ian on the ground, my motorcycle in flames, blood on my hands, and Miranda laughing over us. What the fuck?

"Ian?" I called again. It would calm me the fuck down if I could see the guy to make sure he was safe.

Still no answer. I glanced over at Ian's side of the bed. There was a pair of jeans and light gray sweatpants folded on the pillow, with a piece of paper and set of keys on top. I leaned over and snatched the paper.

> *Scored a meeting with the bishop. Hopefully won't take too long. The house keys are yours. Welcome home. Love you xoxo — Ian*

I smiled and tossed the note on the nightstand, setting the keys on top. He'd set out my medicine and a glass of water for me too. Ian was so freaking sweet.

Massaging my ankle, I decided the pain wasn't bad enough to take meds. Last thing I wanted was to get hooked on pain pills.

I took off the brace and wrap from my leg, then grabbed the crutches from the floor and headed into the bathroom. Carefully, I did my best to take a quick shower. Once done, I made my way back into the bedroom and looked through Ian's drawers for some boxers. Found them. Going back to the bed, I grabbed the sweats and put them on.

Not too bad.

Now all I needed was a shirt. I looked through the closet first, running a hand along the row of button-downs. They smelled like Ian. I extended a sleeve and inhaled. "Mmm."

Back to the dresser, in search of T-shirts. Finally—a drawer that contained a few. I picked one out and slipped it on.

I straightened up the bed, leaving the brace and wrap on top; they'd stay off for a while, partly because I was too lazy to put them back on.

Thanks to Ian letting me use his charger, I checked emails on my phone and made some calls, mainly to the school. Apparently, Ant had let the school know about the accident, so everything was good there. Anna must've told him when she found out, along with Ian.

I made my way to the kitchen to raid the fridge. The quickest thing to make was a sandwich.

Just as I gathered all the fixings onto the counter and began the preparation, the front door opened. Thank God. He was safe. "Hey, baby, I'm in the kitchen," I called.

Ian came around the corner with a cute-ass smile on his face. As he got closer, the smile got wider. "Hi, babe," he greeted, giving me a smooch. "Whatcha doin'?"

"Making a sandwich. I'm hungry. How was the meeting?"

He stared at me up and down, still smiling and looking like he'd devour me for lunch. Not that I would complain. "What?"

"Nothing. Just—you're wearing my shirt."

"Oh yeah." I chuckled as I tugged at it. "Hope you don't mind."

He shook his head. "Not at all. Looks good on you. I like you wearing my stuff."

"Good. Because I'm wearing your boxers too." I pulled the waistband from beneath the sweats to show him.

His eyes skimmed down my body. "And I see the sweats fit."

"Yeah. They're a little long but not too bad."

"They look . . . really good." He placed his hand on my waist.

"I know that look. Let me eat first, then you can sex me up all you want," I teased.

He blushed and chuckled. "Want me to make the sandwich for you?"

"I got it. Tell me about the meeting."

He leaned against the counter. "Well, I got my job back."

"Babe, that's great!" I leaned forward and kissed him. "What about Father Sicko?"

"He's getting fired, apparently. I don't know. The bishop told me not to worry about him, that he was being taken care of."

I listened as Ian recapped everything the bishop had said. "See, I told you they would look at your history at the church. Did you tell him about the death threats?"

"I mentioned there are people at the church that don't want me there and what to do if they accuse me of something."

"And what'd he say?"

"He basically said without proof, any accusation would be worthless."

"Good. But what about the actual death threats?"

He shrugged, grabbing the plate with the made sandwich and

placing it on the breakfast bar for me. "He said to keep him informed. But I really don't think anything will happen. I think those people are just trying to scare me into resigning."

I pressed my lips together. "I hope you're right. But if I catch someone threatening your life—or worse, hurting you in any way—I'll break their face."

He huffed, narrowing his eyes. "Then you'll go to jail."

I stood straighter as I gripped the crutches. "I don't fucking care."

"Well, I do."

"Then they better pray to fucking God I don't find out who they are."

Ian smirked as he shook his head.

"Are you hungry?" I asked as I caressed the side of his face. "Want me to make you a sandwich too?"

"No, it's okay. I can make it. Sit down and eat."

"You sure? I don't mind."

He took my hand. "I'm sure. Eat."

I leaned forward and gave him a kiss. Then I crutched my way to the other side of the breakfast bar and sat.

"How's your leg?" Ian asked as he began prepping his sandwich.

"Not too bad. I haven't taken medicine yet today. I wanna see if I can go without it."

"But the medicine is supposed to help you."

"I'm only supposed to take it as needed. I don't wanna get hooked on that shit."

"Yeah, but if you need it—"

"Babe, I'm good," I said, swallowing a mouthful of food.

Ian's mother hen attitude was simultaneously annoying and cute; it meant he cared. And honestly, I would act the same way. Maybe worse. The thought of him being hurt like this—or any way, for that matter—scared the hell out of me. Like in my dream. It freaked me the fuck out.

I watched as Ian licked the mayo knife before placing it in the sink. He went to the fridge and took out a jar of pickles.

Yuck.

"When do you go back to work?" I asked.

"The bishop said it was effective immediately, but I figure I'll just go in tomorrow. There's work I can do from home, anyway. What about you? When do you think you'll go back?"

"Probably next week. I already called the school and let them know."

"If you want, I could work from home the rest of this week so we can spend time together. I would just want to go in for a little bit tomorrow."

If it were up to me, I would want Ian to work from home forever. Much safer. I smiled as I quirked a brow. "Sure, but I don't think you'll get much work done."

A blush rose to his cheeks as he chuckled. "Oh, I think I'll take that risk."

I smiled as he grabbed his plate and brought it over to the breakfast bar next to me. "You're so freaking cute when you blush."

"Cute? Really?"

"Yeah, cute. Come here." I reached for his hand, pulling him toward me, and kissed him. My lips lingered on his, then moved to his cheek before I sat back.

We finished eating in silence with the occasional glance and smile. After we finished, Ian leaned over and kissed my neck, nuzzling as he stood. I wrapped my arm around his waist before he moved away. I pulled him close and captured his lips in a thorough kiss.

My hand slid to his ass as I leaned back. "My baby."

He smiled, stealing another kiss. "My man."

"That's right. And don't you forget it."

"I won't. Trust me." He laughed as he pulled away and picked up the empty plates, taking them to the sink.

"You want any help?"

"No, it's okay. You seem tired. Is your leg bothering you?"

Crazy how he knew me so well. "Yeah, a little. I'm gonna lie down on the couch."

"Do you want medicine?"

"Nah. Not yet."

I ignored his concerned, disapproving look and crutched my way over to the couch. I stretched out carefully, placing a throw pillow behind my head and getting comfortable. After a few minutes, Ian joined me, positioning my legs on his thighs as he sat.

"Why aren't you wearing the brace?" he asked as he lightly massaged my ankle.

"I didn't feel like putting it back on after my shower."

"I could put it on for you."

"Maybe later. Just keep doing what you're doing. It feels good."

My lids got heavier and heavier until the only thing I felt was my baby boy's amazing, magical hands.

* * *

Ian

It felt good to be working again.

Jake was still asleep on the couch, so I took the opportunity to get some work done. In my home study, I had gone through emails and looked over the songs the choir would perform this upcoming Sunday. Also, I texted Anna, updating her on Jake and my job situation.

Now I was working on the advertisement for the LGBTQ+ support group. The bulletin's wording needed to express everything the group intended to be.

"Ian!" Jake called from the other room.

Instant panic mode. I jumped to my feet, running into the living room.

"Ian! Ian!"

"Babe, I'm right here. What's wrong?" I asked, sliding to the floor in front of him.

He was sitting up, gripping the back of the couch. A look of terror shadowed his pale face. When he finally focused on me, he let out a sigh of relief. "Thank God. Are you okay?" he asked as he grabbed my shoulders.

"Yeah, of course I am. Are you?"

He squeezed his eyes shut and lowered his head into his hands. "Yeah, it's just . . . this fucking nightmare. It seemed so real."

"What was it about? It must've been bad."

Jake leaned back and rubbed his face. "I don't wanna repeat it. God, Miranda has really fucked up my psyche. It's the second nightmare I had with her in it."

"You've gone through a traumatic experience. Maybe it's just welding together."

"Maybe. But thank God it was only a dream. Come here." He took my hand and pulled me on top of him, wrapping his arms around me.

"It's all right. She can't do anything to us."

"I know, but she'll try. And that's what scares me."

I rubbed a finger along his stubble and kissed him. "How's your leg?"

"It's fine. But I could use some water."

"I'll be right back."

I headed into the kitchen and retrieved two glasses of water, then returned to the couch, where I sat next to him and handed him a glass.

"Thanks."

We sipped our waters in silence.

"Hey, babe," Jake said.

"Hmm?" I replied as I took a swig of water.

"What do you think of topping?"

Water almost shot out through my nose. "What?" I choked out the question.

He chuckled. "Do you ever think about it? Like, would you want to?"

"I don't know. I guess I've never thought about it. Why? Do you think of bottoming?"

He shrugged. "Yeah, lately I have."

"Oh. Is there any particular reason why?"

"I just want to experience everything with you. And that includes feeling what you feel."

I smiled. "In that case, yeah, I'd definitely try topping, if that's what you want. The only thing that worries me is what if I can't?"

"What do you mean?"

"Don't you remember ninth grade?"

He huffed, sucking his teeth. "Baby, that was with a girl."

"Yeah, but what if that wasn't the reason? What if it's me?"

He huffed. "I highly doubt that. But if it is, then we'll deal with it. But at least we'll know." I nodded. "Besides," Jake continued as he smacked his own butt, "my ass is hot. No way your dick will limp out."

I threw my head back and laughed. "That is true. Your ass is hot."

Jake laughed, too, as he moved forward, taking my face in his palm, and kissed me. He deepened the kiss, plunging his tongue into my mouth. I kissed him back, matching the intensity.

He leaned back. "What do you say? Ready to pop my cherry?"

"What—now?"

"Sure, no time like the present. Unless you don't wanna."

"No, I do. I'm just nervous, I guess."

"I think I'm the one who should be nervous."

I smiled. "What about your leg?"

"Stop worrying about my damn leg, babe. It's fine. Besides, all I have to do is lie there."

Point made. Leaning forward, I reached for his glass and set it on the table behind the couch, along with mine.

Jake grabbed my face and pulled me forward, kissing me. I felt my shirt slide out of my pants as Jake worked on the buttons. Once almost complete, I lifted the shirt over my head and tossed it. Finding his lips again, I slipped my hands under his shirt and pulled it off him.

I lunged at his neck, licking and kissing. Jake's hand slid up my back and moaned. "Baby, fuck me."

My head snapped up. Hearing him say the words did something to my insides, my cock intrigued and eager to try something new. "Should I carry you to the bedroom?"

"How about I hop on your back?"

I nodded and stood. Jake used my shoulders as leverage as he balanced himself on the couch and got onto my back, piggyback style. We laughed as I took us into the bedroom, where I carefully lowered him onto the bed.

Getting serious, I got onto the bed, kneeling between his legs, and slipped my fingers in his waistband and slid off his pants. I cupped him over the boxers, sliding my hand over the already-hard length of him. I teased him with my fingers and mouth, then the fabric came off as well. I licked my lips as I took him into my mouth, sucking him, slathering him up. Sliding lower, I sucked his balls, then further down, tasting his hole.

He grunted and lifted his legs, granting me full access. I traced my tongue over him, lubricating him thoroughly. Licking my index finger, I dipped the tip inside.

"Fuck," Jake groaned.

That encouraged me to go deeper to my knuckle, then I tried a second finger. He was so tight; I worried I would hurt him. Lubrication would be key.

I rose over him. "Are you sure you want to do this?"

He reached for my waistband, effortlessly unbuttoning and unzipping. "Yes." His hand slipped inside, stroking me.

"'Cause we don't have to. I'm perfectly happy being bottom."

"Baby, I want to feel you inside me. But if you really don't want to—"

"My God, I want to. I'm just afraid I'll hurt you."

"If you can handle it, I can too. Besides, I know you'll be gentle."

I couldn't help but smile. "Until you tell me to go harder."

He bit his bottom lip and smiled. "Take me there."

I was happy to oblige. Putting my fears and uncertainties aside, I lowered to kiss him, then stood, removing my pants and boxers. I leaned across the bed to the nightstand and retrieved a tube of lube. First I slathered myself, then poured it onto Jake, making sure he was nice and wet. Positioning myself, I gently prodded at his opening. It took several tries before I could push my tip inside.

Jake gasped.

"Oh my God," I breathed. The pressure around my cock was nothing like I'd ever felt before. All the sensory nerve endings at the head were awakened and ready to explode.

I held still, allowing Jake to adjust around me. I feared that if I moved, it would be over before it began. But Jake lifted his hips, giving me the uncontrollable urge to pump my hips *fast*.

I fought the urge. Lowering myself on top of him, I buried my face in the crook of his neck. "Are you okay?"

"Yeah. Keep going."

I swallowed hard, holding my breath as I slid in deeper. It was like a ring of ecstasy milking my cock, wanting to squeeze the cum out of me. It was nothing like that time in ninth grade. Maybe it was because that time, it had been with a girl. I had thought my dick was broken. But Jake was showing me that was not the case.

I was hard as hell and ready to explode at any minute. "You feel so good," I whispered into his neck. "So tight."

He gripped my ass and lifted his hips. "Go faster, baby. It doesn't hurt anymore."

I squeezed my eyes shut. "Gimme a sec. It feels too good. I don't want to cum before you."

He brought his hands to my head, forcing me to face him. "It's okay. I know it's intense. It's your first time. Just let it happen." He smiled. "Besides, it's a turn-on, how you're struggling to hold back."

I gasped as he rotated his hips. "Are you trying to make me cum?"

"That is kinda the point."

Okay, I can do this.

I lifted onto my hands and began pumping, slowly at first. Jake moaned, which gave me encouragement. Faster. Deeper. My concentration was on point.

"Yeah, baby," Jake breathed. "Fuck me. Give it to me."

I peeked down between our bodies. Jake's cock glistened at the tip, bouncing stiffly against his belly. I licked my lips. His moans were getting louder, which brought me closer. I couldn't stop now, even if I wanted to.

Jake reached for his cock, jerking it.

Oh my God. My balls tightened. I was going to cum.

"Fuck. Baby—" He exploded, shooting onto his belly and chest.

The strong orgasmic pulses were too much. I cried out, the orgasm ripping through my body like a wave of ecstasy. Every nerve ending vibrated—and it kept going. It was like Jake's ass gripped me, holding me inside, milking me until every last drop filled him.

When it was over, I collapsed on top of him, out of breath. My hair was glued to my forehead with sweat. "Holy shit," I mumbled.

"Yeah," Jake agreed, also out of breath. "That was fucking intense." He chuckled. "Are you okay?"

"I don't know. I'm breathing, I think."

He wrapped his arms around me, chuckling. "Now you know why I like it so much."

"How do you let me cum first every time? Even when we did it for the first time, you seemed to have so much control."

He laughed. "Trust me, it's not easy. But I think I've gotten better over time."

I lifted my head. "How do you feel? Did you like being bottom?"

"Yeah. It was intense. Not as painful as I thought it was going to be. Definitely something I would do again."

"I would top again, but if I'm being honest, I prefer bottoming. But being versatile is definitely something I wouldn't mind being with you."

"I agree. I like topping, but verse would bring the spice of life."

I laughed. "True."

He kissed me. "I love you."

"I love you too. So much."

Chapter 33

Ian

I felt bad. Jake had begged me not to go into work, but it was the start of a fresh week. And what kind of music director would I be if I continued to play hooky with my love?

Sure, I could have worked from home again, but there were things I needed to get done at the church. I did the next best thing: I promised my sexy, overprotective boyfriend that I'd only stay a few hours. And I'd be home before he even realized I was missing.

I'd just settled at my church office when my phone buzzed. It was a text from Jake. **I know you're missing...you're not back yet.**

I chuckled and shook my head. **Baby, I just got here. Get some rest. I'll be back soon.**

I'm bored...and I want you.

I want you too. The sooner I get this work done, the quicker I can return to you.

No response. I got to work. Jake had taken a few more medical days from school to give his leg a little more healing time, but it was obvious he was going stir-crazy.

A few minutes passed and another text came through. Unable to resist, I opened it and gasped.

It was a picture of Jake. Shirtless. Wearing those sexy, clingy sweatpants low on his hips. Laying on the bed. The caption read: **Just a little incentive to make you work fast**.

I wiped the drool off my face and replied: **Omg…so sexy. I expect you to look just like that when I get home.**

Bet.

I got to work again, attempting to concentrate, which, after that pic, was hard. Literally.

After a few rounds on the organ, a couple trips to the rectory, a visit to the copy machine, and some email responses later, I was almost ready to go home.

And another text. **You better hurry if you don't wanna miss out on this**. Attached was another pic. This time, Jake had his hand down his pants, clearly aroused.

Oh my God. I was about to reply with something indecent when there was a knock on the door. My head jerked up as I nearly dropped the phone.

Jake's dad stood in the doorway. While I was holding a half-naked picture of his son in my hand . . . masturbating.

"Mr. Edwards."

"I hope I'm not interrupting."

I swallowed as I glanced down at the phone. The thought of sending Jake a quick text crossed my mind, but instead, I exited out of the texting app and swiftly hit RECORD. If experience had taught me anything, it was to get proof. Nothing good could come from William Edwards visiting me at work. And there was no way I would go through another my-word-against-his situation.

"No, not at all," I answered as I rose to my feet, placing the phone facedown on the desk. "What are you doing here?"

Mr. Edwards stepped forward and shut the door. "I was hoping I could speak candidly with you."

I had a bad feeling about this. "Of course. Please do."

"First, I want you to know I have absolutely no problem with homosexuals. If that's how you identify yourself, then by all means. But I know my son. This isn't who he is."

"Maybe you don't know him as well as you think you do."

"Oh, I know him. I raised him. I know him. It's you who doesn't know him."

"Why exactly are you here, Mr. Edwards?"

"To tell you to let go of my son."

"Or what? You're going to threaten me?"

"I just don't want you to get hurt, Ian."

"And how will I get hurt?"

"When Jake realizes what he feels for you is nothing more than an overblown, affectionate friendship that he's mistaken for having romantic feelings."

"Wow. Do you really think that little of Jake that you think he can't differentiate between friendship love and romantic love?"

"You confused him. You made him curious about your way of life."

"I have never done anything to sway him to my *way of life*, as you put it. He has always sought after me. Even when we were kids."

"Because for some reason, he feels the need to protect you."

"Okay, with all due respect, Mr. Edwards, you know nothing of our relationship, so you're assuming a lot when you say Jake's only with me because of some misguided guardian affection."

"I know Jake was in a committed relationship with Miranda for over eight years, and now he wants to throw it all away because of you."

"He was only in that relationship because she threatened to out him to you if he didn't stay with her."

"Is that the story he's telling you?"

I slipped my hands in my pockets. This conversation was going nowhere quick. "Look, Mr. Edwards, I love Jake. So much so that I tried letting him go. I stepped aside for years because I thought he wanted Miranda. But he has shown me time and time again that it's me he wants. So, until he tells me himself that he no longer wants me, then I will stay by his side, loving him and supporting him."

The man stepped closer until we were face-to-face. "You are making a big mistake."

"How?"

"There are things you don't know about Jake. Things that could get you hurt. I'm telling you one last time—stay away from my son."

"Things I don't know about him, or things I don't know about you?"

He narrowed his eyes. "Is there a difference? Jake is my son. We're family, therefore I come first."

"Really? Then why did he tell me I'm the only family he needs?"

His mouth straightened to a thin line. His hands came up without warning, gripping my shirt collar, and he pushed me against the desk. "You little punk," he gritted between clenched teeth. "Stay away from my son. He is not gay. You hear me? Leave him alone, or you'll regret getting involved with him!"

"Let go of me, or I'll call 911 and tell them everything."

His eyes widened, shoving me away. "What are you talking about? Tell them what, exactly?"

I straightened my shirt. "That you came in here, at my place of employment, threatening and assaulting me." When Mr. Edwards's shoulders relaxed, I added, "I'll have to tell them why. Because we both know why you're really here. The real reason you want me to break up with Jake is so he can go back to Miranda. Keep her happy—and quiet." He remained silent. "But the thing is, he won't do that. Even if I left him, he'd never go back to her, not even to protect you. Sounds to me you're out of luck." I paused. "Like I said, you know nothing of our relationship. We don't keep secrets from each other."

"You have no idea who you're dealing with."

"I think I do. And I think you should leave."

Mr. Edwards shook a finger at me. "Don't say I didn't warn you.

You are letting Jake pull you into a dangerous situation. You think that's love? If he truly loved you, he would want to keep you as far from this as possible."

"And if you really loved your son, you would want him to be happy, even if he didn't fit into your social norms. You wouldn't make him sacrifice his life in an unhappy marriage in order to protect you." I went over to the door and opened it. "Goodbye, Mr. Edwards. We're done here."

Jake's dad pursed his lips and nodded as he strode over to the open door. He eyed me coldly as he stepped out.

I shut the door and rushed over to the desk, snatching up the cell, and pressed STOP. Letting out a deep breath, I played back a little of the recording. I couldn't believe I'd caught all that on audio. I was shaking.

My phone vibrated. I had multiple texts from Jake, asking where I was and if everything was okay because I hadn't responded to his last text.

Trying to control my trembling fingers, I texted back. **Sorry. Unexpected visitor.**

Everything okay?

Yeah. I'll tell you when I get home. I'm packing up now.

Okay. Hurry. But drive carefully.

I will. Love you.

Love you too.

Chapter 34

Jake

Something was up.

It was weird that Ian hadn't commented on the last pic I sent. I could understand him getting busy with whoever had paid him a visit, but I didn't have to hear his voice to know something—or someone—had upset him.

Hopefully it had nothing to do with Father Sicko. Or any of the death threats. Or another vandalism.

Fuck.

Bringing my hands to my face, I rubbed away the negative thoughts. I had to stop thinking the worst. Ian was fine. He was on his way home, and he'd tell me what the holdup had been. He should be here soon.

The doorbell rang multiple times.

Ian had a key, so it obviously wasn't him. Sliding off the bed, I hopped over to the window.

Son of a bitch.

Dad's car was parked on the street.

I yanked the crutches from the wall and made my way over to the front door, not caring that I was shirtless.

"What are you doing here?" I demanded when I opened the door. No sense in asking how he'd found Ian's address. His drug-dealer status must give him certain advantages, like invading people's privacy.

My father pushed his way inside, not even waiting for a fucking invitation. "You told him?"

"What the fuck are you talking about? Told who what?"

"You told your *friend* about my business?"

Wait, was he the unexpected visitor Ian had mentioned? It all made sense now. "Did you go to the church?"

"Answer me, damn it!"

"Yes, of course I told him! I love him. Being completely honest with him was the only way he would forgive me for hurting him."

He laughed, but it was cold and humorless. "Love? Son, my God, enough with this nonsense. What you have with Miranda is love. Not this ludicrous notion of love with your childhood friend."

"What I *had* with Miranda was not love. It was me being a coward and hiding in a relationship that you and Mom wanted because I was too scared to explore these feelings I had for Ian. I was so worried what other people thought of me that I let Ian go and chose Miranda because it was the safer option. Dad, I was miserable with her. Ian was on my mind all the time. Even during sex."

He squeezed his eyes shut, waving a hand through the air. "Oh, please!"

"It's true. Lots of times, it was the only thing that would get me through it."

"Have you ever had these types of feelings for other men?"

"No, but—"

"So, if I showed you a picture of a naked man right now, would it turn you on?"

"Dad, I'm not talking about that with you."

"You're the one who brought up sex. How about a woman? Does a naked woman turn you on?"

"The only thing I know for sure is that seeing anyone naked makes me think of Ian."

"So he's the problem."

"No, Dad! He's my solution. I never wanted to label myself as gay or bisexual. I hate labels. But I can tell you, without a shadow of a doubt, that I love Ian. He is my soulmate."

"Oh, for Christ's sake, *soulmate*?"

"Yes, soulmate."

"Well, your *soulmate* better not say a word about my business."

"He won't."

"How can you be so sure?"

"Because I know him. The person you should be worried about is Miranda. She's the one with the proof. You're directing your anger at the wrong people."

"And you're the only person who can stop her."

"I'm not marrying her. You better start threatening her and stop wasting your energy on me."

He stepped forward, his fists clenched. "You ungrateful—"

The door swung open. "Hey," Ian said as he came in. "What's going on?"

I crutched over to him. "Hi, babe." I gave him a kiss on the lips because, duh, I wanted to shove that shit in my old man's face. "Dad was just leaving."

"What is he doing here in the first place?"

"Good question. Dad?" When he remained silent, I answered for him, "He came to call me out because I told you about his shady business."

"Yeah, I told him we didn't keep secrets from each other," Ian said. "He seemed to have a hard time believing that."

"I told him the same thing." I glanced at Ian. "Honesty is the only reason you're back in my life again. So, you bet your sweet ass I'll always be real with you."

"Aw, baby," he said as he leaned in for a kiss. "Me too."

Dad cleared his throat and stepped toward the door. "Go ahead and continue this charade." He stopped in front of Ian. "And don't come crying to me when he's done playing with you."

"What the fuck does that mean?" I launched forward on the crutches, but Ian stopped me.

"No, Jake. Just let it go."

"I want to know what the old man meant by that."

"You know what I meant, son. We both know this is one dragged-out experiment with a childhood friend."

This time, I dropped the crutches and hopped over. But once again, Ian got a grip on me. "Yeah, that's it. Walk away, old man. And don't ever come back here!"

Once he got in his car and drove away, I slammed the door shut. Ian let go of me as I hopped over to the couch. "Baby, please calm down," he said as he sat next to me. "Don't let him get to you."

"What the fuck did he say to you at the church? Did he threaten you?"

"I'm not going to tell you until you calm down."

I dropped my head into my hands. "I'm trying, baby, but—just please tell me you don't believe him."

"About me being an experiment for you? Of course I don't believe it. I think we're way past the experimental stage," he laughed.

I let out a sigh of relief. "Thank God." I took a few moments to breathe, waiting for my heart rate to slow down. Once I didn't feel like wringing my father's neck as much, I lifted my head and glanced at Ian. "Okay. I'm calm. Now tell me what my crooked father said to you."

"I'll do better than that," he said as he reached into his pocket and pulled out his phone. "You can listen for yourself."

A recording.

It was official. I was in love with a genius.

* * *

Ian

I watched Jake go through the emotions as he listened to the recording. Everything from gasps to his mouth hanging open, to chuckling at my witty responses, to smiling and tenderness in his eyes, to fist-clenching anger.

And his reaction to his father gripping my shirt collar did not come to a surprise.

"I'm going to kill him," he muttered through clenched teeth. It was obvious he was still trying to hold it together. Once the recording ended, he bolted to his feet. "He put his hands on you?"

"Calm down."

"No. My dad is a dead man."

As he hopped forward, I grabbed his hand. "Stop. Sit." He didn't fight me as I pulled him down. "William only grabbed my shirt collar. He didn't hurt me."

"Are you sure?"

"Yes." I pulled my collar down. "See. No marks."

Jake leaned closer, inspecting for himself. He caressed my neck. "I'm sorry my father did that. Sorry he went to the church in the first place."

"It's not your fault." I held up the phone. "But I handled it. Now we have something to blackmail him with. Leave us alone, or I'll tell the police he assaulted me."

He grabbed my face and kissed me. "You're obviously the brains of this relationship. I love you."

"I love you too," I said. "And I see you're still wearing exactly what you did in the picture you sent me."

"Yup. And I would've been in position, had you-know-who not shown up."

"It's not too late. I'll wait."

He smiled, biting his bottom lip as he rose, grabbing the crutches off the floor, and made his way back into the bedroom. After a few moments, he called out, "Ready!"

I pushed off the couch and eagerly joined him. He looked so sexy, stretched out on the bed, his hands behind his head. The sweats were low on his hips, clinging to all the right spots, the strap from the boxers exposed. His eyelids were low, his gray eyes sparkling. He should be a cover model.

So sexy.

Bringing my fingers to my shirt, I leisurely unbuttoned as I kept eye contact. Once done, I slipped it off, kicking off my shoes as well. Then I crawled onto the bed, kneeling in between his spread legs. Running my hands along his thighs and up his hips, I leaned forward and kissed his belly button, then lower, slipping my tongue under the waistband. I dipped my head, kissing his cock over the fabric and outlining it as he hardened.

Jake moaned, "Baby—"

I continued to tease him through his pants until he was thrusting his hips and entangling his fingers through my hair.

Hooking my fingers in the waistband, I pulled them down, exposing his perfect erection. I sat back on my heels, admiring the view for a moment. Still couldn't believe he was mine. He'd chosen me. I pulled the sweats the rest of the way off, then leaned forward again, taking him into my mouth. After slathering him up, I slid my mouth up, letting him slip out, and then I admired him some more. Slick and glistening, his cock jerked for more attention. And I was happy to oblige. I wrapped my hand around him, feeling him up, then lowering my mouth to him again. I kept up a nice rhythm until he sat up, taking my face in his hands, and guided me up. He kissed me.

"You're driving me crazy."

I smiled against his lips. "That's kinda the point."

Jake kissed me with urgency, thrusting his tongue inside, then rolled me onto my back.

"Be careful with your leg," I said when Jake got on top of me.

"Fuck my leg. Right now, I need to build you up so we're even." He kissed me again. "I want us to cum together. With me deep inside you."

I sucked in my bottom lip as he adjusted himself between my legs. He grinded his naked cock against my pants, making me desperate for skin-on-skin contact.

As though Jake had read my mind, he lifted and undid my pants. I helped remove them. With both of us naked, he went back to rubbing our dicks together. He slid down, taking me into his mouth, echoing the same action I'd given him until I was squirming beneath him.

"Jake—" This time, I sat up and brought him up to my mouth. As we kissed, I pushed him onto his back and climbed on top of him.

Straddling him, I positioned his cock underneath me and lowered myself to the base. He gripped my hips as I bounced up and down. I leaned forward, placing my hands on the bed on either side of his head as he thrust his cock into me, meeting my grind. I bent down, meeting his lips as he wrapped his arms around him and pounded into me.

I was so close. Sitting up, I arched my back, throwing my head back as Jack wrapped a hand around my cock. Amazing. He jerked me closer to the edge until I could no longer hold it in. I cried out as I exploded onto Jake's chest and belly.

He moaned as he milked me till the contractions stopped. I fell forward as Jake placed his hands back onto my hips, thrusting into me until he found his own release. He grunted as his cock pulsated inside me. I closed my eyes, savoring the feel.

I nudged my face in the crook of his neck as he held me close, still inside me. As our breathing normalized, his cock slid out and I straightened my legs.

"I love you," I mumbled against his warm skin.

He tightened his arms, his hand sliding through my hair. "I love you, too, baby boy."

After a few minutes, I shifted my weight, snuggling against his side so that I wasn't crushing him. We laid like that for a while, Jake lazily caressing his fingers along my arm. I could fall asleep just as we were.

But I knew Jake's mind was filled with rage and sadness regarding his father. And I wished there was something I could do to help.

"What are you thinking about?" I asked. Maybe talking about it would help.

"I'm thinking how much you mean to me and how grateful I am that you let me back into your life."

"That's sweet. But I know that's not what you're thinking about."

"I might have other things on my mind, but I am always thinking about how lucky I am."

I lifted my head and kissed him. "Aw. Well, I think the same about you." I laid my head back down. "Are you thinking about your dad?"

He sighed. "Yeah. I'm sorry. I can't forget the shit he said and what he did to you."

"Babe, I'm fine. He didn't hurt me."

"What about the lies he told you, huh? He's trying to sabotage our relationship, twisting it in a sick way."

"Our relationship is stronger than ever. No one will ever be able to sabotage us if we don't let them. And I don't believe a word your father says. I believe you. I know you."

"Thanks, baby. I promise you, I will always tell you the truth."

"I know that now. And I will always be honest with you too."

"I know, baby." He took a deep breath. "I need to go talk to him."

My head snapped up. "You're going to beat up your dad, aren't you?"

He sucked his teeth. "I want to, but no. I have a better idea."

Chapter 35

Jake

"**S**on, are you here to apologize?"

I leaned on the crutches at my parents' front door, wondering at what point the man I'd looked up to my whole life had become so arrogant and out of touch with reality. Made me think he was on those drugs he sold.

"No. I'm here to see Mom."

He narrowed his eyes. "Why?"

Shoving one crutch through the doorway, I pushed my way inside past him. "None of your business."

"It is my business if—"

"Relax, Father dearest. I'm not telling her your secret. I'm telling her mine."

His eyes widened. "Jake, I'm warning you. Don't do it. She won't be able to handle that."

"I've had enough of your warnings to last a lifetime. But you can't stop me. She's going to find out eventually. I want her to hear it from me."

"This isn't the right time."

"That's not up to you."

"Son—"

I stepped closer. "Here's a warning for you, Dad. I'm going to come out to Mom, and you're going to support me. You will back me up. If you don't, I'll reveal your secret as well." Wow, this threatening thing was kinda fun. I should've started a long time ago. Why stop there, though? I was on a roll. "And if you ever put your hands on Ian again, I'll kill you."

"Jake, darling, what a surprise," my mother called as she entered the foyer area. She gasped. "What happened? Why are you on crutches?"

"It's nothing, Ma. I just sprained my ankle."

"How in the world did you do that?"

"Minor motorcycle accident. No big deal."

She gasped again as she gave me a hug. "I knew those things were dangerous. Why didn't you tell me?"

"Dad knew. I'm surprised he didn't mention it."

She smacked Dad's shoulder. "William, why didn't you tell me?"

"Sorry, sweetheart. I didn't want you to worry. Besides, like Jake said, it was minor."

"Oh, but still, you should've told me. Are you okay, honey?"

"Yeah, Ma, I'm fine. Promise. I'm here to talk to you. Can we sit?"

"Oh yes, darling, of course." As she led the way into the living room, she asked, "Is this about wedding preparations? I'm so excited to hear about the progress you've made. But why didn't Miranda come with you? I'm going to have to call her. I wrote down the names of some highly recommended caterers, just in case. Have you two set a date yet? Time's passing by, you know—"

"Mom," I interrupted. It was like a game of twenty questions.

She looked at me expectantly, then pouted, sitting when I remained quiet. "Oh, don't tell me you're planning to elope. That would just break my heart. I hope that you—"

"No, Mom," I said as I sat down next to her on the couch, placing the crutches on the floor next to my feet. "This isn't about the wedding. Not really, anyway."

"Well," she prodded when I got quiet again. "I'm waiting." But as I was trying to find the right words to extract myself from the closet, she gasped again. "Does this have to do with the accident? Was Miranda involved? Is she okay?"

"No, Mom. I mean, yes, she's fine, but this doesn't—" I stopped myself from saying it didn't have to do with her, then decided maybe I should start with that. Sometimes you just had to rip the Band-Aid off. But compared to the main news, this was just scratching the surface. "We broke up."

She brought her hand to her heart as her mouth fell open. "Oh no. Why? What happened? Jake Edwards, what did you do?"

"Why do you automatically assume I did something?"

"Because I know she wouldn't be at fault. She loves you too much."

"No, she doesn't. She loves the idea of me."

She shook her head. "Now you're not making any sense."

"I couldn't give her what she needed."

"So it *is* your fault. Stop speaking in riddles and tell me why you broke up with a perfectly fine, good-looking Christian woman."

"Mom, our relationship has been broken for a long time."

"Then why would you get her hopes up and ask her to marry you?"

"I didn't. The whole marriage thing was her idea."

"You led her on. Shame on you. I didn't raise you to be such a user and a coward."

Funny she would say that. "You're right. I have been a coward, which is why I'm here now. To tell you the truth."

"What truth? For heaven's sake, child, just spit it out."

"I'm gay."

Silence.

Mom blinked a few times, then shook her head. "How can that be? You can't—you had lots of girlfriends. You showed no signs of—you were with Miranda for over eight years."

"Actually, I only had a couple of girlfriends in high school. And you're the one who introduced me to Miranda and convinced me to date her."

"So this is my fault?"

"No, Mom, that's not what I'm—"

"He's bisexual," Daddy dearest spoke up.

My mother turned to him. "You knew about this?"

Dad cleared his throat. "I've only just recently found out. Jake wanted to be the one to tell you."

After a moment of processing, Ma sighed. "Okay, so if you're bisexual, that means you can still work things out with Miranda."

"No, Mom—"

"You have to be with a woman."

"Mom—"

"I'm sure Miranda will—"

"I'm in love with someone else."

Silence again.

When I opened my mouth to speak, she put her hand up. "Don't you dare say you're in love with a man."

"I am."

She closed her eyes as she brought her hand back to her heart. "That is not possible."

"What do you mean? Of course it is."

"No. Not the way a man loves a woman. The Bible doesn't allow it."

"That's not true."

"Do you want to go to hell? Is that it?"

"I'm not going to hell. I'm a good person in love with an amazing guy. There's no sin in that."

"Yes, there is. It's not natural."

"Well, it feels natural to me. In fact, it's the most natural thing I've ever felt in my life. And honestly, if feeling this way for the rest of my life means I have to spend eternity in hell, then I'd say it was worth it."

Ma gasped. She brought back her hand and slapped me.

Funny. Same reaction Miranda had when I'd told her.

"Don't you ever say that again. Who is this man you claim you love?"

I thought of withholding that precious info, but I didn't want to hide anything anymore—at least, not when it came to him. Besides, my dad already knew, so what was the point of keeping it a secret? "It's Ian. I'm in love with Ian."

She huffed and let out a dry laugh. "I should have known."

"What does that mean?"

"That boy always had it in for you. Always hanging around here. Being so clingy and needy."

"Oh my God, Mom, just stop. We were best friends. That's why we hung out together. We had each other's backs."

"No. He influenced you. So much so that you don't even realize it."

"You're wrong."

"Jake, I understand you're curious. Maybe you even experimented. God can forgive you for that. But the best thing for you to do is go to therapy. If you believe you're bisexual, then it's a matter of just converting to only females so that you can be normal again."

"That's not how this works. I don't even know if I'm bisexual. I might be gay. Or even pansexual."

"What in heaven's name is a pansexual?"

My parents needed to join the twenty-first century. "It's when you're attracted to people regardless of their gender identity."

"Gender identity? There are only two genders—man and woman."

"No. There are many genders, like being transgender, for example."

"Oh, for heaven's sake—"

"It doesn't matter. My point is, I don't know what I am, and I don't care. I'm not labeling myself just to fit in a box. All I know for sure is how I feel about Ian. It goes deeper than physical attraction and sex. Looking back, I began having more than just friendship feelings for him when we were kids. But it wasn't until after college that I realized I was in love with him. But I couldn't do anything about it because I knew you would react this way."

"Because you knew what you were feeling was wrong."

"No, because I was too scared of what you would think of me. So I chose to be with Miranda. I tried to make it work with her, but Ian is in my blood. I love him. And I don't want to be apart from him anymore."

My mother shook her head. "Poor Miranda."

"She knew, you know. For almost our whole relationship, she knew about Ian. But she threatened to tell you and Dad if I didn't stay with her. And like I said, I was scared back then."

"Because she knew what was best for you. That's how I know she'll take you back if you—"

"I don't love her, Mom. And no amount of therapy or praying or shaming is going to change that. I'm in love with Ian, and he's in love with me. I've moved into his place. We're happy. Please, can't you at least try to be happy for us?"

"No. I can't be happy when my son is blatantly living in sin."

"Dad supports us. Right, Dad?"

Dad straightened, uncrossing his arms like he just got called on in class while he was daydreaming. He cleared his throat. "Well, I wouldn't say *support* per se. But I am processing it, and, well"—he swallowed—"it will take time to—"

I smirked as I let my head hang, then slapping my palms on my knees, I reached down to the crutches and stood. "Thanks a lot, both of you. It's great to know I have such open-minded, supportive parents."

Not.

I crutched my way to the front door. As I opened it, I paused. "By the way, Mom, you should ask Dad about his side business. I'm sure you'll be fascinated to learn the huge secret he's been keeping from you. Turns out, I'm not the only one living in sin. But we'll see who ends up in hell."

Bomb set. I walked away before the explosion.

Chapter 36

Ian

I closed my eyes, resting my head on the rim of the bathtub. How much time had I been soaking in aromatherapy and bubbles? It seemed like forever, but I knew it hadn't been that long. The point was to distract myself until Jake got back.

I sighed, calming my nerves.

He'd taken the loaner to see his parents. I'd offered to go with him, but he'd insisted he'd be fine. And he promised he wouldn't beat up his father.

So I was stuck at home. In a bathtub. Attempting not to worry.

I sighed again.

The noise that came from the other room made me jerk to attention. It was the front door. "Jake?" I called, hoping to God it was him and not a burglar.

"Yeah, it's me. Where are you?"

"In the tub."

A moment later, Jake walked in and smiled. "Hey," he said, using one crutch to shut the door. "Taking a bath, huh?"

I nodded. "I thought it'd help me relax. How'd it go?"

He came closer, taking both crutches in one hand as he leaned on the edge of the tub with the other and lowered to his knees. After placing the crutches on the floor, he gave me a quick kiss on the lips, then rested his forearms on the tub. "Not good."

"Oh no. What happened?"

"Not only did my mom freak out, but my dad stabbed me in the back. Before my mom came in, I warned him to back me up and tell my mom he supported me and our relationship. But when it came down to it, he stumbled over his words, and he couldn't do it."

"Oh, baby, I'm so sorry."

"So, on my way out, I told my mom to ask my dad about his side business." He pressed his lips together, squeezing his eyes shut as he shook his head. "God, even by threatening to reveal his secret, he still couldn't lie and say he supported me." He lowered his head as he gripped on to me tight—and cried. I cradled him, holding him close as he let it out. "My parents hate me," he sobbed. "They don't accept me. My mom wants me to go to therapy."

"What can I do?"

He lifted his head, his tear-stained face glistening in the dim candlelight. "You're doing it. Being here. Just please don't leave me. I have no one. I don't know—"

"Shhh," I whispered, wiping at his tears with my thumb. "I'm not going anywhere. I love you, Jake. You have me. All of me. And the truth is, I need you as much as you need me. So please, lean on me. I'm here for you."

He sniffled as he nodded, then threw his arms around me. "I love you so much."

"I love you too. You'll be okay. Everything will be okay," I whispered.

After a few moments, he leaned back, wiping at his face and sniffling. "You got any room for me in there?"

I smiled. "Of course. Plenty."

He swiftly stripped down and removed his leg brace, then I moved forward as he carefully lowered himself behind me. Once all the way in, he reached for me, and I nestled against him in between his legs.

"Mmm, this is nice," he said, sinking in and wrapping his arms around me.

"I know, right? I was thinking we should utilize this tub more often."

"Definitely." He kissed my shoulder as I rested my head back.

Peaceful silence filled the room as we enjoyed light caresses between us.

Jake was the first to speak. "I don't want to keep this a secret at the church anymore—or anywhere else, for that matter."

I looked up at him. "What about Miranda?"

"I don't care anymore. She and my parents have done nothing to spare my feelings, so why should I do the same? I'm done. From now on, you come first."

"Are you sure? You don't have to do anything you're not ready to do on my account. I'm perfectly happy staying in our secret bubble for a while longer, if that's what you need."

"Baby, I'm sure. I'm ready. The hospital was like a trial run, and it felt good. I don't know why I ever thought it would be weird."

"But that was with strangers. You're talking about coming out to people who know us, who we work with. People at your school. Are you sure you're ready for that?"

"Yes, without a doubt."

I grinned. "Okay. How do you want to do this?"

He shrugged. "I don't think we need to make it a big production or anything like that. I just want it to be natural, you know—like, holding hands, having my arm around you, that kind of stuff. People will talk and ask questions, of course. And then we can just admit we're boyfriends. What do you think?"

"That sounds good to me." It'd be like what I did with Matt, except this time, it'd be real.

Jake lowered his head and kissed me, coaxing my lips open, dipping his tongue in. "Are you cold?" he asked as his hand slid down the front of me, reaching for my cock and wrapping his hand around me.

I moaned. "Certainly not anymore."

He laughed softly as he continued to glide his hand up and down my length. "Maybe we should take this into the bedroom. I don't want you getting sick."

"We could add more hot water." I moved to the other end and turned the hot-water faucet on while I pulled the drain to even out the water. While I waited, Jake slid up behind me and kissed my back and lightly massaged me.

When the water felt hot enough, I spun around on my ass so I was facing him. He slid back again as I put my legs over his on either side of his hips so that we were cock to cock.

And it definitely got steamy.

Chapter 37

CJ

I was in deep shit.

One rule. That was all I'd had to follow. A promise to myself to make life better.

No second dates—and by dates, I meant one-night stands only. Fewer chances of getting attached that way. Fuck the same guy more than once, and it becomes more than just a hookup. Even if you emphasize no strings attached.

I'd broken my rule the moment I agreed to see Matt again. The thought of asking to see him a second time had been whirling in my head—I'd planned to resist, but he had beaten me to it and I couldn't say no. Sure, there were plenty of guys who'd asked to meet up again, and I'd say yes on the spot only to ghost them later. That wasn't an option with Matt. And I didn't know why.

For the first time ever, I'd actually wanted a repeat date with a guy. No one had made me laugh from the get-go. Not only did he match my humor but he also matched my sexual stamina, always willing to play along with witty comebacks. We meshed perfectly. He even went beyond the initiative and had cooked me dinner and come up with a role-play game he'd thought I'd like.

Yup, I was in trouble. Everything surrounding me screamed to get out before I fell in deeper. It had only been two dates; we could easily recover and move on from this with no real bumps. But I wasn't ready to end things. For some reason, Matt made me happy. And I deserved a tiny bit of happiness for once in my life.

But things could get complicated if I wasn't careful, which brought me to why I was standing in front of Mercy Grace Hospital—Matt's hospital. I needed to find out what floor he worked on. Sure, I could've asked him, but where was the fun in that? This gave me an excuse to see the hot doctor and repay him for the delicious meal he had cooked for me.

People knew me in this hospital, and I had to make sure our paths wouldn't cross, especially if I planned to visit him more frequently. But if it proved too risky, I'd limit our visitations to his apartment or nightlife places only. And to clear up any confusion—mostly to myself—this was strictly for sex and companionship. I liked him, but it could never go beyond what I could give.

Bakery bag in hand, I lowered the cap on my head and went straight to the front desk. "Good afternoon. Can you please direct me to where I might find Dr. Matthew Carter, please?"

The woman typed something on a computer screen. "He's in internal medicine, but he could be with patients on any floor. Would you like me to page him?"

"That won't be necessary. What floor is the internal medicine department on?"

"Third floor. If you take the elevator, hang a left and there is a nurse's station in the center. They could help locate him."

"Thank you so much."

I kept my head low as I made my way to the elevator. The third floor was good news; I rarely went past the second floor. Another good sign: Matt's floor was relatively quiet at the moment. I hesitated before heading to the nurse's station. So far, there was no one I recognized.

"May I help you?" the young nurse behind the desk asked.

"Yes, I hope so. Is Dr. Carter around?"

She smiled and pointed behind me. "Perfect timing. He's coming out of a patient's room."

I turned, and sure enough, he was coming down the aisle with a tablet in his hands. Was it possible for the guy to look any more scrumptious? He was wearing blue scrubs with a white lab coat. Pure definition of eye candy.

Stepping away from the desk, I waited until he raised his head and spotted me. His steps slowed as he got closer, and his eyes widened. "CJ? What are you doing here? Is everything okay?"

The fact that his initial reaction to seeing me at his place of employment was concern for my well-being spoke volumes—and proved that I was playing with fire.

I smiled. "I wanted to surprise you and bring you this." I held out the paper bag.

"What is it?" he asked, stepping closer.

"Tiramisu."

"You brought me tiramisu?"

I shrugged. "Yeah. I wanted to give you something in return for the nice dinner you made me. I figured you can't go wrong with a famous Italian dessert."

"Oh my God, that is so sweet of you. Thank you."

He made a move toward me, either for a kiss or hug, so I stepped away. PDA in a place like this was completely off limits. "My pleasure. It's not a big deal."

He backed off, taking the hint. "To me it is. I'm definitely eating this for dessert. Thanks again."

"No problem."

He looked at me expectantly, raising his brows, and smiled. "Is that all you came for?"

I smiled as well and bit my lip. "Not exactly. Is there someplace private we can go?"

"Yeah, of course. Follow me." He led the way down the hall, away from the nurse's station, and entered an empty patient room, placing the bag on the table. As he closed the door behind me, he asked, "Are you on your lunch break?"

The blinds were closed, making it dim inside. "Um, actually, I have the day off." I removed my hat, tossing it on the bed, and ran my hands through my hair to fluff it out. "Do you have some time, or am I keeping you from your patients?"

He looked at his watch. "I have some time. Why? What's up?"

I closed the distance between us, backing him up against the wall. "You, I hope." I cupped him.

He gasped, then gave me a side smile. "Keep doing that, and I will be."

It didn't take long. "Does that door lock?"

He stretched over to the side and locked it. "Yup."

I crashed my mouth to his, demanding he surrender to me. And he didn't disappoint. I loved how responsive he was to me and the way he was always down for anything.

His hands came up to the sides of my face as he pressed his cock into my hand. I wanted him in my mouth so bad. My fingers fumbled with the tie on his bottoms, then found their way inside and stroked him.

"Oh, fuck," he breathed.

"Do you want me to suck it?"

"Yes, please."

He didn't have to beg twice. I dropped to my knees, pulling down his pants easily. I really liked these scrubs; nothing beat easy access. Except nudity.

I sucked his cock deep into my mouth, savoring the taste of him. His fingers gripped my hair, indicating this wouldn't take long. I could taste the precum oozing from him. A hunger overcame me, a thirst for this man. I eased back to build him up more and feasted on his balls. I licked up his shaft, teasing the tip, then sucked him in again, up and down, over and over.

"Fuck, CJ. I'm cumming."

I swallowed it all. Good till the last fucking drop.

Chapter 38

Jake

My eyes popped open to the annoying sound of the alarm blaring from my phone. Reaching over to the nightstand, I hit snooze, then rolled back over, scooting closer to Ian's warm body and wrapping my arm around him. I nuzzled my face into his neck, breathing in his scent as I drifted off again.

"You should stay home one more day," Ian mumbled sleepily.

"Only if you stay home too."

He muffled a laugh. "So you can distract me all day? I'll never get any work done."

"Exactly." I chuckled into his neck. "But my leg is better, so I really should get back. My students are even emailing me."

Ian moaned that cute little moan he did when he was half asleep. "Your students are lucky."

"Yeah? Why's that?"

"Because they get to be with you all day."

"Aw, baby." I kissed him on the cheek and tightened my hold on him. Closing my eyes, I drifted off once again.

Fucking alarm. I grunted as I flipped over to turn it off.

As I plopped onto my back, Ian rolled into my side. "Five more minutes," he pleaded.

Reaching for my phone, I checked the time. "Okay. Five more minutes." I set the timer 'cause I could never say no to my baby boy. I settled back under the covers and wrapped my arms around him.

Five minutes went by in a blink of an eye. With a heavy sigh, I shut off the timer and tried not to wake Ian as I slid from the bed. Limping around the room, I gathered my clothes and headed for the bathroom.

Once dressed, I put on the medical boot that I now had to wear instead of using crutches and made my way into the kitchen. I quickly made some coffee and grabbed some cereal. I had just finished the last bite when I got a text from Ant saying he was outside. Thanks to him, Ian could stay in bed and not have to wake up early just to take me to work. I couldn't wait until my leg was completely healed and the motorcycle was fixed so I wouldn't have to rely on others for rides.

After sending a quick reply saying I'd be right out, I gulped down the rest of the coffee, then headed back into the bedroom. Ian was still lying on my side of the bed, hugging my pillow.

So freaking cute.

"Hey, baby, I'm leaving now. Ant's here," I whispered.

His eyes fluttered open. "Okay. He's still taking you to the music studio after school?"

"Yeah. I'll let you know if that changes. But he said it was no problem."

"Okay. I'll pick you up from there, then."

"Sounds good. I'll see you later, baby. I love you." I gave him a kiss.

"Bye. I love you too. Have a good day back."

"I will. Have a good day too. Let me know if my father or anyone else starts any more shit with you."

"I will."

Heading back into the living room, I threw my satchel over my head and guitar case on my back and went outside. Once I was at Ant's car, I tossed the stuff in the back and hopped in the passenger seat. "Hey, man. Thanks for doing this."

"It's no problem," Ant answered.

As Ant drove to school, I asked, "Any chance you and Anna would consider going to St. Pius this Sunday?"

He frowned. "Why?"

"Because Ian and I are planning to reveal our relationship, and I thought maybe you guys would want to be there. I know it would mean a lot to Ian if Anna was there. I mean, we're not going to make it this big hoopla event, but people will notice."

Ant smiled. "Wow. That's great, Jake. I'm happy for both of you. As far as us going, I'm not sure. I have a feeling people will have stronger reaction to me and Anna showing up than to you and Ian coming out."

He had a point. The dude had broken his chastity vows with Anna and gotten her pregnant before actually leaving the priesthood. I couldn't imagine there would be a welcome bandwagon for them at the church. "I understand. It was just a thought."

"I'll talk to my wife about it. But I'm not promising anything."

"Okay, cool. Thanks. Just tell her not to say anything to Ian. I want it to be a surprise. You know how those two tell each other everything."

Ant huffed, then laughed. "Yes, I'm very aware of that. I'll tell her."

* * *

It was great seeing my students again.

After Ant dropped me off at the music studio, I had just finished setting up shop when I got an incoming call. I answered without checking the ID, expecting it might be my student. It wasn't.

"Hello, Jake? It's Miranda. Please don't hang up."

Every part of my body tensed up, ready to tell the bitch off. "What the fuck do you want?"

"I need to talk to you. Can you come over?"

"Are you insane? Why the fuck would I do that? I have nothing to say to you."

"I promise you it's not for anything bad. I—I want a truce. Please give me a chance to apologize."

"Why can't you do that over the phone?"

"Come on, Jake. You know I hate doing these things over the phone. Please. Your father has me spooked. I want a chance to explain things face-to-face."

I hesitated. "I can't now. I'm working."

"Well, come over after. And you can pick up a few of your things you left behind."

I sighed. "Fine. I'll take an Uber over there after my session."

"Great. Thank you. I'll be waiting."

There were still a few minutes before my student was due to show up, so I called Ian.

"Hey, babe," I said when he answered.

"Hi. Everything okay? Did you make it to the studio?"

"Yeah, everything's good. Hey, something weird just happened. Miranda called me."

"Why?"

"She wants me to come over after my session. Says it's important. She wants to talk about my dad and wants to apologize."

"Really?"

"Yeah, I'm just as surprised as you, but I'm curious. I'll just take an Uber over there after I'm done here, and I'll text you to come get me at her house when I'm ready."

"Are you sure?"

"Yeah. I'll be fine."
"Please be careful."
"I will. I love you."
"Love you too."

Chapter 39

Jake

"Thanks for coming," Miranda said when she opened the door.

I nodded as I stepped inside. "I don't have a lot of time, so just get to the point."

"Jake, you said you would hear me out, so please sit down."

I rolled my eyes as I placed my guitar case and satchel on the floor, then went over to the couch and sat. "What is this about, Miranda?"

"How's your leg?" she asked as she sat next to me.

"It's fine."

"Good." She paused. "This isn't easy for me. I-I'm sorry. For everything. I don't plan on causing you any more trouble. And I won't be going to the police."

"Why the change of heart?"

"To be honest, William said some things that scared me."

"Like what?"

"He threatened me. He said if I turned him in, he would hire a hitman from prison and kill me and my family."

"And that's all it took?"

"I'm serious, Jake. He really gave me chills—and it made me wonder if it was worth it. I mean, either way, I've lost you." Her face scrunched up, and the tears fell. I sat awkwardly, not really knowing what to say or do.

Then her head fell on my shoulder. Damn it. Sometimes I wished I was a meaner bastard who didn't have a heart. I raised my hand to her shoulder, patting it. "It's okay. You'll be okay. I promise."

Her head came up and her tear-stained eyes searched mine. "Can you forgive me? For all the blackmails and threats?"

I just wanted this nightmare to be over and move on with my life. Besides, I'd never seen her like this. She seemed sincere and not a cold bitch for once in her life. "Sure. Forget about it. Let's move on and call it a day."

She smiled. "Thank you. It means so much to me." After a moment, she said, "Let me get you a beer for old times' sake."

"Oh no, that's okay. I should really get back."

She stood, heading for the kitchen. "Please, just one. Then you can leave. I still have your favorite brand."

I didn't have the heart to protest. Truth was, I was a little parched. Just one wouldn't hurt.

"Here you go." She handed me the beer and had a wine cooler for herself.

As we drank, she chatted about her friends—what they were up to, her plans for the future, and a bunch of other bullshit I had zero interest in. I couldn't gulp fast enough. When I was done, I stood. "Well, hate to drink and run but I should go."

"Wait," she said, standing as well. "That box with your stuff is upstairs in the bedroom."

"Oh, okay. If it's alright with you, I'll just go grab it."

"Of course." As I went up the stairs, she said, "Hey, while you're up there, do you think you can change the lightbulb in the fixture? I've been meaning to do it but just haven't gotten around to it."

"Um, sure."

In the bedroom, I grabbed the stepladder from the corner of the room and brought it under the light. She handed me the bulb, and I replaced it. "There. Easy peasy."

"Thank you so much."

As I lowered to the last step, I lost my footing and nearly fell. What the fuck? The room began to spin.

Miranda grabbed my arm. "Are you okay?"

"I don't know. I got dizzy all of a sudden." My speech was slurred. This couldn't be from one beer. "What's going on?"

"Here. Sit down." She led me to the bed.

My eyes shot to her. "What did you do to me?"

"What?"

"Did you drug me?" Things darkened. I blinked. My heart quickened. "What—why—" I fell back onto the bed. My head spun.

Miranda leaned over me, then . . . blackness.

* * *

"I can't. He's too out of it."

I slowly opened my eyes. *Blurriness. Voices.*

"Did you try rubbing yourself on him? For stimulation?"

"William, it's no use. He can't get it up."

"Well, how much did you give him?"

Dad?

"The full amount you gave me."

Miranda—and my dad?

"The full amount in one bottle of beer? You idiot. You were supposed to split it up."

"Well, how was I supposed to know that? It's not like I go around drugging people all the time."

I moaned and tried to move. I couldn't. It was like I was in sleep paralysis.

"Is he waking up?"

"Impossible. But just in case, he can't see me here. You're going to have to undress him."

"What?"

"Get him naked. And get naked with him."

"What's the plan? How am I supposed to get pregnant with him in this state?"

What the fuck were they talking about?

"We'll worry about getting you pregnant later. For now, it'll be enough to make him think you slept together. The important thing is to separate him from that homo."

Ian? They had better not hurt him.

* * *

I wasn't sure how much time had passed when I regained consciousness, but it was quiet. My eyes flew open. I was still in Miranda's room. In her bed. The last thing I remembered was changing the lightbulb—and discovering I'd been drugged. Everything was fuzzy. I couldn't speculate right now, though. I had to go home. Ian was probably worried sick.

I sat up and immediately grabbed my head. Throbbing pain. I groaned as I swung my legs to the side of the bed, throwing the covers off me.

What the fuck?

Naked. How was I naked . . . in Miranda's bed?

My boot was even missing.

"Honeybun, come back to bed. It's warmer under the covers."

I whipped my head back. Miranda was in bed, too—naked. "What the fuck happened?"

"What do you mean, silly? Do you want a play-by-play?"

"Yes. What the fuck did you do to me?"

"Do you really not remember? It was beautiful. You'd never made love to me like that before."

"What the fuck are you talking about? There's no way. You put something in that beer."

"Okay, you're starting to concern me. You had more than one beer, but you assured me you knew what you wanted. And you forgave me for all the hurt. You said you made a mistake leaving me, and you wanted us to get back together. Do you really not remember any of this? It's the only reason I let you back into my bed."

"You're lying." I bolted to my feet and immediately regretted it. Nausea and dizziness knocked me to my knees. I found my jeans and slipped them on, then crawled in search of the rest of my clothes.

"How dare you insult me," Miranda cried. "Why would I lie? I apologized to you."

I ignored her as I got dressed. My phone—it was still in my pocket. Thank God. I pulled up Ian's number and texted **Help** and sent my location. After getting on my boot, I held on to the wall as I stood.

"Jake, let me help you," Miranda said as she got up from the bed.

"Get away from me."

She took another step toward me. "Jake—"

"Stay away! Don't touch me." I backed away and stumbled out of the room.

Chapter 40

Ian

I hadn't realized how late it'd gotten. When I'd finished up at the church, there was still no word from Jake. I went home, sure I'd receive a text from him soon. I couldn't imagine he'd want to hang out with Miranda more than necessary.

By the time I got home, still nothing. I was getting worried. Had I remembered where Miranda lived, I'd have gone there. Maybe his phone had died, or he'd decided to take an Uber home.

I was sure he'd walk in through the door at any minute.

After putting away my things, I began prepping dinner. My phone dinged. Hoping it was Jake, I swiped my phone off the counter.

Not from Jake.

It was from Jake's dad. A message with an attachment. **I warned you**.

My hands shook as I clicked on the link. Pictures—of Jake and Miranda.

No. This can't be real.

Don't fall for it. Don't fall for it.

But pictures don't lie. Or do they?

The whole thing was weird. Sure, it appeared they were naked in bed . . . but how would William get these pictures?

Spy?

NO!

He wouldn't do that to me. Would he? My mind raced to all his promises, his actions. His fight with his father. There was no way these pictures were real.

And yet doubt still crept in.

I dropped my phone onto the counter and braced myself, taking deep breaths. I stood that way for a few minutes, trying to control the bad sinking feeling in the pit of my stomach and think of what to do.

My phone vibrated. This time, I was slower to reach for it.

From Jake. **Help.**

Along with his current location.

* * *

I'd never driven so fast in my life.

Jake had sent an updated location, which was down the street. On my race over, I had decided to take Jake's side. We'd promised to be honest and have each other's back, and that was what I intended to do. Until he told me otherwise, we were in this together. I would not turn my back on him again.

It took me a while to find him, but when I did, he was sitting on the curb. He looked like he was throwing up.

He squinted up at my headlights and got on his hands and knees. He was struggling to stand. I jumped out of the SUV and ran over to him.

"Jake, are you all right? What happened?" I lifted him, draping his arm across my shoulders, and grabbed his guitar case.

"Thank God, baby. I was scared you wouldn't come. You didn't answer my text."

"Sorry. I rushed over as soon as I got it." I helped him into the car, then went around and hopped in. "Jake, what happened?"

"Drive. We have to get out of here."

I stepped on the gas. When we were a couple miles away, I said, "Okay, you're freaking me out. What happened?"

"I was drugged."

"What? Miranda drugged you? How? Why?"

"I don't know. Last thing I remember is drinking one beer and changing a lightbulb for her."

"Oh my God." This wasn't good. I grabbed my phone and pulled up Matt's number.

"What are you doing?"

"I'm calling Matt. We're going to the hospital."

By the time we made it to the hospital, I still felt like shit. High as fuck, but not in a good way. Like, high with a hangover.

I leaned on Ian on the elevator ride up to Matt's floor. Everything was still spinning, and my head was pounding.

Matt was standing there with a wheelchair when the doors opened. "Thank you so much for seeing him," Ian said.

"No problem. Hi, Jake. Have a seat."

I let Ian help me into the chair and tried to keep my head from falling back as the doctor wheeled me down the hall. He brought into an examination room, and Ian helped me onto the exam table as Matt shut the door.

"So, Jake, can you tell me what happened?" he asked as he flashed a little flashlight in my eyeballs.

"I don't remember everything."

"That's okay. Take your time. Tell me what you do remember." He paused when I didn't answer. "Would you like Ian to leave us? Whatever you tell me will be confidential."

"What? Fuck no. Ian stays."

"Okay. Tell me everything you remember. The more I know, the more I'll be able to help you."

"I went over to my ex-girlfriend's house because she told me she wanted to apologize for all the shit she's put me through. She seemed sincere for the first time in her fucking life. She said she wanted to put everything behind us." I glanced at Ian. "We even hugged it out. She said she would leave us be."

"What happened after you hugged it out?" Matt asked.

"She offered me a beer. I said no because I wanted to get home, but she insisted. Something about it being for old times' sake and having my favorite brand. I thought one beer would be okay, and I'd text Ian to pick me up." I paused, trying to remember everything I could. "We chatted while we drank. Well, mostly she chatted. When I was ready to leave, she told me there was a box full of my stuff upstairs in the bedroom. She said I could grab it. She followed me upstairs and asked if I could replace the lightbulb while I was there. That's it. That's all I remember."

"And where did you wake up?"

I glanced at Ian again. I knew what he would think once I said it. I didn't want him to think I did anything. My eyes watered. I squeezed my eyes shut and let my head hang.

Ian came closer and squeezed my shoulder. "It's okay. Whatever it is, say it. You've done nothing wrong."

I let a sob out and thanked God for his words. "When I came to, I was in her bed. Naked." I couldn't stop the tears. "I'm so sorry, baby. I don't know what I did. She said we had sex, but I don't remember—"

His arms came around me. "Baby, it's okay. I believe you. I'm not going anywhere. Hey, Matt, can you give us a minute?"

"Of course. I'll order a tox screen so we can pinpoint what we're dealing with and what our next course of action should be."

"Okay. Thanks." When the door closed, Ian leaned back. "I need to show you something." He pulled his phone out. "I received something a few minutes before you sent me your text."

In front of me, he held a picture of me and Miranda naked. "What the fuck?" I said as I grabbed the phone. "Where did you get this?"

"Your father sent them, along with a message telling me he warned me."

"I don't remember this. Please believe me."

"I do believe you. I was hoping seeing these would jog your memory."

I took a moment. "Wait. My father sent you these?" He nodded. "I think . . . my dad was there."

"William was at Miranda's house? Did you see him?"

I shook my head. "I may have dreamt it. But I thought I heard his voice. Miranda and he were arguing."

There was a knock on the door, and a nurse came in. They drew my blood, then hooked me up to an IV to sober me up and hydrate me.

"I'll put a rush on that toxicology report," Matt said. "Just rest for now. Let me know if you need anything."

* * *

It felt like hours later when I woke up again. Ian was sitting on a chair next to my bed, his arm draped over my waist, his head resting on me. I was relieved he was still with me—and that my head wasn't pounding anymore.

There was a knock on the door, and Matt walked in. Ian popped his head up and rubbed his eyes. "Hey, you two. Jake, how are you feeling?"

"Much better."

"Did you get the results?" Ian asked.

"I did. We found traces of GHB in your system."

"Roofies? That bitch roofied me?"

"Usually, GHB doesn't stay in the system that long. The fact that we were able to detect it shows how high a dose you were given. There was also ketamine in your bloodstream, which can explain your deep sedation and confusion."

"Special K. What the fuck?"

"Jake, due to these results and the circumstances involving your memory loss, along with the nature of your undress, I recommend you do a sexual assault evidence kit. And I highly encourage you to file a report with the police."

"You think I was raped?"

"I don't know, but it's a possibility. Regardless, you were drugged and undressed against your will. The only way to know for sure what happened is to have this kit done. You don't have to do all the steps, just the ones that are relevant, which can detect DNA and other evidence."

I looked at Ian. "What if I wasn't forced? I mean, what if there's evidence of sex, but I did it willingly?"

"You were drugged," Ian said. "If you had sex with her, it wasn't because you wanted to. You were under the influence. You didn't know what you were doing."

"Ian's right," Matt agreed.

If what they were saying was true, and my father was somehow involved, then that motherfucker was going down. I was done being Mr. Nice Guy. "Okay. I'll do it. And I want to talk to your brother. Ian said he works in drug enforcement?"

"Yeah. Okay. I'll call him. And we'll get that kit started."

* * *

After I'd been swabbed, prodded, scraped, and poked, the only thing I wanted to do was take a long, hot shower and crawl into my own bed with Ian's arms around me and forget tonight ever happened.

Fuck Miranda and William. If I ever saw them again, it'd be too soon.

Another knock on the door interrupted my alone time with Ian. He'd been awfully quiet during this process. I wanted to know what he was thinking. I guess it was good news that he'd stuck around the whole time.

"Hey, guys," Matt said as he entered with a man who looked like he could be his twin, except with broader shoulders and shorter hair. "I promise you'll be able to leave soon. This is my brother, Luke."

Ian stood, stretching out his palm to shake the guy's hand. "Hi, Luke. Thanks so much for coming. I'm Ian."

"So, you're the infamous Ian. Glad to finally meet you. The one who broke my little brother's heart."

Matt covered his face with his hand. "Oh my God, Luke." He turned to Ian and me. "Please don't listen to him. I never said that."

"You didn't have to say it, little bro."

"Luke—"

Ian cleared his throat and came over to stand next to me. "This is my boyfriend, Jake. He's the one who wanted to speak to you."

The smartass came over and shook my hand. "Hey, Jake. Sorry to be meeting under these circumstances. My brother told me a little about your case. I'm not sure if I'm the right person to help you, but I'll do my best."

"You're DEA, right?"

"That's right."

"Then you're the right person. I have information regarding a drug crime. And I'm not only talking about the roofies I was subjected to."

"Okay. You have my undivided attention."

"I'll give you guys some privacy," Matt said and left the room, closing the door behind him.

"Should I leave too?" Ian asked.

I grabbed his hand. "No. Stay."

He sat again in the chair next to the bed, not letting go of my hand. I needed his strength. He must've sensed my hesitation because he leaned close, resting his head on my forehead. "You've got this. I'm here. I'm not going anywhere."

I nodded, then took a deep breath. "William Edwards. He embezzles money from the company he works for to buy drugs. In turn, he sells to other businesspeople, then he puts money back in the company's funds and keeps a hefty profit for himself."

The agent took out a small notepad and pen. "And how do you know this William Edwards?"

I paused. "He's my father."

"Well, shit. Okay, hold up." He grabbed a chair from the corner of the room and brought it near the bed. "I need to sit for this." Once he got comfy, he said, "I'm ready. Start from the beginning."

And I did—everything from Miranda's blackmails to my father's threats and everything in between, including the threats to Ian and my suspicions of my dad supplying the drugs that fucked me up to Miranda. I held nothing back. Surprisingly, it felt good to get it all off my chest.

After a moment of the agent tapping his pad, seemingly going over his notes, I asked, "So . . . what happens now?"

"Now we open up an investigation and see if we can dig up some solid proof to bring him down. If the strategy you say he used is accurate, I might have to involve other jurisdictions. As far as what your ex-girlfriend did to you, I can hook you up with my friends in the police department. Once your kit results come back, we'll know if we should add sexual battery to her assault charge. Unfortunately, in the state of Georgia, male rape victims aren't treated the same as females.

The best they'll be able to book her with is aggravated sodomy, if she indeed sodomized you in some way."

That was some fucked-up shit, but at least she'd go down for something. "I understand. Thank you for your time."

"No problem. Thank you for the information. I'll get started on this right away."

"Hey, I have a question," Ian said. "Regarding that list of so-called clients Miranda had—"

"We can't touch that. The only way we can go after them is if they are caught buying."

"Okay. Thanks."

Good to know Ian's dad was in the clear. Just as long as what he'd told Ian was true—that it was a one-time deal years ago.

Luke stood. "By the way, I'm sorry for what I said earlier about the heartbreak thing. My intention was to mess with my little brother, not make you two uncomfortable."

I shrugged. "No discomfort on my part. Babe?"

Ian glanced at me and smiled, then looked back at the agent. "Nope. Look, Matt always knew the extent of my feelings for Jake. I'm sorry if he was saddened by our breakup, but I'm glad we're able to remain friends."

"Me too. You seem like a nice guy." He backed up toward the door. "Okay, well. We'll be in touch."

Chapter 42

Ian

As I cut the engine of my finally repaired SUV, I glanced at Jake. It had been two weeks since the whole fiasco of Miranda drugging him. The good news was that the results of the sexual assault had come back negative, meaning she didn't rape him. What a relief.

So, putting two and two together, the whole thing was to make us think they'd slept together. To break us up.

Wow.

If anything, it had made us stronger. I never for one second believed he'd slept with her on purpose.

"Are you sure you're up for this?" I asked.

Today was the day we planned to reveal our relationship at church, but I was worried it would be too much, facing everyone after the trauma he experienced. I mean, there was a possibility he'd see Miranda.

He placed his hand on my thigh. "Yes. I've never been more sure of anything in my life. I want everyone to know we're together."

"I know, but if you need more time—"

"I don't. I know who I am and who I want. I need this, babe. Just like we talked about. No big production. Just chill, like us."

"Okay. Let's do it then."

We got out of the car and headed across the parking lot. Some more good news: Jake no longer needed the boot for his leg.

Jake put his arm around me, but we were still early, so there weren't that many people yet. Sliding his arm away as we walked inside, he took my hand and made our way down the aisle. The few people who were there eyed us, but there were no strong reactions. When we got to the altar, we genuflected, then Jake squeezed my hand before letting go and continuing to the sacristy located behind the altar to change into his choir robe as I headed for the organ.

After a few minutes of warming up, I played soothing music as the parishioners filled the pews. Two songs in and a squeal echoed from the gathering area. I glanced over—

Anna and Ant? What in the world were they doing here? The squeal had come from Rosemary, excited to see her former boss and friend.

Once I finished up the current song, I headed down the aisle. "Anna? What are you doing here?"

"Jake asked us to come."

"He did? Why?"

"Support. He mentioned coming out and revealing your relationship."

I covered my mouth. "Oh my God, he did?"

She nodded, flashing a wide grin. "He thought you might want us here."

"And you came? You didn't have to do that."

"It's okay. It was about time we showed our faces. Right, baby?" she said as she looked up at Ant.

"That's right. We no longer have a reason to hide. Just like you and Jake."

"Thank you. This means a lot."

"Thank Jake. He's the one who convinced us."

"Oh, I will. Trust me."

There was a loud *hmph* that came toward the entrance. Jake's mother and Miranda stood there.

"Well, well, well," Mrs. Edwards said. "If it isn't the gathering of sinners."

"Mrs. Edwards." I swallowed as a bad feeling crept in, but I had to show respect. She was Jake's mother, after all. "It's good to see you."

She stepped closer, facing Anna. "You must be the infamous Anna Ward."

Anna lifted her chin. "It's Anna Martin now."

"No, it's not."

"I beg your pardon?" Anna proclaimed as Anthony got in front of her.

"Not in the eyes of the Church or God."

"Actually, we were married in the church. Right inside that chapel," she said proudly, pointing in the chapel's direction.

Mrs. Edwards lifted a brow as she *hmph*ed again. "Everyone involved in that ceremony will burn in hell, including that bastard child in your belly."

"How dare you!"

"No, how dare *you*! Showing up in the house of God with the work of the devil growing inside you!"

Anna gasped and Ant stepped forward. "That's enough! Do not disrespect my wife and child," he said in a low tone.

"Oh, you mean like you disrespected your vows and God, *Father* Anthony. You have some nerve showing your face here again after what you did. I'm sure God has a special place for you in hell!"

People were staring. I needed to put a stop to this. I stepped forward. "Mrs. Edwards, mass should begin soon. Shall I help you find a seat? Or did you want me to find Jake for you?"

"You stay away from my son." She narrowed her eyes. "All these years, I trusted you. I thought you were a decent young man with morals. I opened my home to you. But you betrayed us. You infiltrated your sick perversions onto my boy. You poisoned him against us. He was in a good, honest relationship, about to get married, and you took that away from him."

"I didn't—"

Her arm swung back, slapping me across the face so hard, it whipped my face to the side and made me see stars.

"What the fuck!"

I jerked back to the sound of Jake's voice. His expression of shock quickly turned murderous as he marched forward, aiming for his mother.

I launched ahead, blocking his path. "No, Jake. She's your mother."

"No, she's not!"

"Jake, stop!" I smiled past the sting on my cheek. "You can't beat up your mother."

Jake stopped pushing and shifted his eyes to mine. "Are you okay?" he asked, lightly touching the side of my face.

"Yeah, I'm fine."

"Sinners!" Mrs. Edwards shouted.

By now, the whole congregation had gathered around, trying to get a front-row seat to the drama ensuing.

Father Kevin stepped forward. "Excuse me, folks. Mass is about to begin. Do I need to contact the authorities?"

"Father, how can you allow such wicked behavior in the house of God? First, a priest disobeys his vows and has an affair with a young woman, whom he impregnates. And you allow them to get married here, in this church! And now, that man has come between my son and his fiancée. He has influenced him to take part in his wicked ways."

"Mom, I'm warning you, stop it!" Jake shouted.

"I will not stop until you let go of this bisexual nonsense and see a therapist."

"No."

"See, Mrs. Edwards, I told you he's been brainwashed," Miranda chimed in.

Jake glared at her. "You need to get away from me."

"Jacob, that's no way to talk to your fiancée," Mrs. Edwards said.

"Have you told my mother what you did to me?"

"I told her the truth. You came over and we reconciled, and yet you still ran to Ian."

"Are you fucking kidding me? You left out the part where you roofied me?"

"I did no such thing."

"What are you talking about, Jake?" his mother asked.

"Mom, your precious Miranda drugged me to get me to sleep with her."

"That is not true. He's just saying that because he doesn't want Ian to know we slept together."

"I have proof," Jake said.

Miranda's eyes widened. "Well, I have proof too. Jake, I think I'm pregnant."

The color drained from Jake's face. "Holy shit. That's why." He turned to me. "I remember now." He turned back to Miranda. "My dad was there. You roofied me to have sex with me, only you gave me too much and I couldn't perform. So you undressed me and had my dad take pictures to make it look like we had sex. And he sent them to Ian, thinking he'd believe we'd slept together." He laughed. "You wanted to trap me with a baby and break me and Ian up. Well, guess what? It didn't work. Ian trusts me. He's too smart to fall for your bullshit."

"Jake, lower your voice. You don't know what you're saying."

"I do know what I'm saying. Do you have any idea what you've subjected me to? Because of you, I had a rape kit done. You violated me. But I got those results. We did not have sex, thank fucking Jesus. But you are going down for assaulting me. I've already filed charges against you."

"You told the police about this?"

"Come on, Jake," I said, taking his arm. "We have to go."

Jake's mom grabbed my arm. "Let go of my son."

Jake shoved her away. "Don't touch him."

"Jacob, I don't fully understand what happened with Miranda, but this obsession Ian has with you is clouding your judgment. You're choosing him over your family."

"He *is* my family. Mom, I'm an adult. You can't tell me who to be with. And if you ever lay a hand on him again, I swear to God, I will forget you're my mother."

"You're threatening me? Your own mother? Look what he's converted you to! Violence against me!"

"Who said anything about violence?" He stepped closer to her. "Anybody—and I mean *anybody*—who causes harm to him is dead to me."

I pulled him back, then turned to Father Kevin. "I'll start the music now." I took Anna's hand and said, "I'm sorry about all this. We'll talk after mass."

As I pushed through the crowd, Jake stopped me. "Wait, are you okay?"

"I'm fine. Look, we can't do this right now."

"I'm sorry for the things my mother said."

"Jake, I hate that I've come between you and your parents. They hate me. I never wanted to cause you so much pain."

"Hey, wait a second. None of this is your fault."

"Still. I feel bad." I shook my head. "I have to get to the organ. We'll talk after, okay?"

I continued past the nave, ignoring the stares as people returned to their seats. I was more than halfway up the aisle when—

"Marry me."

I froze.

Clearly, I was hearing things. Just how hard did Mrs. Edwards hit me? Jake couldn't have said what I thought I heard. But, gauging by the gasps and murmurs cascading among the crowd, something mind-blowing must've been said.

Slowly, I cranked my head around. "What?" I breathed.

"Marry me," he repeated with a small smile.

"Jake, what are you doing?" I whispered, waiting for the just-kidding punch line.

"I love you. I want to spend the rest of my life showing you just how much. You're my best friend, my world, my everything. And I can't think of a better way to live life than with you by my side. I don't give a fuck what people think, or what they say, or what obstacles they put in our way. This is my life, and I choose you. I'm sorry it took me so long, but I realize now that you're my better half. I can't breathe without you. Just please say you'll marry me. I want you to be my husband, and I'll be yours. For forever. Will you? Marry me?"

I blinked twice—no, three times—and swallowed as I took a step toward him. Then, another, one foot in front of the other until we were face-to-face.

My mouth opened but no sound came out. I cleared my throat and tried again. "So much for not making a big production, huh?"

He chuckled and shrugged. "What can I say? Go big or go home." The silence stretched. I was in shock. "I'll get down on one knee if—"

"Yes," I breathed.

"Yes?"

I nodded. "Babe, you fucking had me at *marry me.*"

His smile widened and he threw his arms around me. We hugged as applause and whistling erupted throughout the congregation. Pulling back, Jake caressed my face and kissed me in front of everyone—and not just a quick peck either. It was a thorough hot, wet, tongue-involved sort of kiss. I was sure that if Mrs. Edwards had stuck around this long, she was probably having a heart attack.

Leaning back, Jake grinned. "I love you."

"I love you too."

"Congrats, you guys," Anna said with tears in her eyes. She hugged us both. Ant was right behind her, congratulating us as well.

Father Kevin came up to us. "Congratulations to you both. Now, can we get mass started? We're already about twenty minutes behind."

"Yes, of course." I took my spot at the organ and, with the biggest smile on my face, played the opening hymn.

Chapter 43

I couldn't stop smiling, and by the looks of it, neither could Ian.

As soon as mass ended and the choir receded, I detoured back up the side aisle to the backroom and quickly changed out of my robe. Once that was done, I went over to the organ, where Ian was finishing up the final song.

He smiled, his cheeks turning pink. "You changed out of your robe quick. Why the rush?"

"I wanted to see my fiancé."

His smile got bigger. "Did that really happen?"

"You bet your sweet ass it did."

He shook his head. "I can't believe it. I feel like it's all a dream."

I put my arm around him and kissed him. "It's not a dream."

"Did you plan it?"

"Honestly, yes and no. Yes, I planned to propose, but I didn't plan for it to go down the way it did."

"What was the plan, then?"

"I hadn't ironed out the details. I just knew I wanted to do it. I was thinking sometime after mass, which was why I wanted Anna and Ant here. I wasn't planning on doing it in front of everyone. But when you walked away feeling bad, I panicked. I wanted to show everyone I'm serious about you—that this isn't some phase."

"And by everyone, you mean your mother."

"Pretty much."

He placed his hand on my cheek. "I love you. And your mother does too. She'll come around. She just needs time to process."

I shrugged. "Whatever. I love that you believe that, but I'm not holding my breath. And I'll never forgive her for hitting you."

He pressed his lips together as he gathered the music sheets. Anna and Ant came up to us. "Congratulations again, you two," Anna said as she hugged Ian first, then me. "I am so happy for you guys. Jake, the things you said . . . oh my God, so beautiful. You made me cry."

I smiled. "It was all true. I just spoke from my heart."

"So, you guys had no idea he was going to do that?" Ian asked.

"Nope. That was all him."

"Wow. I'm engaged to a romantic."

We laughed.

As Ian gathered his belongings, some people came over to congratulate us. Others gave us dirty looks as they shook their heads, while the rest ignored us, as if they had other things to worry about than a couple of dudes getting engaged in a Catholic church.

* * *

I could not wait to get my fiancé naked and in our bed. That sounded weird in my head: *fiancé.* But I did it. I popped the question. And it felt so right.

The last couple of weeks had been hell. Not knowing the extent of Miranda's violation made my skin crawl to the point of diminishing my sex drive. There had been a lot of cuddling, though. I loved Ian even more for his patience and support, but now I wanted to rip his clothes off and fuck him until the sun came up—with his consent, of course.

"You're staring at me again," Ian said, smiling as he drove us home.

"I know. I can't help it."

"What are you thinking about?"

"Getting you naked."

His cheeks turned pink. "Really? And what are you going to do once I'm naked?"

"Lick and kiss you everywhere. Want me to elaborate?"

"Please do."

"I'm going to suck your dick till it's rock hard and ready to cum. More?"

He hooded his eyes, slanting a smile my way. "Yeah."

"Next, I'm going to lick your ass till it's nice and slathered in wetness so you're ready for me. More?"

He licked his lips. "Mm-hmm."

"Then I'm going to slide my dick inside you nice and slow until you squirm and beg me to go faster. But you know what?"

"Hmm?"

"I'm going to keep going slow until your cock is about ready to burst. Until it's glistening with precum. Until it's shaking with need."

"Fuck, babe—"

"That's exactly what I'm going to do to you. Fuck you. Slow . . . then fast . . . then slow again. Until every part of your body is quivering with need. And then . . ."

"And then what?"

I leaned closer, placing my hand on his leg. "Is this making you hard?"

He smiled as he bit his lip. "Why don't you see for yourself?"

No need to ask me twice. Sliding my hand up his thigh, I cupped him. He gasped, and I smiled. "Yup. You're hard. But you still have room to grow."

He laughed, and I kissed his neck. "You are crazy."

"Are you just now finding that out?"

"Nope. I've always known. And you did the ultimate crazy thing today."

"Were you surprised?"

"Uh, yeah."

I bit his earlobe, then slid to his neck. Now that everyone knew about us, we could mark each other up with hickeys all we wanted. I made a mental note to add that to my list of things I planned to do to him.

"Hey, you didn't finish."

"Hmm?"

"What happens next?"

"Where did I leave off?"

"My body quivering with need."

"Ah, yes." I purposely didn't answer as I continued licking his ear.

"Well?"

"Oh, you're going to have to wait and see what happens next."

He giggled. "Oh my God, what a tease."

"I assure you, you will be thoroughly and completely satisfied."

The car stopped, and he faced me. "Good. Because we're home."

A beat later, we simultaneously hopped out of the car and raced inside. Ian was still jiggling the key out of the door when I tackled him, kissing him, and pressing myself against him, attacking the buttons on his damn dress shirt.

After tossing his bag and keys on the floor as the door shut, Ian was finally on board, grasping my shirt, pulling it over my head, feeling me everywhere.

His damn shirt. Fuck it. I forced it apart, causing buttons to fly everywhere. "I'll buy you a new fucking shirt," I breathed, ripping it off him.

He snickered as he claimed my lips, holding me to him as he

moved his hips against me. I needed to get him to the bedroom, but I didn't want to pause what we were doing.

Time for plan B.

I trailed kisses down his neck, pausing at his chest to nip at the tight, small buds, then I dropped to my knees, tasting his flat belly, feeling him everywhere. I leaned back and eagerly undid his slacks, almost tearing them like the shirt. Luckily, they were fastened by one of the sliding clip thingies. Much easier to remove.

I hooked my fingers in his waistband and pulled the pants off, along with his underwear. Finally, I had him naked.

Mission one: complete.

His cock jetted out, begging to be played with. Ian cried out as I engulfed him in my mouth, sucking and licking. He tasted so damn good. If we did nothing else all night but this, I'd be happy. I slid him back into my throat, not caring that I almost gagged, and he moaned. I savored him as I built him up. I gripped his ass, pulling him closer, taking in more of him. Mmm. Hello, precum.

I sat back on my heels, admiring my handiwork. My fiancé was rock hard and so ready to cum.

Mission two: done.

On my knees, I hooked my palms on Ian's waist and spun him around, pushing against his upper back so that his chest was flat against the door and his ass stuck out. Then I got to work, burying my face in his ass, licking him and slathering him with my spit. I separated his butt cheeks to fully explore, fucking him with my tongue.

"Jake," Ian moaned.

I slipped my hand between his legs, rubbing his balls, then slid up the length of him, feeling the wet tip. Leaning back slightly, I inserted a finger in his ass, then two.

So wet and ready.

Mission three: check.

I rose, swiftly removing my pants and boxers and freeing my eager cock. My arm wrapped around Ian's waist as I moved close to his ear. "Don't cum until I tell you." Then, spreading his legs wider, I positioned him just right, and—

Holy fuck.

We both moaned.

I moved nice and slow. It was a struggle not to pound him like a dog in heat, but I had to stick to my plan. Nice and slow . . . until Ian begged for release. But I might cum first if I didn't pace myself.

Ian arched his back, pushing his ass into me. "Oh my God, baby," he breathed as he rotated his hips.

I dug my fingers into his hips to keep him still. I was calling the shots here. With control, I thrust into him, picking up the pace. He cried out, dropping his head against the door. I slowed down again, sliding almost all the way out and back in deep, inch by inch.

My hand snuck around to the front of him and circled around his cock.

Still hard AF.

Ian shuddered and moaned, leaning his head back on my shoulder. "Please, baby," he whispered.

"Please what?"

"Please fuck me faster and let me cum."

I grinned.

Mission four: hell yes.

I pulled out and swung him around to the couch, tossing him onto it. I plunged into him. Back into his moist heat. Home.

Ian panted, latching his heels onto my lower back. "Yeah, baby— oh my God."

I kissed him as I thrust harder, faster, bringing us both closer to the edge. "Do you want to cum, baby?" I breathed.

"Yes. Please."

"Then cum for me, baby," I commanded, leaning back as Ian reached for his cock and did what he was told.

He shouted as he exploded a fountain of the glorious white fluid, hitting him in the face and chest.

"Holy fuck."

He was still pulsating around my cock when I poured myself into him. The contractions were intense and never-ending, it seemed. I didn't stop pumping until I was thoroughly milked.

When I could finally form a coherent thought, I leaned over him and licked the cum off his face before I kissed him.

"Baby, that was so hot," Ian slurred, obviously satiated.

"You're so hot." I kissed his neck, tasting some cum there as well.

"I could go to sleep just like this."

"I take it you're thoroughly satisfied?"

"Oh, yeah, definitely."

"Good. But don't go to sleep yet. I want us to go out tonight to celebrate."

"I thought we were celebrating. Right here. In the comfort and privacy of our home."

"Our home?"

Ian drew his eyebrows together. "Uh, this isn't news, baby. You have a key, you're wearing my underwear, and we're engaged. This is your home too."

I chuckled. "I know. I just like hearing you say it. I'm still getting used to it. But I do want to go out, now that we're official. I want to show you off." I reached for his left hand. "By the way, I should get you an engagement ring."

Ian smiled. "Or we can go ring shopping together and pick out our wedding bands. I don't think we need an extra ring."

"Okay. But I want to get you something to symbolize our engagement. Maybe a necklace or a watch or something. I want people to know you're taken."

He laughed. "I like that idea. But trust me, people will know—with or without a symbol."

I kissed his neck again. "Oh yeah? What, you're gonna tell everyone you meet?"

"Yup. And if they try anything, I'm gonna say, 'Better watch out, my husband-to-be will kick your ass.'"

"Damn straight."

"What about you? What will you say if some hot girl or guy comes on to you?"

"First of all, no one in this world is hot except you."

"Oh, please." He laughed.

"And second, I'll tell them to fuck off. I'm taken by a sexy, gorgeous, blue-eyed hottie who I can't wait to call my husband."

"Aww. I'm not sure about sexy and gorgeous—"

"I am."

"—but I can't wait to call you my husband too."

That made me smile. I pressed my lips to his. "Good. Now that that's settled, let's go shower because tonight, we're celebrating."

"Are you ready for this?"

Ian's lips curled into a smile. "Baby, I've been ready for this moment for a long time."

I grinned and took his hand. Together, we walked down the streets of downtown. My heart almost beat out of my chest. Excitement and nervousness ignited inside me. But I was ready to kick some ass to defend our love, if need be.

But none of that came. It was like no one paid attention to us. Everyone was so busy doing their own thing that two guys holding hands was far from their focal point. Huh. Who knew?

"So where are we going first?" Ian asked.

Up ahead, the place I'd been thinking of taking Ian came into view. Hopefully, he would be on board. "It's a surprise."

"A surprise? Can I get a hint?"

"We're almost there."

He furrowed his brow as he focused on the stores ahead. Then I stopped.

Ian looked confused as he glanced at the establishment before us and narrowed his eyes. "A tattoo parlor? Seriously?"

I chuckled and clasped both his hands. "I want to get your name tattooed on my heart. And I was hoping you'd get mine on yours. Right here." I placed my palm on his chest. "I thought we could do this as a symbol of our engagement and commitment to each other. You know, instead of an engagement ring."

Ian smiled, placing his hand over mine. "Baby, that's the sweetest thing."

There was hesitation in his voice. "But?"

"But . . . a tattoo? Can't we do something less painful?"

I laughed. "Come on, babe, please? Our names are short. The pain won't last that long."

"Easy for you to say. My name is shorter than yours."

"Yeah, by one letter. I'll have him draw a heart or something after your name so it'll be even."

"I don't know. What if something happens?"

"What do you mean?"

"With us. What if—"

"Hold up. Let me stop you right there. We will be together forever, unless there's something you're not telling me."

"Stop. Of course not. I just feel like this is all too good to be true. That you'll wake up tomorrow and realize this isn't what you want."

I reached for him, closing the gap between us, and grabbed his collar. "You listen to me, Ian Cooper. That will not happen. I love you. And I will always love you. This is real for me. The only way it'll end is if you end it. And if you do, I wouldn't care that your name is etched permanently on my skin because you're already etched in my heart. And nothing could ever remove you from there."

He blinked as his eyes glistened. "You're etched in mine too. So much that it hurts."

I caressed his cheek, catching an escaped tear. "I'm not going anywhere, baby."

He nodded and sniffled. "Neither am I."

I kissed him softly, keeping it short. Not only were we in public but we were also in front of the tattoo parlor, most likely being watched.

Ian pulled back. "Let's do it. Let's get tattoos."

"Are you sure?"

"Yeah. I do like the idea. It'll be like permanent hickeys."

"Exactly. I'll go first if you're nervous. And if you decide you don't want to go through with it, it's okay. I want to get your name tattooed on me whether or not you get mine."

"I'll go through with it. I promise. But you can go first. I want to see how painful it's going to be."

I chuckled as I took his hand. "Ready?"

"Yes."

Two hours later, we had fresh ink on our skin.

"That actually didn't hurt that bad," Ian said.

"Are you kidding? That hurt like a mother. I was trying to be brave for you, but goddamn."

Ian laughed as he kissed me. "I'm glad we did it. Thanks for thinking of it—and talking me into it."

"Absolutely. I'm glad we did it too. Even though it freaking hurt. It felt like a cat was clawing the shit out of me."

"So overdramatic," he said, lightly caressing the area where the bandage hid his name. "I'll kiss it all better later."

"Is that a promise?"

He laughed. "Yes, promise. Now, can we go eat? I'm starving."

I draped my arm around his shoulders. "Yeah, babe, of course. What do you feel like having?"

We settled on a casual Italian place not too far down the road. My mouth watered as soon as we walked in and got a whiff of the aroma of brick-oven pizza.

There was a five-minute wait, so I gave my name to the hostess, and we sat on the bench to wait.

After a moment, Ian leaned close to my ear and whispered, "I think that lady in the corner by the door doesn't approve of us."

I glanced over. It was an older woman with a scowl on her face. "Fuck her." I put my arm around him. "Might as well give her something to really judge us for." I kissed him, nice and thorough.

The woman huffed. I looked over as I pulled back. Her eyes were wide as she shook her head.

"Oh my God. You two are so cute together!" a young woman with short black hair and glasses chimed as she walked over to us.

"Well, thank you," I answered.

"Yeah, thanks. That's so nice of you to say," Ian said.

"You're welcome. I saw you guys and I just had to come over and say something. How long have you been together?"

I glanced at Ian. "Officially? A few months. But we've been friends since we were twelve."

"We're engaged," I added, "as of today."

The girl's hands shot to her mouth. "Oh my God, congratulations! That is so sweet!"

"Thanks. I don't know how I got so lucky."

"Aww, I'm literally going to cry. That is so cute."

"Yeah, he has a habit of saying the most unexpected sweetest things. I think I'm the lucky one," Ian replied.

"Oh, my heart," she said, placing her palm over her chest.

"Jake, party of two, your table is ready," the hostess called.

"Oh, that's us," I said, taking Ian's hand as I stood.

"Thanks again for coming over. It means a lot to have your support."

"Oh, yeah, definitely. I know how cruel and unaccepting people can be. I wish you all the best. Congrats again."

"Thanks so much."

Chapter 45

Matt

Sometimes you had to do things yourself around here.

On my way back from the lab to drop off a blood sample of my patient—no one was around to do it, and I wanted it ASAP—I stopped by the second floor to check on a couple patients who began dialysis today.

It was going well. At least, as well as you could expect from dialysis.

After spending some time with them answering questions, I got a nonemergency page. They needed me back on the third floor. I said my goodbyes and headed toward the elevator. As I waited, a group of people came out of the chapel, inclusively known as the meditation room.

I did a double take. CJ?

He had on clothes that I'd never seen him wear before, a big cross around his neck, and . . . a collar?

"CJ!" I called.

He stiffened but didn't look back as he continued on with his group. Maybe he didn't hear me.

I caught up to them and tapped his shoulder. "CJ?"

He turned that time, his eyes wide. "I'm sorry. You must have me confused with someone else."

What the hell?

I had never been so confused—and pissed—in my life. I stood watching them leave for a good minute before I remembered my page.

CJ . . . a priest?

No, no, no. That couldn't be. But why else would he be coming out of a chapel with a collar and acting like he didn't know me?

I couldn't dwell on this right now. My patient was waiting for me.

Chapter 46

Jake

Life was fucking good.

Almost three weeks had passed since I'd popped the big question, and I had never been happier. Ian seemed happy, too, and that made my chest puff out with pride. After all, Ian's happiness took priority.

We fell into a nice routine over the weeks. I'd wake up before Ian, get ready for school, eat something quick, and head out, but not before kissing my man goodbye. After school, I'd give guitar lessons, then, depending on the day, I'd either meet Ian at the church for choir practice or go home for our private duet rehearsal, which would often lead to a hot sex sesh. Actually, that part happened regardless of the night.

Not to brag or anything.

On some other news, my motorcycle was finally fixed, good as new, which made our routine easier now that I didn't have to keep spending money on Ubers or rely on Ian and Ant for rides. Ian was concerned with me hopping back on my bike—he was so cute, how he worried about me—but I promised to never drive in fog again. And I promised to ride carefully every time I left, and I would text him when I arrived at my destination.

The DEA was still investigating my father, and Miranda was facing sexual assault charges for drugging and undressing me. They hadn't been able to prove my dad was involved yet.

I hadn't heard from my mother since that day at the church, and I couldn't have cared less. I'd never forgive her for hitting Ian.

The death threats against Ian had died down, but I wasn't letting my guard down. I made sure he wasn't alone at the church for too long.

Tonight was the first LGBTQ+ support meeting at the church. I'd promised I'd be there as soon as I finished the guitar lesson I had scheduled. This was a big night for Ian, and I wouldn't miss it for the world. Words could not express how proud I was of him for making this support group happen.

There were a few cars in the parking lot as I pulled into a space. That was good news. After securing my helmet, I sprinted to the church hall basement, where the meeting was being held. I glanced at my watch. Fifteen minutes late. Fuck.

I opened the door quietly and slipped inside. Ian's eyes met mine instantly. His whole face lit up as he smiled and waved, which caused everyone to turn their heads toward me. Mostly teenagers and a few adults were sitting in a half circle.

"Everyone," Ian addressed the crowd, "in case you haven't heard, that beautiful man who just walked in is Jake, my fiancé."

I smiled and waved. Some whistles and clapping erupted from the crowd.

"Did you want to pull up a chair and join us or just observe?" Ian asked as everyone quieted down.

"I'll join you." I wanted to support him in every way, and to me, that meant participation.

For the next forty minutes, I was in awe of the amazing stories told by the group. Some were frustrating and some were sad; others contained a glimmer of hope. I now understood how Ian felt: helpless, wanting to help these people in some way. It wasn't like they could confront their families and order them to accept them.

If only.

"Anyone else want to add anything before we end tonight's meeting?" Ian asked. After a moment with no responses, he continued, "Okay, then. Just know that those who didn't get a chance to speak tonight will get that chance next week. We will all have the opportunity to share our stories. And, like I said earlier, this is a support group. We are here to listen and share. Unfortunately, that's all I can offer, but I hope it brings peace of mind, knowing we are like-minded people. We are here for you."

Applause erupted.

I smiled as I clapped as well. A sense of pride washed over me. The luck I scored in life with him was mind blowing. I couldn't wait to get him alone.

"Thanks, everybody," Ian said. "But I would like to applaud every single one of you as well. If not for you guys, this support group wouldn't exist. Thanks so much for joining me tonight. And remember, be who you are. God loves you no matter what. Don't let anyone tell you differently. See you next week."

I watched as people surrounded him, giving him hugs and shaking his hand. A few people even came up to me to congratulate me on our engagement, which, of course, I proudly accepted.

Thirty minutes later, we were finally alone. "That was awesome, babe," I said, standing and walking over to him.

"It was, wasn't it?"

"Hell yeah." I gave him a kiss. "It was very moving. I think I'll share my story next week."

"Yeah?"

"Definitely. You've really made a comfortable atmosphere here. I'm proud of you."

"Thanks, baby. That means a lot. Help me put away the chairs?"

"You bet."

About ten minutes later, we were done and shutting off the lights.

"I can't wait to go home. I am beat," Ian said as he locked up. "I think all the excitement leading up to this night is crashing down."

I swung my arm around him. "When we get home, I'll make you some dinner, then give you a back rub. How does that sound?"

"Oh my God, that sounds like heaven."

"Good."

We held hands as we walked outside.

"Well, well, well, if it isn't the homos of St. Pius."

My heart dropped as we stopped dead in our tracks. Donald, Andrew, and two other men walked toward us. One man had a stick, the kind police officers carried.

I squeezed Ian's hand, pulling him closer to me. "What are you doing here, Donald? Vandalizing cars again?"

Donald sneered. "You're pretty funny for a fag."

My instinct was to move forward, but Ian's grip didn't allow me to. "Jake, no," he whispered.

"Yeah, listen to your boyfriend, Jakey. Or should I say *fiancé*." He laughed as he shook his head. "What a joke. Two men getting hitched. What has this world come to?"

"It's a free country. We have the right to be with who we want. We're not breaking any laws. Unlike you."

Donald put his arms up. "We're not breaking any laws. Are we, fellas? At least, not yet." The group laughed.

"What's your plan, huh? Rough us up with that stick? Why not be a real man and fight me, one on one, no weapons?"

Donald laughed. "Real man? You say that as you hold hands with a dude. That's hilarious . . . for a fag."

My jaw clenched as I narrowed my eyes. "Fucking call me that one more time."

He stepped closer. "Or what? You're gonna risk making your

fruitcake here cry?"

Before I could stop him, Ian moved forward. "What do you want, Donald?"

"You know what I want. But you haven't heeded any of my warnings."

"It was you. So, what, you're here to kill me? Isn't 'thou shalt not kill' a commandment?"

"Thou shalt not kill the innocent. You aren't exactly innocent, are you? You're a sicko who mocks the house of the Lord. You think Jesus died so you can do perverted shit with other faggots?"

That did it. I shoved the bastard away from Ian, then punched him across the face, knocking him down on his ass. I went down after him, grabbing him by his jacket collar and punched him again and again. No demands to stop from Ian, so I took that as a go-ahead.

"Get this queer off me!" Donald shouted.

"No!" Ian yelled.

The blow on my back knocked the wind out of me, allowing iron fists to grab my arms and pull me to my feet. I fought against them, but a second blow to my stomach caused me to cough and gasp for air.

"Let go of him!" Ian shouted.

I lifted my head. One of Donald's goons held Ian back. *Get your fucking hands off him.* The words wouldn't come out.

"Please!" Ian struggled against the arms holding on to him. "I'll do anything! You want me to quit? Fine, I quit! Just stop hurting him!"

No! Don't quit because of me!

"I'm afraid it's a little too late for that, fruitcake."

"Why? You'll never see us again. Promise!"

"Tempting, but no." Donald reached for something in his back pocket.

Fuck.

The unmistakable sound of a knife flipping open followed.

"What are you going to do with that?" Ian asked, the panic

evident in his voice.

"Teach you two a lesson."

My breath came back, and I fought against the assholes holding me. I got them to loosen their hold, but they gained the upper hand once again, locking me in a hold with the baton across my neck.

Ian's fear-struck face made my heart ache. *Don't worry, baby.* "Let go of him," I bit out, warning the motherfucker who had his hands on my man.

The guy snickered. "Or what? Trust me, I'm not trying to feel him up."

My eyes shot to Ian, hoping he'd come up with the same idea as me. His expression confirmed that he did.

"Are you sure about that?" Ian asked his captor. "I'm pretty sure that's not a pencil in your pocket pressing up against my ass."

"Aw, hell no!" the guy shouted over a collective *eww.*

It was enough for Ian to slip free—only he was supposed to run away to safety, not toward me, where all the danger remained.

I watched in horror as Donald turned, knife in hand, and plunged right into Ian, stopping him from any rescue attempts.

"NOOOOOOO!" I screamed, the word ricocheting through my head. I somehow managed to gain hold of the baton and knocked the knife from Donald's hand. In some out-of-body experience, I chased the fuckers away.

I turned to Ian, running to him. He was on the ground, holding his stomach.

"Baby," I cried, skidding to my knees. Blood oozed from his right side, soaking his shirt and hands.

I ripped off my jacket and pulled off my overshirt. Replacing Ian's hands, I applied pressure with the fabric.

"Help!" I shouted, praying that someone would hear me at the rectory. My vision blurred with tears as I glanced down into Ian's pale face. "Baby, hang on, please. Can you reach your phone? I don't want to stop applying pressure."

His hands moved, retrieving the phone. "Jake," he whispered. "I'm sorry."

"No, don't do that. Don't fucking do that. You are going to be okay."

"I love you."

"Stop. Press the emergency call button on your phone."

I heard footsteps approaching, and I immediately shielded Ian the best I could while still applying the needed pressure. I was prepared to protect him with my life.

Thankfully, it was only a priest. Not one I'd recognized. "What happened? Oh, dear God!"

"Call 911. Please—hurry!"

The priest took out his own phone and made the call.

Shortly after, we heard sirens. Thank God.

The police showed up first, immediately starting first aid until the paramedics arrived. I explained everything that had happened to the best to my ability while monitoring Ian. I gave Donald's name and descriptions of the assholes with him. When they put Ian in the ambulance, I followed, not caring that I left an officer midsentence.

Inside the ambulance, I held Ian's hand, not liking the look of his blue lips.

"He's stable right now. We're doing everything we can for your friend."

"He's my fiancé," I said, running my fingers through Ian's curls.

"Oh. Very cool. Congratulations."

Ian's eyes opened slightly. His blue eyes, which were usually filled with brightness and shine, were dull and almost lifeless. The thought nearly killed me.

I knew what he wanted to say. I could see it in his eyes. "Baby, don't say anything. I already know. Just save your strength."

He squeezed my hand as a tear escaped the corner of his eye. He tried to speak beneath the oxygen mask, but I didn't want him making the effort. I knew everything he could possibly want to tell me.

"Shh . . . I know. I love you too. But you're not going to leave me. Do you hear me? You are not leaving me after everything we've been through." My voice cracked, and I cleared my throat. "I need you here with me. I can't do this alone. So, you fight. Okay, baby? I'm begging you, please fight." I wiped at the tears streaming down my face. "Because I'll die. If you—I'll just die."

I reached up, wiping the tears from his temple as he closed his eyes. Lifting Ian's hand to my lips, I kissed his knuckles.

Please, God. I beg you, help Ian through this. He has to make it. Please. I can't live without him. Please don't take him from me. I'm not ready. The time we've had together hasn't been enough. Please. I need more time with him. If you have to take someone, take me instead.

Chapter 47

Jake

Fucking surgery.

They had taken Ian to surgery to check the extent of the damage the knife had caused. In other words, if any major organs had been affected by the knife, he'd more than likely be a goner.

Fuck.

And if Ian died, I would grab the nearest sharp object and off myself. He was the only good thing in my life. Without him, my life would be meaningless.

Once they wheeled him away, I found the closest garbage can and threw up. My weak-ass stomach couldn't handle this shit. I ignored the stares as I pulled out my phone. Only, it wasn't mine. It was Ian's. I had placed it in my pocket after the police had come. Passing my fingers over it, a picture of the two of us popped up on the lock screen. It was a recent photo of us in bed, smiling at the camera, Ian's curly hair in disarray. We had just finished making love, our new tattoos visible. I would give anything to go back to that moment.

I wiped the tears from my face, sniffling as I put the phone back in my pocket and pulled out mine. Another picture of Ian. This one was only him, a snapshot I had taken of him on our official date. He looked so happy. And beautiful.

Fuck.

I wiped at my face again as I searched for Anna's phone number. Ian would want her to be here, and she would want to know as well. She was his best friend, after all.

"Hello?" she answered. From her voice, I could tell she was already aware that something wasn't right.

"Anna—" My voice cracked, sounding rough to my ears.

"Jake? What is it? What's wrong?"

I tried to speak but couldn't get the words out.

"Are you all right?" Anna persisted. "Talk to me, Jake. What happened? Is it Ian?"

I cleared my throat, steadying it as I spoke. "Yeah. Um, he's hurt. Bad."

She gasped on the other end of the line. "Where are you?"

"Hospital. He's in surgery."

"Oh, God, okay. Anthony and I are on our way. Okay? We'll be there as soon as we can. Just hang tight."

"Okay."

After ending the call, I dragged myself over to the chairs against the wall and collapsed. I should've called Ian's parents, but I couldn't. Not yet. This would devastate them.

My hands shook as I put my phone away. It was cold. I wrapped my arms around myself, rocking back and forth to generate some heat. My mind drifted to a time in our bed where it was warm, where we made heat together.

And just like that, my mind was back to the present, in this icy-cold hospital, all alone with my heart lodged in my throat. Feeling like I would puke again.

My future was unknown.

* * *

"Jake," Anna called, Anthony right beside her.

I was unaware of how much time had passed. The concerned expression on Anna's face was enough to make me tear up again. It was obvious she had been crying; her eyes were red rimmed. The relationship she had with Ian made me feel closer to her, almost like being with her was like being with him.

Weird, but I'd take it.

Throwing myself into her arms, I fucking let it out—the anguish I'd been feeling, the frustration, the fear. She cried with me as Anthony wrapped his arms around us.

After a few minutes, Anna pulled back, wiping at her eyes as I did the same. "Tell me exactly what happened."

I cleared my throat. "Tonight was the first LGBTQ+ support group meeting."

"I know. Ian told me about it."

"It went great. Ian was amazing, as usual. You would've been proud. But as we were leaving, Donald, Andrew, and two other guys showed up."

"Who are Donald and Andrew?"

"They were members of the choir. Ian kicked them off for disrespecting him after he came out at the church."

"I see. Why were they at the church tonight?"

"They, uh—they had a police baton. They threatened us. Ian had been receiving threatening emails. He got Donald to admit it was him. Words were exchanged . . . I can't remember what exactly, but he called us the F word. That is one word I've never tolerated, so I punched him. I fought him until one of the other guys hit me with the baton. They knocked the wind out of me, once on my back, then again in my stomach. They restrained me. Another guy had Ian in a headlock. Ian pleaded with him to let me go. He promised to quit the church, but Donald said it was too late. And that's when he took out a knife."

Anna gasped, bringing her hands to her mouth. "Stabbed? Ian got stabbed?"

I squeezed my eyes shut, blocking out the image of Ian's face as he lay bleeding. "He managed to slip out of the guy's hold, but instead of running away, he tried to help me. And that's when Donald stabbed him."

"Where? Jake, where did he get stabbed?"

I showed her on my stomach. "Right here."

She swayed and Anthony caught her. "Love, are you all right? Come, let's sit down," her husband said.

"No, I'm fine."

Anthony placed a hand on her swollen belly. "But the baby—"

"The baby is fine. I'll sit in a minute." She glanced back up at me. "The surgery is to see the extent of the damage. To see what organs were involved."

I nodded. "And to repair them. If they can."

Her chin quivered as her face twisted. "Have you called his parents?"

I shook my head. "No, I—uh, I can't. I mean—"

"I'll call them," Anthony said.

Anna let out a sigh of relief. "Thank you, baby. Here." She took out her phone and handed it to him. "His mom's number is in my contacts."

He nodded and kissed the top of her head. "I'll be right over there if you need me. Just sit."

"I will."

I followed her to the chairs. "I'm sorry. This is all my fault. I should have protected him better."

"No. Nobody protects Ian better than you. This wasn't your fault."

"I should have taken hold of that stick sooner. I should have fought harder."

"Don't do that to yourself. You were outnumbered. If you would have done anything different, you could've been stabbed."

"Good. I should've been. It should be me in there."

"You men, I swear." She placed her hand on my knee and smiled. "I remember when I got shot, Anthony said the same thing—that he wished it would have been him instead of me. It's the love you guys have for us. But you know what? I was glad it was me and not him. And I bet Ian would feel the same way."

"Yeah, but you wish it were me. Don't you?"

"Jake, don't. Okay? We may have had our differences, but you have done a lot to prove your love for Ian. And he loves you, so that means I love you too. I don't want either of you to be hurt."

"Sorry. I just—" I covered my face with my hands. "Anna, I can't live without him. If he doesn't make it, I'll kill myself."

"Jake, don't say that!"

"It's true. I have nothing without him."

"You have me. And Anthony. What do you think Ian would do if he heard you say that?"

"I know he wouldn't like it, but—Anna—"

She wrapped her arms around me as I let it out again. "Let's try to think positively, okay? We have to have faith that he's going to make it."

"He has to."

"I know. He will."

Ant came back and sat next to Anna. "Ian's parents are on their way."

"Thank you for calling them."

"No problem."

We sat for hours, it seemed. Ant grabbed coffee for himself and tea for Anna. I refused everything that was offered to me.

Ian's parents showed up and immediately hugged me. They had been so happy and accepting of me when Ian told them we were engaged, so supportive. The way parents should be.

I gave them the gist of what happened at the church. It was a hate crime, which the police were aware of. His mom was, as expected, distraught and crying.

"How can people be so cruel? My son only wants to help people."

Ian's dad hugged her, trying to calm her down.

"I'm so sorry, Mr. and Mrs. Cooper. I should have protected him better."

"Oh, Jake. This wasn't your fault. We know you love Ian and would do everything in your power to protect him. He loves you so much, and so do we."

I nodded. "I love you guys too."

"All we can do now is pray. I have faith God will protect our son."

They went to the chapel to pray, leaving Anna, Ant, and me waiting for any news.

"Jake, have you been checked by a doctor?" Anna asked.

"No, why? I'm fine."

"You don't look fine. You're pale, and I can tell you're in pain because you keep rubbing your stomach."

"Well, yeah, those motherfuckers hit me with a goddamn police stick. Fucking cowards couldn't use their fists like real men. And if I'm pale, it's because I'm worried sick that my fiancé is gonna die."

She squeezed my hand. "You were throwing up when we got here. You could have internal injuries."

I shook my head. "I have a weak stomach. I always throw up when I'm upset. Been like that my whole life."

"Okay, but just to be safe, please—I don't want to have to tell Ian that the man he loves died because he was too stubborn to get checked out."

My eyes snapped to hers. She had a point, even though I was sure nothing was wrong with me except fear. "Okay. I will as soon as I know he's okay."

"Jake—"

"Ian Cooper," a surgeon called out.

A rocket shot out from under my ass. I had never stood up so fast. I stared wide-eyed, scared to death as the doctor walked over to us. His expression was hard to read. Thank God Anna and Ant were here because I couldn't speak.

"Are you Ian Cooper's loved ones?" the surgeon asked.

"Yes," Anna answered, holding on to my hand. "How is he?"

"He made it through surgery."

"Oh, thank God!" Anna and Anthony said.

I exhaled and fell to my knees, hugging the doctor's legs. "Thank you so much, Doc."

Hands pried me up. "Jake, stand up. The doctor has more to say," Anna said, giggling.

"Sorry." I wiped the tears of joy from my face. "I'm just so relieved. You did say he's alive, right?"

The surgeon chuckled. "That's quite all right. Yes, Ian is alive. He did suffer a laceration to his liver, but it was minor and we were able to repair it. All other organs are intact. He lost a lot of blood, so we had to give him a blood transfusion. We will continue to monitor him, but I expect him to make a full recovery. He is incredibly lucky."

I threw my arms around the man, again. "Thank you so much. You have no idea what this means. I will forever be grateful to you."

He patted my back. "I was just doing my job, but you're very welcome."

I pulled back and turned to Anna, throwing myself into her arms. Then I did the same with Ant.

"I'll go tell Ian's parents," Ant said.

"Thanks, Ant."

"Um, Doctor, do you think someone can see Jake? He suffered a blow to his abdomen, and he's been vomiting. I just want to make sure there are no internal injuries."

"Oh yes, of course."

"You promised, Jake," she said.

I nodded. My man was going to be okay. I'd do anything anyone wanted right now, I was so happy.

"When can I see him?" I asked the doctor.

"Well, they're prepping him to take him to recovery. By the time you're checked out, he should be ready to be seen, but keep in mind that it'll take a while for him to wake up."

"How long?"

"Everyone reacts differently. It could be a few hours or a few days. His body went through trauma, so he needs time to recover."

"But he will wake up, right?"

"Yes, that's what we expect."

"Then that's all that matters."

Chapter 48

Jake

After going through the wringer of tests and shit, I waited impatiently for the doctor to come in to tell me if I was dying or not.

"What the fuck is taking so long?" I asked Anna, who kindly sat with me while they poked and prodded me, even though I told her she didn't have to. She probably wanted to make sure I went through with it.

"Hopefully it won't take too much longer."

"I want to see my fiancé."

"I know, but Anthony texted me saying they just brought him to his room. His parents are with him now."

"Good. I don't want him to be alone when he wakes up."

There was a knock on the door, and the doctor entered.

Fuck me. "Just what I fucking needed," I murmured.

Matt looked up from the tablet he was holding, and his eyes widened. "Jake?" He glanced back down at the chart. "It didn't even register with me that it was you I'd be seeing."

"Lucky me."

He looked at Anna. "Hi, Anna."

"Hi, Matt. It's good to see you," she said as she kissed him on the cheek.

"You look beautiful. How much longer till the due date?"

"About six weeks."

"Oh, wow."

"Hey, can we get on with this? I have somewhere to be."

Matt sighed. "Let's see here—it says you were hit in the stomach by a baton?"

"Yeah. So, give it to me straight. Am I gonna live?"

"Yes, Jake, you're going to live. Other than dehydration and low blood pressure, you're fine."

I hopped off the table. "Thanks. Bye."

"Hold on. What exactly happened? Was Ian with you?"

Of course he had to ask about Ian. He was probably hoping Ian was the one who hit me. "What, you didn't hear? Don't you work here?"

He pressed the corners of his lips together. "I don't get notified of every admission. Plus, I haven't worked the ER in the last couple of nights. What happened?"

Anna placed her hand on my arm. "Jake and Ian were attacked. Ian got stabbed."

The guy's mouth gaped open. "Oh my God. Is he . . . ?"

"He's fine," I answered.

He closed his eyes, letting out a deep breath. "Thank God."

"His liver was lacerated slightly, but they were able to repair it," Anna said. "He's in recovery now."

"What a relief."

"Am I free to go to my fiancé now?"

"Fiancé?"

I may or may not have called Ian my fiancé on purpose. "That's right. I asked Ian to marry me, and he said yes."

"Wow. Congratulations."

"Thanks. So can I go?"

He nodded. "Just make sure you get fluids in you as soon as possible. And eat something."

"Will do."

As I moved to leave, he grabbed my arm. "Regardless of what you might think, I *am* happy for the both of you. Believe it or not, I was rooting for you. All I ever wanted was for Ian to be happy."

Something about his tone and the look in his eyes told me he was being sincere. Ian would want me to be nice to the guy. I sighed as I extended my hand out to him. "Thank you. It's my life's mission to make him as happy as he makes me. And I'll spend the rest of my days making up for lost time."

He nodded as he shook my hand. "That's the kind of love I hope to find one day. Ian is lucky to have you."

Out in the hall, I raced to find Ian's room.

"Jake, slow down. Pregnant woman here, remember?" Anna laughed behind me. "Are you going to get something to drink and eat before you see Ian?"

"No. I need to see him first. I will after, promise."

She grabbed my arm, stopping me. "Okay, listen. You go ahead to his room. I will find Anthony, and we'll bring you a drink and maybe some food."

"Are you sure?"

"You need to be with him. Go. I'll meet up with you in a little while."

I took her face in my hands and kissed her on the cheek. "Thank you, Anna." I turned, taking off in a sprint.

After many wrong turns and stopping for directions at least twice, I finally stood in front of Ian's room. Taking a few deep breaths, I pulled on the latch and walked inside. Ian's parents were standing by the bed. His mom seemed to be crying.

She wiped at her eyes when she saw me. "Jake, come in."

My stomach churned at the sight of Ian lying in that hospital bed. After taking a step closer, I could see how pale he was. His lips were missing their pink color. If it weren't for the steady beep of the heart monitor, I'd have thought he was dead. The thought had me running to the small trash can to hurl once again, but all I managed was dry heaves. There was nothing left in my stomach.

Ian's mother came over to me and rubbed my back. "Jake, are you all right? What did the doctor say?"

When I was done gagging nothing but air, I straightened. "I'm fine, Mrs. Cooper. The doctor just said I was a little dehydrated, but Anna is bringing some fluids."

"I'm sure the nurse can bring you something."

"It's fine," I said, rushing over to Ian's bedside. "Why does he look like this?"

"Oh, sweetie, he lost a lot of blood and just got out of surgery. His color will return soon."

I extended my hand, reaching out to him, but hesitated. "Can I touch him?"

"Of course. The nurse said we can. You should also talk to him. Maybe hearing your voice will wake him up."

My fingers shook as I touched his hair, then rested my palm on his head. Leaning forward, I whispered, "Baby, it's me, Jake. I'm here, waiting for you to wake up. I'm not going anywhere."

The door opened behind me, but I didn't bother taking my eyes off Ian. Ian's parents greeted Anna and Ant, then Anna came and stood beside me. She placed her hand on Ian's leg as she slipped an arm through mine. "He'll wake up soon. Just keep talking to him. He'll come back to the sound of your voice."

I nodded as I brushed away the tear that had slipped from my eye.

"I brought you a couple of bottles of water and a juice. And a sandwich. It's the best I could do."

"Thanks."

"Anthony and I are going to leave. Do you want me to get anything for you? I could stop by the house. Maybe a change of clothes? For you and Ian?"

"Um, yeah, I'd appreciate that. Ian will need clean clothes to wear when we go home."

"And you, too, right?"

I shrugged. "I guess." I dug into my pocket and pulled out my keys. "Here, this one is the house key."

She smiled as she took the keys. Leaning over Ian, she said, "Ian, it's Anna. Anthony and I are going to say good night, but we'll be back tomorrow. I love you." She gave him a kiss on his cheek.

Ant came over, placing his hand on Ian's shoulder. "Hey, Ian, it's Ant. I'll see you tomorrow. I'm praying that you'll wake up soon. Good night."

"Remember to drink and eat," Anna said as she gave me a hug.

"I will. Thanks for everything."

"We'll see you tomorrow."

After Anna and Ant left, Ian's mom said, "Well, we're leaving as well. We'll be back in the morning."

"Okay." I hugged them both.

"Try to get some rest."

I nodded. And just like that, I was all alone with Ian.

After pulling up a chair close to the side of the bed, I held his hand. "It's just you and me, babe." I kissed his knuckles. "Baby, please wake up. I love you so much. I want to see your gorgeous blue eyes. I need to see that you're really okay."

I stood, leaning over him, and I lightly brushed my lips against his. Then I straightened and grabbed one of the bottled waters Anna got for me. I downed it in four gulps. I drank the second bottle more slowly.

The nurse came in, letting me know that there was a built-in guest bed by the window if I wanted to spend the night. But it was too far away from Ian. I wanted to be near him so that when he opened his eyes, he would see me.

Lowering the safety railing on the left side of the bed, I carefully moved Ian's hand, resting it on his stomach. Then, making sure no wires were in the way, I climbed into the small space, curling up next to him on the bed. I buried my face in his neck as I draped my arm over him. "Good night, baby. I love you."

I kept my eyes on his chest as it moved up and down. My lids got heavier as the sound of the heart monitor lulled me closer to sleep, until eventually, I couldn't fight it anymore and dozed off.

Chapter 49

Matt

I couldn't get the image out of my head.

Before leaving the hospital, I had stopped by Ian's room. What I had walked in on was the sweetest thing: Jake had gotten into bed with Ian and cuddled up to him. They were both sleeping.

Well, as far as I knew, Ian hadn't awakened since surgery, and that was somewhat concerning. I had asked the nurse to page me as soon as he opened his eyes.

But Ian and Jake were the real deal. Something I was starting to believe wasn't in the cards for me.

I wanted to erase the last couple of days, beginning with CJ's rejection. I still didn't know what the fuck that was about, but whatever. He had texted me and left voice messages, but I hadn't bothered to check. One, I was too busy, and two, it didn't matter. It wasn't like we were dating. I'd said it a million times before and I'd say it again: we were just fucking. Nothing more.

Then why couldn't I stop thinking about it?

As I sat on the couch, stiff drink in hand, I reached into my pocket and retrieved my phone. Just out of curiosity, I read the texts.

I'm sorry. Let me explain.

I called, but you didn't pick up.

You're ignoring me. I get it.

Please answer me.

Fine. I'm coming over.

Fuck.

Right on cue, there was a knock on the door. I thought about ignoring it, but if it really wasn't a big deal—which it wasn't—I should give the guy a break. But not without making him squirm a little first.

I got up, put my drink on the counter, and took my time answering.

CJ stood there with a sheepish look on his face. "Matt, I—"

"I'm sorry, do I know you? You must have my apartment confused with someone else's."

"Okay. I deserved that. May I come in so I can explain?"

I turned, letting him follow me inside. "You don't have to explain anything. It's not like we're a couple or anything."

"True, but I still want to explain. I feel like I need to."

I crossed my arms over my chest. "Fine. If it'll make you feel better. I'm listening."

"I volunteer at the church, giving Communion. We go to the hospital weekly to give to the sick. Nobody at the church knows about my lifestyle, and I want to keep it that way, so when you called out my name at the hospital, I panicked. I didn't want any of my colleagues asking questions about who you were. I'm sorry."

"Why couldn't you just tell me that? I would've been prepared and not bothered approaching you, had I known there was a possibility of running into you at the hospital."

"I didn't know how you'd react to me working at a church. Like you said, we're not a couple. I had no idea if it'd be a major turnoff or what. I mean, that's not exactly a selling point in the dating app bio."

I rubbed my face. "Okay, true about the bio, but I thought we were past the selling point."

He came closer. "We are. I'm sorry. I just really like you and didn't want to freak you out."

"You freaked me out more by acting like you didn't know me."

"Sorry. Let me make it up to you." He kissed my neck.

I tilted my head, allowing him better access. "I don't think I can. I'm so beat."

"You don't have to do anything."

I wanted to ask him if he knew Ian and about the stabbing, but I couldn't because of HIPAA rules. "CJ?"

"Hmm?"

"I really like you too."

He lifted his head and smiled. "Good. Now that we've established that, let me fuck you."

I put my hands out, stopping him from kissing me. "Just so you know, I would never out you or anyone. Ever."

"Thank you. I believe you."

"And I know we're just having fun here. No strings, just hooking up, whatever you want to call it. But there is one thing I can't stand, and that's being lied to. Whether we're dating or just fucking."

He nodded. "I understand. I'm not lying about giving Communion."

"I know. But there is one thing I need to know before we can continue this. And please be honest."

He swallowed. "Okay. Shoot."

"Are you a priest?"

His eyebrows shot up and he laughed. "What? Hell no, I'm not a priest. Why would you think that?"

"Because of the collar thing you were wearing."

"It's just part of the uniform. I swear I'm not a priest."

Good enough. "Okay, then. Take off your clothes. Tonight, I'm fucking you."

Chapter 50

Jake

I woke with a start. A nurse was in the room checking the monitors. "Good morning. Sleep well?"

She was obviously referring to me sleeping on the bed with Ian. I slid off and glanced at Ian's face. Still asleep.

"Why hasn't he woken up yet?"

"Some patients take longer than others. His vitals look good. He'll probably wake up soon."

"When's his doctor coming to check on him? I want him to look him over."

She nodded. "The doctor will make his rounds soon. I'll let him know you wish to speak with him."

"Thanks."

As the nurse left, someone else entered. "Hello, pardon me. I hope I'm not interrupting."

I glanced over my shoulder. It was the priest from last night, the one who may have saved Ian's life. "Father, please come in."

"Do you remember me? I was there last night."

"Of course. You called 9-1-1."

"That's right. I wanted to come down to see how the patient was doing and, well, to introduce myself. I'm Father Drew. I'm the new priest at St. Pius."

So he was the one taking over for Father Jackass. Bypassing the priest's outstretched hand, I threw my arms around him instead. "Thank you, Father. Thank you so much for hearing my cry for help. For coming when you did. For making the 9-1-1 call. You saved my fiancé's life. I don't know what we would've done if you hadn't shown up when you did."

He rubbed my back. "Oh, there now. God was sure to place me there at the right time and place. I'm glad I could help."

I pulled away, wiping my face. "He still hasn't woken up from surgery, but he's going to be all right."

"Thank God. You said he's your fiancé?"

"Yeah. You'll be working with him. His name is Ian Cooper. He's the music director at St. Pius."

"Ah, yes. I've heard great things about him. And you are?"

"Oh, I'm sorry, I'm Jake Edwards. I'm part of the choir and band."

"I'm sorry we met under these circumstances. I hear Ian is striving to make positive changes at St. Pius."

"Yes, he is. I'm proud of him."

"As you should be."

"Listen, Father, Ian had an issue with the previous priest. Is he going to have any problems with you?"

"I heard about that. I can assure you, there will be no such issues with me. I'm excited for the changes Ian is making. St. Pius is becoming quite the progressive church of acceptance, and I'm all for it. I'm aware last night was the first LGBTQ+ meeting and that the attack was part of some hateful crime. It angers me that such violence still exists. You and Ian can count on my full support."

"Thank you so much, Father. That means a lot. I know it'll mean a lot to Ian as well.”

“You’re very welcome. I hope Ian wakes up soon so I can meet him formally and we can talk.”

“Me too, Father. Me too.”

As Father Drew was leaving, Anna and Ant arrived. “Oh, sorry. We didn’t realize you had company.”

“Oh no, that’s quite all right. I was just leaving,” Father Drew said.

“Guys, this is Father Drew. He’s the new priest at St. Pius. He’s the one who called 9-1-1 last night.”

Anna gasped as she threw her arms around the priest. “Thank you so much, Father.” As she pulled away, she said, “Ian is my best friend, and I will forever be grateful to you.”

“God put me there. I’m glad I could help.”

“I’m Anna Martin. This is my husband, Anthony.”

Ant extended a hand to the priest. “Nice to meet you, Father. God bless you for helping our friends.”

“Please don’t mention it. I just did what any good Christian would have done. Anthony Martin? The name sounds familiar. Do I know you from somewhere?”

Ant smiled. “Not personally, I don’t think. I used to be a priest at St. Pius. I believe you’re my official replacement.”

It took a moment for Father Drew to put the pieces together. “Oh, dear, that’s right. I remember now. I was intrigued by your story. How are you both?”

“We are great, actually. Preparing for this little one to arrive soon,” Ant answered as he rubbed on Anna’s baby bump.

“Wonderful. Well, you’ve left me with big shoes to fill. I hope I’m able to do as good a job as you did.”

“I’m sure you will. You’re off to a good start.”

We all laughed.

“Well, I must go. So good to meet all of you.”

“You too, Father.”

After he left, Anna went to Ian. "He still hasn't woken up?"

"No, the nurse said he should wake up soon. I told her I want the doctor to look him over."

"Okay, well, I brought your guitar. I was thinking maybe hearing you play will stir him awake."

"That's a good idea."

"Also, in that bag, there's a change of clothes for you and Ian, along with a bunch of toiletries. I think I was able to figure out whose clothes were whose. But the bathroom stuff, forget it, so I just brought everything."

"Thanks, Anna. I'm sure it's fine."

"Here," she said, handing me a coffee cup and a paper bag. "This is for you. You need to eat."

I ate the breakfast sandwich as we hung out for a bit longer. When I finished the last of the coffee, I took out my guitar from its case and made myself comfortable on the chair next to Ian.

"Let's see if this works." And I played our song.

Chapter 51
Jake

Three songs later, and Ian still hadn't opened his eyes. I was losing hope. Everyone kept saying he was fine and he would wake up soon, but I was starting to think he'd slipped into a coma or something.

Frustrated, I walked over to the window ledge and sat. Tears filled my eyes as I glanced through the glass. I was lost at what else to do, so I prayed.

My head whipped back to Ian. Did he just moan?

Fuck. Now I was hearing things.

I threw my head back against the wall and closed my eyes.

"Baby?"

My head shot to Ian again. The word was mumbled, but I definitely heard it. "Ian?" I said cautiously.

"Why—why'd you stop playing?"

I flew off the window ledge, bolting to Ian's side like a missile. "You're awake!" I caressed his face and hair.

"Mmm."

He was groggy. "You had me so worried. I should call someone to check you out."

As I reached for the call button, Ian stopped me. "Wait."

"What is it?"

He lifted a hand to my cheek. "You're okay?"

I smiled. "Yeah, babe. I'm perfect, now that you're awake."

His beautiful blue eyes, still dull from the trauma, filled with tears. "I was so scared I would never see you again."

I turned my face into his palm, kissing it. "Me too."

"I'm so sorry. I should have taken the threats more seriously."

"No. This isn't your fault. You did everything you could do. You went to the police. They're the ones who failed you."

"I should have stayed fired."

"No, baby. I'm so proud of you for sticking to what you love and believe in. I'm the one who should have protected you better."

"How?"

"I could have fought harder."

Ian shook his head. "No, no. Donald would have stabbed you instead. Then I really would have died. If anything happened to you—I would just—" Tears flowed down his face.

I wrapped my arms around him and wept right along with him. "Aw, baby. Don't think about that. We're both alive. God, I love you so much."

"I love you too. Jake, please don't ever let go of me."

"Never. I got you, baby boy. Always and forever."

* * *

Ian

The right side of my stomach burned, but I'd refused the drugs offered. And I was so tired, but I didn't want to go to sleep.

As the doctor looked me over, I kept my eyes on Jake. Never wanted to stop looking at him. He hadn't gotten much sleep; the dark circles under his eyes gave that away. I hated that I'd put him through such a scare. Heck, I'd put myself through a scare; thought I was going to die. I was so lucky and blessed. Never again would I take my life for granted. Every moment with Jake would be even more appreciated than before.

"So, Doc, how is he? Is my man going to be okay?" Jake asked the doctor.

"Yes, everything looks great. Like I said before, some patients take a little longer to wake up from surgery due to how they take to the anesthesia and the medications given while under. But it's nothing to worry about. He's awake now and seems to be doing fine. We'll keep him one more night for observation, just to make sure there are no adverse effects. If he continues to show improvement, he can go home tomorrow."

Jake smiled as he leaned over me, running his fingers through my hair. "Did you hear that, babe? We'll be able to go home tomorrow."

I nodded, smiling as well. "Yes. Can't wait. Thanks so much for everything, Doctor."

"No problem. You get some rest."

As the doctor left, the nurse came in. "You have a visitor out in the hall. Should I let him in?"

"Him?" Jake asked in that territorial voice of his. "Who is it?"

"I didn't ask. Would you like me to find out?"

"Yes."

I grabbed his arm. "No," I told the nurse. "That's not necessary. Please send him in."

As the nurse headed back out, Jake turned to me. "You can't just let anyone in here. What if—"

"Babe, stop worrying. I'm sure it's no one bad."

"You can't know that."

Someone cleared their throat. "I hope I'm not interrupting."

Jake and I raised our heads. Agent Carter. I looked up at Jake and gave him the I-told-you-so look. "Not at all. Please come in."

"You guys taking turns being in the hospital or what?" he chuckled.

I glanced at Jake as he narrowed his eyes.

Luke's laughter faded when he realized he was the only one laughing. "Sorry. Bad joke."

"Yeah, you seem to be full of those," Jake said.

"So I got a dry sense of humor. Sue me." He came closer. "Anyway, I'm here to give you an update on your father's case. But first, how are you doing, Ian?"

"I'm good, thanks. Feeling very lucky."

He nodded. "Good. Glad to hear it." He looked around and gestured to the chair in the corner of the room. "Shall we sit?"

We nodded and Jake grabbed a chair, sitting next to me as Luke pulled the other chair close to the end of the bed.

"Well, it looks like your story checked out. Your old man is ass deep in some illegal drug shit." He paused and smirked. "Uh, excuse the pun."

Yeah, Matt's brother was nothing like Matt.

Jake rolled his eyes. "So, what the fuck are you going to do about it?" He was clearly losing patience with the guy.

"The investigation is still ongoing."

"What does that mean?"

"It means we are gathering as much proof as we can to take him down."

"How much more proof do you need?"

"It turns out, the more we dig, the more we discover."

Jake let out an exasperated sigh. "Get to the fucking point. What aren't you telling me?"

"Jake, your father isn't working alone."

"Who else is involved?"

"Miranda Sullivan."

Dead silence. Jake looked at me, then back at Luke. "Miranda is helping my dad? How?"

"Her salon is a front to launder money. I shit you not."

Jake shook his head. "I can't believe this. She was bluffing. All that time she threatened to expose my dad, she was—" He turned to me. "Five months. I lost five months with you because of that bitch."

I reached for his hand. "Baby, it's okay."

He bolted to his feet. "No, it's not okay. I'll never forget the look on your face the day you thought I betrayed you. The day I *did* betray you."

"You didn't know. You were protecting your father."

"And he didn't deserve my protection."

"You had no way of knowing that. Besides, you thought my dad was involved. You were protecting us."

He sat again, leaning over the bed as he took my hands. "I'm so sorry."

"It's okay. We're together now. That's what matters."

Luke cleared his throat. "Don't mean to interrupt this Hallmark moment, but there's more."

Jake snapped his head to face him. "More?"

"We have reason to believe your father's connections extend to the men who attacked Ian."

"What the fuck are you saying?"

"I'm saying we are investigating William Edwards involvement with Ian's attackers."

"Did my father give the order to hurt Ian?" Jake's voice was cold and deadly.

"No," I said. That couldn't be true. I had to diffuse this situation before Jake did something crazy. "That's not what you're saying. Right, Agent Carter?"

"I'm not gonna lie—it's a possibility. We're just checking all the boxes."

Jake shook as he rose, gripping the bedsheet. "I'm going to fucking kill him."

"I'm sorry? Did you just—"

"No. He didn't." I said, putting my hand out so Luke would give me a chance to calm Jake down. "Baby, we don't know if your father did this." I reached up, squeezing his shoulder. "Please calm down. Let DEA handle this. I can't lose you. Please."

His eyes met mine, then he nodded and kissed my forehead. "I'm sorry. I'm not going anywhere." He turned to Luke. "I want you to get to the bottom of this and punish all those involved to the fullest extent of the law. Do you hear me?"

Luke stood. "Loud and clear. Trust me, everyone mixed up in this shitshow will pay. I promise you that." He looked past Jake. "Ian, I hope you have a speedy recovery. I'll keep you two posted."

After he left, Jake came over to me again and sat. He didn't have to say anything for me to know what he was thinking. He felt guilty and responsible for his father's actions. "Baby," I whispered as I reached for his hand. There were unshed tears in his eyes. "You know I love you, right?"

He squeezed his eyes shut and shook his head. "How could you after—"

"You are not responsible for your father's actions. I don't blame you for any of it. I've loved you since we were twelve. Nothing is going to change that."

"Why do you still love me? After everything I've put you through?"

"Because you protect me. Because you have always been there for me. Because I know your heart better than anyone. And honestly, because you're sexy AF."

He smirked and leaned closer, caressing my cheek as he rested his forehead on mine. "I love you more than my own life. Thank you for believing in me."

"Of course. You are my world, Jake. I'm sorry I ever doubted you."

After a few minutes of holding each other, Jake pulled back and kissed me. "What are you thinking about?"

I hesitated. Just like I knew what he was thinking, he knew when there was something on my mind. "I'm thinking about your mother."

He scoffed. "Why the fuck for?"

"Aren't you the least bit concerned for what she's going to go through when your father gets arrested?"

"Not really. And I'm sure I'm the last person she wants sympathy from."

"That isn't true."

"Well, she's the last person I want to support."

"Baby, she's your mother."

"She made her feelings for me clear when she refused to accept who I am—and when she raised her hand to you."

"I love that you love me with such intensity, but it didn't even hurt that bad. Hey, at least she didn't stab me."

He narrowed his eyes. "That's not funny."

I smiled, pulling him down to me. "I'm sorry. I just don't want to be the reason you don't fix things with your mom."

"You're not the only reason. And you know that."

I sighed. "I'm so sorry she hurt you."

He wrapped his arms around me, burying his face in my neck. "You're all I need."

"And I'm here for you. Forever."

After a moment, Jake sniffled as he leaned back and wiped at his eyes. "Let's get married as soon as possible. As soon as you're better."

"Really?"

"Yeah. I don't want to waste any more time. Almost losing you made me realize life is too short. I want us to be husbands—like, right now."

"But we need some time to plan it all out. Like, where and when. And then there are the invitations and the food and—"

"We have people that can help us. Anna and Ant, your parents—I'm sure they'd love to help."

My stomach fluttered with excitement at the thought of Jake as my husband. My smile widened. "Okay."

"Yeah?"

I nodded. "Yeah."

Jake grinned. "I'm going to be the best husband to you. I promise."

"Baby, you already are so good to me. I hope I make you just as happy."

"You do. I've never been happier."

And he genuinely seemed happier. "Can I ask you something?"

"Of course."

"How do you feel about kids? I mean, we've never talked about it. And with Anna giving birth soon, it just got me thinking."

"I don't know. I never really thought about it. Do you want kids?"

"Maybe. I love kids."

"Then we'll have them."

"Really?"

"If having kids will make you happy, then fuck yes. As many as you want."

I laughed. "But do *you* want kids?"

"Babe, I'm around kids every day at school and at the guitar shop. They're great. I just never thought of having my own. I would love to have kids with you someday."

"Someday?"

He smiled as he ran a finger along my jaw. "I want you all to myself for a while."

I sucked in my bottom lip between my teeth. "You know the process to adopt is a long one, right?"

"Honestly, I don't really know how it all works."

"Me either, but I do know it can take a long time."

"We'll have to do research, then."

"Definitely." I yawned. "And there are other options, like surrogacy, but I'm sure it's more expensive." My eyes were getting heavy.

"We'll figure it out." He kissed my forehead. "For now, get some rest."

I yawned again. "Will you be here when I wake up?"

"What kind of question is that? Of course I'll be here."

"Can you play your guitar for me?"

"Absolutely. What would you like to hear?"

"Our song."

Chapter 52

Matt

Never thought I'd be here again.

At church.

This is what my life had come down to: spying on a guy who wasn't even at the very least a boyfriend because he'd pretended not to know me. He'd sworn he wasn't a priest, but he'd been wearing the whole priest getup. Well, not exactly, but he'd had the white-collar thing and he'd been in the chapel. Kinda looked like a priest to me. But since he wouldn't elaborate and I had caught him in a lie, I'd succumbed to stalker status.

If he wasn't a priest, why the secrecy? We weren't official, but I liked the guy. I wanted to keep seeing and fucking him, but not if he couldn't be honest. And definitely not if he had some secret life as a priest. I wasn't religious, but I had to draw the line somewhere. I was in enough hot water with the big guy upstairs. I didn't need fucking one of His chosen ones added to the mix.

And if I was just being paranoid, then I could slip out before he even discovered I was here, and we could continue fucking like I wasn't an insecure, untrusting asshole.

Walking inside was easier than the first time. I didn't stall; I just walked right in. I hesitated in the atrium this time, but then realized I'd forgotten to grab one of those pamphlets the man was handing out. It might come in handy for locating CJ's name.

I backtracked to the guy. "Excuse me. Can I grab one of those?"

"Oh, sure." He handed me one. "Here you go, sir."

"Thanks."

I glanced at it. No CJ Miller listed anywhere. That was good, but—*Chester J. Miller* was listed as the deacon.

What the fuck was a deacon? Was that another word for a priest?

I was jumping ahead of myself. CJ never told me what his initials stood for, and I never asked. It could be a coincidence.

Taking a deep breath, I continued into the main church part and sat in the very last row, toward the right. I didn't want to be seen until I made sense of all this.

Ian was at the organ playing soothing music, and the church was filling up quickly. Thankfully, a few people sat in my row, so that would help camouflage me. I didn't know how I would explain to Ian why I was here.

The music stopped, and Ian walked down the aisle toward the atrium to meet with the choir. I turned my head away, pretending to read the pamphlet so he wouldn't see me. A few minutes later, he went back to the organ, and Mass began.

I stood along with everyone else as the music sprang to life, Ian's voice leading the singing. I did not sing. My stomach was in knots as the procession started down the aisle. First, the choir. I saw Jake, but luckily, he didn't see me. Next, some kids—altar servers, I guess, were what they were called. Then some other people followed. Then—

There he was.

He was holding a red-and-gold book high above his head. He had on robes, but they were different from those of the guy who followed behind him. I recognized him from the last time I came; Ian had introduced him to me. I didn't remember his name, but he was the priest.

After they all made it to the altar, the music died down and the priest began speaking. Eventually, we got to sit. I paid no attention to the words spoken. I stood when it was time to stand and sat when it was time to sit, all the while keeping my eyes on CJ.

Then he spoke. He stood at the pulpit and read the gospel. Afterward, he spoke some more. I didn't recognize him. He was different, not the CJ I knew. It was weird watching him speak about godly things, considering all the things we'd done. The mouth that had done unspeakable, ungodlike things to my cock and ass also spewed words of Jesus the Savior.

Make it make sense. Who was he?

I remained in shock for the rest of Mass.

When it was over, I hid my face as the group exited down the aisle. I stayed seated as everyone left and the music and singing died down. When most people had taken their leave, I slipped out of the bench and snuck to the back wall, carefully peeking through the crack of the open door. CJ stood by the front doors next to the priest, greeting people as they left. How was I going to get out of here without him seeing me?

"What the fuck are you doing here?"

I almost jumped out of my skin at the sound of Jake's voice behind me. With my hand on my racing heart, I turned to face him. "Jesus, Jake. You scared the hell out of me."

"Answer the question."

"What?" I turned back to peeping through the door crack.

"Does Ian know you're here?"

Confused, I faced Jake again. "Huh?" I drew my eyebrows together when his question registered. "No. I'm not here for Ian." I turned back to the crack.

"Then why are you here?"

"You know—church."

"What?"

I sighed. "I'm here for the same reason you are, Jake."

"To sing in the choir and support my fiancé?"

"What? No."

"Why are you whispering? And what the fuck do you keep looking at?"

"Hi, Matt. What are you doing here?"

Great. Ian had joined us. I turned my attention to the couple and shrugged. "I thought I'd give churchgoing a try."

Ian quirked a brow. "Really?"

"Sure. Why not?"

"Because you hate churches and are terrified of them."

I waved a hand through the air. "That's in the past. I wanted to give it another chance and learn more. For example"—I pulled out the pamphlet, unfolding it and pointed to the list of names—"who are these people? Were they here today?"

They both looked at me like I was insane. But then Ian answered. "Well, yeah, some of them were. Father Kevin was the presiding priest, Chester was the deacon—"

"Deacon? What's that?" I asked, trying to hold it together.

"A deacon is an ordained minister of the church."

"What does that mean? Is it like a priest?"

"No. The deacon assists the priest and can't perform certain sacraments alone."

So, not a priest. What a relief. I turned to the crack again. There was a woman standing next to CJ now. "Is that the deacon right there?"

"Yup. That's Chester."

The woman was tall. Maybe it was because she was wearing heels, but she was almost the same height as CJ. Her skin was bronze, and her hair was in a short bob. They laughed and conversed with Father Kevin and a few other people. Then CJ's arm slipped around the woman's waist. "Who's the woman standing next to him?"

"Lola, Chester's wife," Jake answered.

My head whipped back. "Wife?" The word puffed out of my mouth. "Are you kidding me?"

"Did I stutter? What the fuck is wrong with you?"

"Unlike priests, deacons can be married," Ian explained, clearly misinterpreting my reaction. "But they have to be already married before they're ordained. Otherwise, they must stay single and celibate."

What the fuck?

"I heard she's a model from some European country," Jake said. "She's got the legs for it."

"Italy," Ian confirmed. "Should I be jealous?"

"Absolutely not. She's not my type."

"What is your type?"

"You."

Ian chuckled. "Matt, are you okay?" he asked. "You look a little pale."

I was going to be sick. This was way worse than I thought. Adultery was not something I could ever be down with, not even a little. Especially with a closeted straight man who was pretending to be gay so he could fuck guys on the down low. Or was he a closeted gay pretending to be straight? Shaking my head, I pushed away from the wall. "I've got to get out of here."

Before lunging myself into the atrium, I froze. I wanted CJ to see me. I wanted him to know that I knew.

He was fucking married? To a woman?

It wasn't the time to lose it. I collected myself, straightening my cuffs and standing tall, then I strode toward the exit. CJ's smile faded when he saw me, his eyes widening. I held his gaze as I walked past him, hardening my jaw. Then I rolled my eyes and punched the door open and got out.

Chapter 53

Ian

Today was my wedding day. I was marrying the man of my dreams.

I couldn't believe it.

But what didn't surprise me was the massive boner poking me in the ass and the warm hand stroking my cock over my boxers. We'd been sleeping in underwear instead of our usual birthday suits to avoid any temptation, and we'd agreed to refrain from sex until after we were married. The concept sounded good. However, following through was definitely proving to be challenging.

"Jakc..." I mumbled into the pillow.

"Baby..." he moaned.

"Babe," I scolded as I rolled back into him. "What are you doing?"

"Feeling your dick get hard."

"Jake!"

"Hmm?" he purred, kissing my neck.

"We agreed. No sex until after the wedding."

He sucked his teeth. "No, *you* agreed. I just went along with it to make you happy."

I narrowed my eyes.

"Come on, babe. We've been abstinent for an entire week. Isn't that enough? I'm dying here." He kissed my neck again. "Just a little taste. A little sample of what's to come later." He smirked at the pun. "Literally."

"But you've already sampled. You know what it tastes like."

He pulled back and gave me a side smile. "I know. And that's exactly why I want more. I'm addicted."

"You can wait a few more hours."

"No, I can't."

He moved close again, resuming the rubbing. I squeezed my eyes shut. Tempting, indeed. "Jake," I pleaded, losing my resolve. "Please stop stroking my penis."

"But I like your penis. Doesn't this feel good? It must. You're almost completely hard."

"I knew I should have slept at my parents' house," I sighed.

"What? No way. I would have died."

"No, you wouldn't have."

"Yes, I would have, and you would've too. We need each other to sleep."

"Okay, yeah, that's true."

"You're my air. I need you to breathe."

"Aw, baby." I kissed him. "But seriously, stop rubbing my cock or I'm gonna cum."

"Go ahead. I won't mind. In fact, let me slip my hand inside and give you a proper hand—"

"No!" I laughed, grabbing his wrist as I pushed him onto his back and got on top of him, straddling him.

"Oh, baby, I like this position." He rotated his hips, causing my cock to jerk.

I giggled. "Me too. But baby, please. I want our wedding night to be special. Please don't make this anymore difficult."

He grunted. "That's not fair. You know I can never deny you. But fine, we'll do it your way."

I grinned. "Thank you. I promise you won't be disappointed."

"Well, I know that. Can I at least have a kiss?"

"Absolutely." I lowered to meet his lips and kissed him. "I can't wait until you're my husband."

"Mmm. I can't wait till you're *my* husband."

After one last kiss, I pushed off him. "There's so much to do before we head to my parents' house. Time to get up."

"Fine. I'll start breakfast while you shower."

"Just coffee. I think I'm too nervous to eat. Besides, my mom said something about brunch."

"Yeah, I'm nervous too. Instead of breakfast, want some help soaping your back?"

"Uh, no. I'm good, thanks," I chuckled.

"How about washing your hair?"

I smiled as I leaned over the bed and kissed him. "I promise you can do whatever you want to me on our wedding night."

"Yeah? Anything?"

"Anything."

He grinned like a mischievous child coming up with a plan. "Okay."

I kissed him one last time, then forced myself into the bathroom. For a cold shower.

* * *

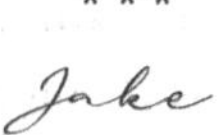

The butterflies had started. They fluttered up a storm in my stomach. All over my body. I swear they were in my toes as well.

Ian's parents' house looked amazing. Anna and Ian's mom, Katherine, had outdone themselves. The ceremony would take place outside in the backyard, and I couldn't wait to get this show on the road.

The guests were arriving, which made me more anxious. If it were up to me, I'd have kidnapped my boy to city hall and skipped all this extra shit, but it was important for Ian to get married in front of his parents and Anna. And who was I to deny my love?

"Is he ready yet?" I asked Ant, aka my best man.

"Jake, it's been two minutes since you last asked."

"So? He can be done in two minutes."

"I have explicit instructions from my wife not to text her again unless it's an emergency."

"This is an emergency. I'm dying here. I was ready in ten minutes. What's taking him so long?"

He laughed at my exaggeration.

"Fine. Twenty minutes. But still, I'm worried he'll wise up and realize he could do so much better than a loser with a deadbeat criminal for a father."

He laughed harder. "I can guarantee Ian will not bolt."

"How can you be so sure? Anna could be up there helping him escape as we speak."

He placed his hands on my shoulders. "Ian loves you. He would never leave you on the day he's dreamed about almost his whole life."

I smiled and sighed. "I will never understand why he chose me."

"We don't choose love. Love chooses us."

I nodded. "True. I certainly didn't expect to fall in love with Ian as deeply as I have."

"Exactly. Ian is up in his old room right now, getting fixed up for you. He simply wants to look his best for you. And my wife is helping him. That's all."

"Thanks, Ant. You've really been a great friend."

He patted my back.

A moment later, there was commotion at the front door. Ian's mother was greeting guests as they entered, but she seemed to be arguing with someone. I walked over to get a closer look.

"Ma?" Aw, hell no. There was no way she was ruining this day for me. "Leave. Right now. Or I swear to God I'll call the cops."

My mother put her hands up. "Jacob, please. I didn't come here to cause trouble."

"Then why did you come? Do you realize what day it is? I will not let you ruin it for Ian and me."

She hesitated as she shook her head. "My son. So handsome."

I did not see that coming. I narrowed my eyes at her, waiting for the punch line.

"I have dreamed of this day since the moment you were born. Well, it's a little different from I imagined, but—"

Yeah, still wasn't following.

"What I'm trying to say is—look, I'm—it's just the two of us now. With your father gone, for Lord knows how long, I . . . well, I don't want to lose you as well. I can't stand here and tell you I'm okay with"— she glanced around, slicing her hand through the air—"all of this. But I'm willing to try. If you'll let me."

It wasn't exactly acceptance, but I supposed it was a start.

"Jake, I'm sorry. I know I hurt you. Please, I—"

"I'm not the only one you should apologize to."

Her eyes focused on something behind me as a collective hum vibrated throughout the room. I turned, and my breath caught.

Ian stood at the top of the stairs looking like a hot-ass angel who'd descended from heaven. All he needed was a fucking halo and wings. He wore a white tux, which outlined his sexy body perfectly. His hair fell in natural ringlets from the top of his head. Even from this distance, his deep blue eyes glowed, outlined by black eyeliner. I couldn't see his hands since they were tucked in his trouser pockets, but I was sure his nails were painted.

Scraping my jaw off the floor, I waltzed over like a magnet drawn to my groom as he sauntered down the stairs. When we met at the bottom of the last step, I had no words. He was so beautiful. He'd rendered me speechless.

"Hi," he said, smiling.

"Hi," I replied, finding my voice. "You look amazing."

"Thanks. So do you."

"Thanks." I was grinning like a fool standing in front of his crush. All I wanted to do was backtrack him up the stairs to his childhood room and devour him.

"What is your mom doing here?" he whispered.

Oh yeah. People. Still around. Wedding. I blinked. "I don't know."

"You don't know? Are you okay?"

"Yeah." I clasped his hands, pulling him in. "I just want to—"

"Hey now," Anna interrupted. "None of that until the officiate says you can."

I grunted. Ian chuckled. God, I loved him. Someone cleared their throat behind me.

My mother.

I instinctively got in front of Ian, shielding him behind me.

She surrendered her hands up. "I come in peace. Ian, can we talk?"

"Whatever you have to say to him, you can say in front of me."

Ian placed his hand on my shoulder. "Babe, it's okay. I want to hear what she has to say."

Mom shook her head. "I could say it here. This won't take long."

I stepped forward. "You better watch what you say."

She gave me The Look, like when I used to talk back as a kid. Ian's warm hand rubbed my back, grounding me. I would lose my shit a thousand times over if it weren't for him.

"What is it, Mrs. Edwards?"

"I owe you an apology. I see now how wrong I was about you, uh, influencing my son. It turns out Miranda was manipulating us all. I shouldn't have hit you. I'm truly sorry."

"I appreciate that. Thank you."

"I can see how much you mean to Jake. And he means a lot to me, so like I told him, I am willing to keep an open mind about your relationship. I would like to attend your . . . ceremony. If you'll let me."

"Yes. Of course." He put his arm around me. "We'd love for you to stay. Right, babe?"

I wasn't completely convinced of my mother's change of heart, but Ian was clearly happy, and who was I to deny him? I nodded. "Right. As long as she stays seated and doesn't speak up at any point."

"I won't object, if that's what you're worried about. I want to be a part of your life, so I will not do anything to jeopardize that."

We'll see.

After we hugged it out, it was time to get the show on the road. The guests headed outside and took their seats. Once the music began, Ian's parents kicked off the procession down the aisle. Then, because of Ian insisted my mother should be part of this, she headed down next, followed by Ant and Anna. And finally, me and my man.

My palms were sweaty and my heart was beating out of my chest as the officiant began. I barely registered the words spoken until it was time for our vows. Ian went first.

"Jake, you know me better than anyone else in this world. You are my best friend, my lover, my protector, my hero, and the love of my life. We've been through some ups and downs throughout the years, but in the end, we've come out stronger. We've beat the odds, knocking down every obstacle that came our way. We survived. Because of this, I know we will make it. And I can't wait to grow old with you. I promise to love you, cherish you, and respect you. I will be faithful and loyal. And I will always be there for you, in sickness and in health, in good times and in bad. You are my everything. I love you. Forever and always."

Okay, time to dry the eyes. I cleared my throat. "Ian, when I first met you, never in a million years did I expect we'd be standing here. Hell, I had no idea I liked dudes." There was some laughter. "I never knew it was possible to love someone with so much intensity that nothing else mattered except for their well-being. Because of you, I've discovered who I am, and I will forever be grateful for that because it means I get to do life with you. You are truly my best friend, my inspiration, my rock. You make me a better person. You are my better half, my soulmate. I promise to protect you with my life. I promise to support you and be there for you, in good times and in bad. And I promise to help make your dreams come true because my dream already came true the day you said you'd marry me. I promise to love you and cherish you every second of every day because tomorrow is never promised, and I don't want to miss a moment with you. I promise to always put your needs before my own because your satisfaction is what I live for. I promise to hold you, in sickness and in health. I promise to always give you the best of me because you deserve only the best. I promise to be faithful to you and trust in our love. And above all, I promise to love you forever, till I take my final breath and beyond."

Not a dry eye in the house, thank you very much. But I meant every word.

Chapter 54

Ian

One Month Later

"Baby, slow down," Jake called behind me.

I stopped at the elevator, smacking the button several times. We'd just landed from our beautiful honeymoon when I got the text that Anna had her baby, and we'd come straight to the hospital. "Sorry. I'm just so excited to meet the little princess."

His arms slipped around my waist. "I know. Me too, but they're not going anywhere. No need to rush."

My husband was not wrong. I smiled. "You're right. I'm so glad you're here with me."

"Where the fuck else would I be?"

I chuckled as the elevator doors slid open. We hopped on and cozied up against the back wall once I clicked on the correct floor. "I love you."

"I love you too." He kissed me. "By the way, our honeymoon is not over."

"Oh, I'm counting on that."

The elevator dinged and, hand-in-hand, we headed down the hall to Anna's room. I knocked.

"Come in," Anna called.

Anthony was holding the precious bundle. It took a lot not to squeal and eat that baby up. I went to Anna instead, hugging her. "Oh my God, Anna, congratulations."

"Thank you. But did you guys really come straight here from the airport?"

"Of course. This is my niece we're talking about. I had to meet her."

"Congratulations, Anna," Jake said, giving her a hug as well. "I was eager to meet her as well."

Anthony came over. "Well, guys, I introduce you to Faith Rose Martin."

I gasped. "What a beautiful name. Can I hold her? Please?"

"Of course you can."

I squirted some hand sanitizer into my hands and rubbed it in. "Okay, ready."

Faith squirmed a little during the transfer, but once I swayed her a little, she cooed and snuggled herself back to sleep. I lowered myself into the chair, and Jake knelt beside me.

"She is precious," he said, caressing a finger along her cheek. "And so tiny."

"Your hand is as big as her head," I laughed.

I felt his eyes on me. "You look good holding her."

I glanced up. There were unshed tears in his eyes, as there were in mine. "I do?"

He nodded. "Let's do it."

"Do what?"

"Let's have a baby."

"What happened to wanting me all to yourself for a while?"

"It's a long process, right? We should get it started. We'll have plenty of alone time."

"Are you sure?"

"Baby, I want to give you the world. And I can see how much you want to be a dad."

I lowered my head against his. "Thank you. I love you so much. You're the best husband, and I know you will be a great dad."

"So are you. I love you too, baby boy. Always and forever."

Thank you so much for reading! I hope you enjoyed Jake and Ian's journey as much as I loved writing about it. They are for sure my favorite couple so far in this series. And there is so much more to tell. So don't worry, you haven't seen the last of them. I have something special in store for them.

Sign up for my newsletter at www.tmamat.com to keep up to date on this and other projects, announcements, and release dates.

And stay tuned for the continuation of Matt and CJ's story. It's not over.

Don't forget to head on over to Amazon to post a short review. It really does make a difference.

Thanks again for your support!

T. M. AMAT writes steamy, contemporary romance. She spends her free time dreaming up sexy realistic characters and the scenarios to put them in. She lives in Georgia with her family.

To sign up for her newsletter, visit www.tmamat.com

www.facebook.com/tmamatauthor
www.instagram.com/tmamatauthor

www.ingramcontent.com/pod-product-compliance
Lightning Source LLC
Chambersburg PA
CBHW011030190726
48290CB00011B/2772